FAMOUS

QUANTUM SERIES, BOOK 8

BY: MARIE FORCE

Famous
By: Marie Force

Published by HTJB, Inc.
Copyright 2019. HTJB, Inc.
Cover Design by Moonstruck Cover Design & Photography
Interior Layout by Ashley J. Lopez, Designing Women
ISBN: 978-1950654468

www.marieforce.com

The Quantum Series

CHAPTER 1

Marlowe

I've planned this night for weeks, down to the last detail. I want it to be perfect. Bringing someone new into my private life is not something I do lightly, having learned the hard way over the years that celebrity has a dark downside that I go out of my way to avoid whenever possible. But Rafe is different. We've been together for months, and I feel ready to take this next step with him. In the dungeon that's accessible only to Quantum partners and our guests, I take a careful look at the items I've set out—a blindfold, a flogger, the smallest plug, a bottle of lubricant and a cock ring. I'm starting him off easy until I can get a sense of whether he shares my appreciation for the lifestyle.

While I'm mostly satisfied by the sex I have with Rafe, there's still something missing, and thus the reason I'm trying to add a little spice to our relationship.

Before I met Rafe, I confessed to my closest friends and business partners that I was feeling out of sorts and off-kilter. Spending time at the clubs we own here in LA and in New York City had become boring, especially since my buddies found love and more or less gave up the clubs. Getting naked in public lost its luster for each of them after they found "the one." In our world, we're always one tabloid photo away from disaster, so I get that they feel the need to protect their significant others from that kind of exposure.

We go to enormous lengths to protect the members of our clubs, including the requirement of a one-million-dollar entrance fee for new members and airtight nondisclosure agreements. But that didn't stop someone in Devon Black's equally exclusive club from taking photos of our partner Jasper Autry that were later used to blackmail him. We're all a little gun-shy after that episode.

Rafe understands the celebrity culture because he works in our industry. As an executive for Cirque, the company that distributes Quantum films—and many others—in France, he travels frequently between Paris and Los Angeles, hobnobbing with celebrities and working deep inside the business. From the beginning, I've felt comfortable being myself around him, because he understands the pressures I face. It's been a long time since I've felt this way about a guy, and even though I can tell my friends don't love him, I do, and that's all that matters.

Or so I tell myself.

Truth is, their opinions matter to me, even if I wish they didn't.

Especially Flynn and Hayden, who have been my closest friends for years. It's so rare for me to be out of sync with either of them, let alone both, but from the outset, they've been rather obvious in their dislike of Rafe. I wish I knew why, but they won't even give him a chance. Flynn's wife, Natalie, and I talked about it over the holidays when we were all together for four memorable days in St. George, Utah, of all places.

As I light the candles in the dungeon, I think about that conversation, as I have so many times since then.

"It's not that he doesn't like Rafe," Natalie said. "It's more that he doesn't like him for *you*."

"*Why?*" I asked and immediately hated myself for the question as well as the desperate-sounding tone in which it was asked. I'm Marlowe Sloane. What do I care if Flynn Godfrey or anyone else doesn't like my boyfriend? Except... I care, and I hate that I care.

I could tell Nat chose her words carefully. "It's just that he thinks you can do... better." She cringed as she said that last word, and I realized I'd put her in a terrible position by bringing it up at all. The guys had gone off to find a Christmas tree for Aileen's kids and had grudgingly invited Rafe to join them. That's what had led me to ask her what the fuck Flynn's problem was with him.

Be careful what you wish for. Flynn thinks he's not good enough for me, which means Hayden, Jasper, Kristian, Emmett and Sebastian probably agree with him.

"Does everyone feel that way?" I asked Nat.

"I'm not sure." She rolled her bottom lip between her teeth, which is a "tell" for her. She knows but doesn't want to say. Fair enough. None of them like him.

"Does it matter to anyone that *I* like him?"

"Yes! Of course it does. That's all that matters. If he makes you happy, we're happy. You know that."

I eyed her skeptically. "I'm happy with him."

"Okay, then."

"Okay."

We changed the subject, but the uncomfortable conversation has stayed with me ever since. Natalie tried to be diplomatic, walking a fine line between keeping Flynn's confidences and trying not to hurt my feelings. She failed in the latter account. My feelings were hurt, and they still are. It's been five freaking years since I dated anyone seriously, so I sort of feel like the guys could at least *try* to give me a break with Rafe.

I glance at the ornate clock on the wall. He's going to be here in fifteen minutes. Time to get changed and stop thinking about why my friends don't like him. Everyone is entitled to their opinion, even if they're wrong.

I remind myself again that they're not in this relationship. Only Rafe and I are, and we're the only two who matter. I'm the only one who needs to like him and trust him and love him. It's my life, and no one else is going to live it for me, no matter how much I love my friends. I'm going to prove how wrong they are by making this relationship work.

I've decided it's time to bring Rafe into my lifestyle because I know we can't succeed long term unless I let him all the way in. Each of the guys has had to do the same with their significant others and did so with stunning success if their happy, dopey grins are any indication.

That's what tonight is all about for Rafe and me. Taking that next step. Depending on how this goes, I might be ready for what comes next, whatever that may be, for a couple juggling a transatlantic relationship.

I'm nervous about tonight because I'm not entirely sure how he'll react to my desire to dominate him. But I won't know until I broach the topic with him. He already knows I'm adventuresome in bed, but he has no idea just how adventuresome I can be. Tonight, he's going to find out, so I'm excited *and* nervous.

I dart into the women's changing room, take a quick shower and dress in one of my favorite outfits—a red leather bustier with a matching thong and sexy stockings with a flower pattern running through them. I've cut myself short on time, so I put my hair up in a bun and go with a smoky cat eye and basic lip gloss for makeup. By the time my phone buzzes with the text I'm expecting from him, I'm ready.

After donning a red silk robe and black stiletto Louboutins with the fabulous red soles, I give myself a quick once-over in the full-length mirror and take a deep breath, letting it out slowly. *Here goes nothing...*

In the lobby, I press the button for the elevator and take it up one floor to the main entrance to the Quantum office building. Most of the people who work here have no idea what's in the basement. When the doors open, Rafe is facing away from me, looking out at the parking lot.

"Hey."

"Why'd you want to meet here?" He turns to face me, his eyes widening when he sees me in the silky robe and heels. "Is this some sort of office fantasy or something?"

"Not quite." I extend my hand to him. "Will you come with me and keep an open mind?" He's absolutely beautiful, with thick wavy dark hair and brilliant blue eyes that crinkle at the corners when he smiles, which is often when we're together.

He seems hesitant, but he takes my hand, links our fingers and kisses the back of my hand. "I shall happily follow wherever you lead, love."

Now imagine that said in a sexy French accent. I'm not one to swoon, but that accent does it for me.

He watches as I place my palm on the scanner that opens the elevator to the basement. "This all very cloak-and-dagger," he says as we descend.

"Not really."

We step out of the elevator, and the first thing we encounter is a reception desk. "This is where I have to ask you to sign a nondisclosure agreement that says you won't discuss anything you see here."

"Seriously?"

"Very seriously. If you need a minute to review it, I'm happy to wait."

Giving me an odd look, he takes the pen I hand him, scans the NDA that spells out the lengths the Quantum partners will go to in order to defend the privacy of everyone who steps foot in our clubs and then scrawls his signature on the line provided. "What's this all about, Marlowe?"

"Come with me, and I'll show you."

Taking him by the hand, I lead him through the double doors with our distinctive Q logo etched into the glass. To the casual observer, the big room we enter might be mistaken for a nightclub, especially now, when there's no one else here. On a regular night, the place would be pulsing with people, energy and sexual tension. Scenes would be unfolding on the three stages, and potential partners would be negotiating hard and soft limits in the various seating areas and at the bar.

"What is this place?"

"Club Quantum."

"How have I never heard of it?" Before we met, he was active in the LA club scene when he was in town.

"Because it's private."

"Still, with you and your illustrious partners involved, how does it stay a secret?"

"You read the NDA. That's how."

The face he makes indicates his skepticism that even an airtight NDA can keep the lid on anything in this day and age, and perhaps he's right. Didn't we learn that when Jasper was blackmailed?

On the far side of the big room, I place my hand on another scanner that opens the door to the dungeon. As we descend the stairs, I begin to feel seriously anxious. Am I doing the right thing? Will he understand? What if he doesn't? Can I stay with him if he doesn't get this or doesn't even *try* to get it?

Don't jump ahead of yourself. One step at a time. You've done this before, and it's been fine.

Rafe stops short at the entrance to the dungeon. "Holy shit. Are you fucking kidding me?"

"You promised to keep an open mind." A trickle of unease travels down my backbone as I begin to wonder if I've seriously miscalculated.

He strides over to the table where I set out the implements of my craft and picks up the flogger, turning to me, his brow lifted and his mouth set in a hard expression I've seen only once before. "What the hell is this, Marlowe?"

I normally love the melodic way he says my name, but there's no melody to it now. His harsh tone frightens me as I realize no one else knows where I am or what I had planned for tonight. Not even my assistant, Leah, who always knows where I am. As he stalks toward me, his blue eyes blazing with anger, I take a step back, furious with myself for being so stupid. I'm thirty-five years old. I should know better by now than to ever put myself at the mercy of a man.

They're usually at *my* mercy, and I wouldn't have it any other way.

"Stop." I hold up my hand to keep him from coming any closer to me. He doesn't stop. "Rafe, I mean it. Take a pause."

"Don't tell me what to do when you're springing this kinky bullshit on me *months* into our relationship." A vein in his forehead bulges as he spews the harsh words at me. "Why didn't you tell me before now that you want to be tied up and flogged and whatever else?"

He's spitting mad, and I'm trying to figure out why as I think about what I should say.

"Marlowe! What the fuck? You owe me an explanation!"

This is why Flynn and the others don't like him. They could see he has this in him while I was too busy being besotted to see beyond the glossy surface, the French words of love and the romance of it all.

He's played me for a fool, and the only thing I want now is to get as far away from him as I possibly can. Immediately.

"I'm sorry, Rafe. Obviously, I've made a mistake, and I'll understand if you'd rather not see me again."

"Not see you again? Is that what you think is going to happen here?"

"I'm not comfortable with the way you're behaving."

He doesn't like that, and I quickly realize I've only made him angrier.

"Isn't that *rich*, darling? You're not comfortable with the way *I'm* behaving. After spending months together, you decide to show me you're a kinky whore, and you don't like the way *I'm* behaving?" He lowers his voice. "You want me to beat you before I fuck you, is that it?"

"No," I whisper. "That's not it at all."

"Then please illuminate me, because I don't get it."

The rebellious part of me, the part that fought and clawed her way to success in one of the toughest businesses in the world, rears up inside me. Fuck this shit. "I'm a Dominatrix. *I* wanted to beat you before I *let* you fuck me, but that's not what I want anymore. What I really want now is for you to get the fuck out of here and never contact me again."

His shock is apparent in the way his face loses all color and his lips go tight before he speaks again in a much lower tone. "That's it? After everything we've shared, you're going to dismiss me like I'm some kind of servant?"

"I'm asking you to leave."

"Fuck you if you think you're going to treat me like I'm nothing." He moves so quickly, I don't see it coming until my head snaps back, hits the wall behind me and my face explodes in pain that rattles my teeth. Then he grabs my hair and drags me across the room. I fight him with everything I've got, but I'm no match against him physically. He outweighs me by seventy pounds.

Before things go from bad to worse, I have the presence of mind to realize I'm in big, big trouble.

CHAPTER 2

Sebastian

I love Mondays at the club, one of the two days a week we're closed. I usually take care of a week's worth of paperwork, inventory and cleaning in one day so I can take Tuesday completely off. My friends tell me I'm weird because I'm the only person in the world who looks forward to Mondays, but whatever. That's just one of many ways they think I'm weird.

I'm okay with that, because thanks to those same friends, I have the world's most unbelievable life, and I'm thankful to them for making me part of the Quantum family.

As I cut in and out of rush-hour LA traffic, dodging slow-moving vehicles and people who'd rather text than drive, I think—as I do almost every day—about how my life should've ended up versus where I am today. I was heading for trouble with gangs when my best friend from childhood, Hayden Roth, intervened and offered me a job with his fledgling production company.

At first, I turned him down. Then he ratted me out to my mother, Graciela, who also helped to raise Hayden while she worked as his father's housekeeper. Once she got ahold of me, I had no choice but to take Hayden's job offer or risk my mother's hot Mexican temper. My *madre* is a doll, but you don't ever want to piss her off. Hayden and I learned that lesson early on.

I took the fucking job, in which Hayden basically made me his bitch on the West Virginia location of his first film. Going from the mean streets of LA to the rolling hills of West Virginia was a shock to my system, to say the least, and I hated the job with a passion, almost as much as I hated him for tattling on me.

I grunt out a laugh as I think about how young and stupid I was. Of course I couldn't have known then that Hayden would grow up to be one of the hottest and most celebrated directors of our time. Back then, he was just the son of washed-up stars trying to make his mark on an unforgiving business, and he'd made up his mind to bring me along with him, kicking and screaming.

Thank God for Hayden. Without him, I'd probably be dead or in prison. I was heading nowhere fast when he intervened, and as much as I resented him for it at the time, now I have nothing but the kind of gratitude that comes with age and maturity.

I have that same thought just about every day as I drive from my condo outside Malibu to the Quantum office building that houses the exclusive club I manage on behalf of the partners. Though I'm not in any way as successful as they are, they never treat me like anything other than a full-fledged member of their family, and for that, I count myself as one of the luckiest guys who's ever lived.

There's nothing I wouldn't do for any of them—or their partners. Watching them fall in love, one right after the other, has been incredible. First Flynn met Natalie, then Hayden finally admitted he'd been in love with Addison for years— duh, we all knew that—and then Jasper and Ellie decided to make a baby together. Aileen and her kids moved to LA to live closer to Kristian, and now they're one big happy family. The one that surprised me the most, though, was Quantum's chief legal counsel, Emmett, falling for Marlowe's sassy, mouthy assistant, Leah. Got to admit, I didn't see that one coming, but the two of them are as happy as two pigs in shit, and all they do is laugh.

The only one of us besides me who's still single is Marlowe, and she's face-first into something with the prissy Frenchman. Can't stand that guy. None of us can. He's fucking pretentious and has a stick jammed so far up his ass that I'm surprised you can't see it when he opens his mouth. He's no fun to be around, that's for sure, and I suspect he's got a dark side, not that I have proof of that. Just a sixth sense I have from my years of running the streets, which is something I've kept to myself. I can't go around accusing the guy of something without proof, but I keep my eye on him.

Flynn and Hayden can barely stand to be in the same room with him, but they try to pretend otherwise for Marlowe's sake. For all his formidable acting skills, Flynn sucks at hiding his disdain for the Frenchman.

Marlowe doesn't seem to care what they think, which I find somewhat remarkable. The group of them are tight, and it's unusual for them to be so far out of sync with each other. Love does funny things to people. I reminded Flynn of that over Christmas, when we were stuck in Utah for a few days due to a blizzard. I pointed out that he was so intent on marrying Natalie last year that he hadn't wanted anyone telling him he needed a prenup. None of us could believe he'd marry anyone—even a sweetheart like Nat—without protecting his sizable fortune.

Flynn conceded the point, but he said his and Nat's relationship had nothing in common with Marlowe and Rafe's. I didn't disagree with him or point out that Marlowe feels for Rafe the same thing he does for Nat. Although how she feels that way about *him* is hard to fathom. But who am I to tell someone else how they should feel? That's so not my style. I'm a live-and-let-live kind of guy, and as such, I keep my opinions to myself, even when I see my friend making a questionable decision.

She's a grown-ass woman who clawed her way to the top of her profession. She doesn't need me or anyone else telling her how to live her life. If, however, she were to look my way for once, I might be tempted to... No, forget I said that. It's never going to happen, and I gave up on that possibility years ago.

Like I said, love makes fools of people, which is one reason why I've studiously avoided the kind of commitments my friends have been making lately. The thought of being shackled to one woman for life, even the most spectacular woman I've ever known, makes me break out in hives. Variety is truly the spice of life, and through my role as the manager of the club, I have a regular buffet of variety laid out before me on a nightly basis. I'd be crazy to give that up to have one woman in my bed forever.

No, thank you. Monogamy is not for me. Don't get me wrong. I'm thrilled for my friends. I can see how happy they are with their partners and how excited they are about a future that includes kids for most of them.

I shudder at the thought of bringing kids into this fucked-up world. I barely knew my own father when I was growing up and had Hayden's disaster of a father around to give me a front-row example of what not to do. I've spent a lot of time in the company of Flynn's dad, Max Godfrey, and have benefitted from the fatherly wisdom he hands out to anyone who needs it, but it's not like I pretend that's enough to make me worthy of being anyone's father.

Why am I even thinking about things that're never going to happen? I ask myself that question as I take a right turn into the Quantum parking lot, where I see that, for once, I'm not the first one to arrive on a Monday morning. Marlowe's white Bentley is the only car in the lot, although she's the last person I'd expect to see there at seven o'clock on a Monday. Marlowe jokes about needing her beauty sleep, and we rarely hear from her before ten when we're on vacation together.

She texted me yesterday that she was planning a private party and wanted to let me know she'd be using the club. I reminded her that she owns the joint and doesn't need my permission to use her own club. What's she doing here so early? Maybe she went home with Rafe.

I park my black Ford F-150 next to her Bentley and head toward the main door. When I insert my key, I'm shocked to find the main door unlocked. Marlowe wouldn't forget to lock up, or was she so caught up in her douche of a boyfriend that she overlooked basic security? If so, I'll need to remind her. Flynn and Hayden would lose their collective shit if they knew the door was unlocked all night. They're freaks about security, and with good reason.

None of us will ever get over Flynn being stabbed on a rope line in London a couple of years ago. People are crazy, especially when it comes to celebrities of any kind, and after the incident in London, Flynn and Hayden ramped up security big-time.

I place my palm on the scanner to summon the elevator to the basement. While I wait, I dash off a text to Marlowe. *You left the door unlocked last night.* I note that the text was delivered as I step onto the elevator.

In the downstairs lobby, I walk through the double doors into the club, where the lights are on. What the fuck? Was she so swept off her feet that she couldn't even turn off the lights?

I cringe at that possibility and then freeze when I see the door to the dungeon is open. There's no way in hell Marlowe would ever leave that door open—or the main door unlocked, for that matter.

I start running before I'm even aware of what I'm doing. Adrenaline pumps through me as I cross the expansive main room of the club and dash through the door that leads down one more level, to the private area available only to the Quantum principals. I pound down the stairs and stop short at the sight of horror. That's the only word to describe it, and even that may not be adequate.

Marlowe, beaten and bloody, suspended from the ceiling in ropes tied in such a way that if she so much as breathes too deeply, she'll be strangled, if she hasn't been already. I can't tell at first if she's alive. Her chest doesn't appear to move, but I can't be certain with the way she's trussed up.

"Oh my God," I whisper as I move toward her, fear pounding through me and making me lightheaded. I'm going to kill that son of a bitch, and after he's dead, I'm going to kill him again.

My mouth is dry and my hands are shaking as I try to decide what I should do first—free her from the ropes or call for help. "Marlowe. Sweetheart…" Tears fill my eyes, and my heart beats so fast, I have to force myself to breathe so I don't pass out or break down. She needs me to keep it together.

I sweep my fingers over her forehead, noting she has a big bruise on her left cheek. "Marlowe."

Her low moan is the best sound I've ever heard.

She's not dead.

"Let me get some help."

"No." The word is softly spoken but emphatic.

"Marlowe, you're seriously hurt."

"No police."

With fumbling fingers, I untie the knot around her neck and then, cradling her in my arms, I use my free hand to work on the other knots holding her suspended. It takes much longer than it should, but I finally release the last of the knots and gather her naked, battered body into my arms.

She trembles so violently, I fear she might be having a seizure.

"You gotta let me call someone, Mo. Please. I'm way outta my league here."

"Call Addie." Marlowe grits her teeth and sucks in a breath before whimpering. "She'll get help. N-no cops or hospitals." Her fingers dig into my arm. "Please, Seb."

"Okay, honey. No cops or hospitals." I take her to sit on one of the sofas and grab a blanket from a basket on the floor, gently putting it over her before withdrawing my phone and calling Addie.

"Hey," she says, chipper as always. "What's up?"

"Where are you?"

"Just got to the office, why?"

"Come down to the club. By yourself. And hurry, Addie. It's an emergency."

"I'm coming."

While we wait for her, I hold Marlowe's trembling body as close to me as I dare, fearful of adding in any way to her pain. "Did he do this to you, love?"

She doesn't reply, which says it all. I'm going to kill him, and I'm going to enjoy it. I'm going to do exactly what he did to her first, every last thing. When Flynn and Hayden hear about this...

"Don't."

The single word is filled with pain, so much I can barely stand it.

"Whatever you're thinking, just don't." Each word seems to cost her.

"Shhh, just breathe, sweetheart."

I hear Addie calling for me upstairs.

"Down here."

Her heels click on the stairs as she comes down quickly. "What's wrong, Sebastian?"

"Over here."

She walks across the room, unable to make out much in the low lighting until she sees the distinctive color of Marlowe's hair and gasps. "What happened?"

"She was beaten and left suspended from the ropes all night."

"Did you call for rescue?"

"No." Marlowe keeps her eyes closed. "No rescue. No press."

"She told me to call you. She said you'd know what to do."

"Marlowe." Addie bites back her shock and dismay to take charge. "What hurts?"

"Everything."

"Do you have broken bones?"

"Don't know."

Addie looks up at me. "We need to be very careful with her until we know that for sure." She caresses Marlowe's hair. "Can I call Dr. Breslow to come see you?"

"Yeah."

"Let's get her upstairs to one of the private rooms." I can hear how upset and worried she is with every word she says. Marlowe is one of Addie's closest friends.

I'm trembling like a newborn, but I hold Marlowe close to me as I stand to walk upstairs.

She cries out in pain that guts me. I hope that son of a bitch is on the run, because I want to track him down and make him pay for what he's done to her. I want to make him *hurt* the same way she does.

"I'm sorry, sweetheart."

"Not your fault." Her words are garbled.

Not once, in all my life, have I ever wanted to actually murder someone the way I do now. I can't imagine how Flynn and Hayden will feel. They go all the way back with Marlowe, the three of them as close as siblings. Following Addie, I carry Marlowe up two flights of stairs to one of the private rooms. I'm thankful for the cleaning team that was here over the weekend, leaving the room smelling like lemons and fabric softener.

Addie pulls the quilt and sheet down and makes a pile of the pillows.

I place Marlowe, carefully, on the bed and get my first look at the bruises on her torso.

Sucking in a deep breath to calm myself, I glance at Addie, whose face has gone white with shock. "Call the doc, Addie."

She shakes off the horror and pulls out the iPhone that runs her life—and Flynn's.

I gently place the covers over Marlowe, sit on the edge of the bed and brush the hair back from her face. "What do you need?"

"Advil."

"Besides that."

"Water."

"I'll get it."

She stops me when I would've gotten up. "Seb."

"What, honey?"

"Don't tell Flynn or Hayden. They'll kill him."

"They won't kill him. He'll already be dead if he comes near me—or you."

Her eyes fill with tears that break me. "Please."

I can't bear to see our strong, powerful Marlowe hurt this way. I want to go outside and howl from the rage that grips me. "I won't tell them."

"She's on her way," Addie reports when she ends the call with the doctor. She sits gingerly on the other side of the bed and places her hand on top of Marlowe's.

"I'm going to get her some water." I leave the room and rush downstairs to the bar, where I pour her a tall glass of ice water. It's been years since I've felt the way I do now—out of control, enraged, thirsty for vengeance. I love every member of the Quantum family as much as I love my own mother.

But Marlowe... I love her like I've never loved anyone, and I'm the only one in the entire world who knows that.

CHAPTER 3

Marlowe

Everything hurts, and I'm so cold, I can't stop shaking.

Addie puts another blanket over me and bathes my face with a warm washcloth that feels heavenly.

"Mad at myself."

"Don't you dare go there. This is *not* your fault."

Her fierce words bring new tears to my eyes. "Should've listened to the guys. They didn't trust him."

"It's not your fault, Marlowe."

"How is it not my fault? I put myself in a dangerous situation."

She feeds me a sip from the water Sebastian brought. "Had he ever given you reason to fear him before this?"

The cool water feels like heaven to my parched throat. "Once, but... I should've known better."

"Stop it, Marlowe. You did *nothing* wrong."

"I fell for the wrong guy."

She runs the washcloth over my face, mopping up my tears. "I'll give you that, but not the rest. That's on him. *He* did this. Not you."

"Flynn and Hayden will kill him."

"*I* want to kill him."

"I don't want anyone to know."

"Shhh, don't worry about anything. We'll take care of you. You know that."

I close my eyes and force myself to focus on breathing through the pain. Just breathe. That's always been my mantra when things get to be too much for me, and I'm hoping it'll help now. I must've dozed off, because I awake suddenly to realize Dr. Breslow has arrived.

"We'll be right outside," Addie says as she and Sebastian leave the room.

"Tell me what happened," Breslow says without preamble. Her blonde hair is pulled back in a ponytail, and her blue eyes are filled with concern. It occurs to me that we've let her into the club without an NDA. I almost laugh from the foolishness of such a thought. What does that matter now?

"I brought my boyfriend to our sex club, and he freaked out when he realized I'm a Domme. He beat the shit out of me and left me hanging in the ropes overnight."

If I've shocked her, she does a good job of hiding it from me. "I'd like to have you transported to the ER."

"No. If we do that, it'll be all over the internet that Marlowe Sloane was beaten up by her boyfriend at a sex club."

"You may have internal injuries, and there's no way for me to know that without X-rays."

"No hospital."

She sighs with resignation when she seems to get that I'm not going to change my mind. "You can't let him get away with this, Marlowe."

"He's probably halfway to France by now, and in the time it would take to extradite him for a trial, the internet would be on fire with my business."

Her mouth sets with displeasure, but she doesn't pursue it further. For that, I'm thankful. "I need to examine you."

"Go ahead."

She pulls down the covers that were tucked around my shoulders and, like Addie did, she gasps when she sees the extent of my injuries. "Marlowe..."

"I'm okay."

"You're *not* okay. You're badly hurt."

"I just need to rest. Please... Just do what you've got to do, give me something for the pain, and if it gets any worse, I'll go to the ER. I promise."

Breslow carefully examines my arms, ribs and abdomen while I bite back shrieks from the pain of even the lightest touch. She asks if I can sit up so she can look at my back.

"He used a whip on you?" She sounds like she's trying not to cry.

Biting my lip, I nod. I blacked out during that part of the assault, but the pain is the worst there.

She helps me to lie back down. "Did he rape you?"

"No." I don't tell her that he said he was so disgusted by my perversions that he couldn't believe he'd ever gotten it up for me in the first place. Thank God for that.

"I'd like to take photographs of your injuries in case you change your mind about pressing charges."

"I'm not going to change my mind."

"You don't know that right now."

"Yes, I do." My plan is to ruin him every other way I can—and there are several ways that can be done without exposing myself and my life to the relentless media scrutiny that would ensue from reporting something like this to the authorities.

"Let me take the photos in case you change your mind about pressing charges. Please."

"Fine." Whatever it takes to get this over with that much faster.

She takes the photos and gives me a shot for the pain.

I'm sure Addie, Sebastian and the doctor assume I'm in shock and not thinking clearly, but there's nothing wrong with my brain. I'm thinking clearly and had a very long night in excruciating pain to plot my revenge.

Not only am I going to make him sorry he fucked with me, I'm going to make him sorry he was ever born. I'm going to ruin him. That'll satisfy me far more than any long, protracted, public airing of this incident ever could.

Planning my revenge makes it possible to withstand the pain.

Sebastian

"I need to tell Hayden and Flynn," Addie says. "They'd want to know."

"She said not to tell them."

"We can't keep this from them."

"Why not?"

"Because!" Addie throws her hands in the air. "They see her practically every day when they're all in town. How're we supposed to hide this from them?"

"I'll take her home with me. You'll tell them she got called away." I have no idea what the hell I think I'm doing. All I know is that she should have whatever she wants right now, and what she wants is privacy—even from her closest friends. The more I think about this idea, the more committed to it I become.

"Please don't take this the wrong way... Marlowe loves you. Of course she does, but she's going to need her girlfriends."

"Come visit her any time you want. Just you until she asks for someone else. We have to take our lead from her, Addie."

I can tell she's not happy about it, but she concedes the point with a small nod. "I'm not comfortable with keeping something like this from my husband."

"Hell, neither am I. Your husband and the rest of the partners are my bosses, not to mention my closest friends. Keeping something like this from them is not cool for me either. When we tell him we were doing what Marlowe asked us to do, what choice will he have but to understand?"

"You know how he can be."

"Better than anyone, but that doesn't mean I'm going to put him ahead of her when she's the one who's been so badly hurt—in more ways than one."

"You're right." She sighs deeply. "Of course you are. But I do think we need to loop Gordon in, not just so he can put security on her, but in case the piece of shit decides to do something with the info he obtained here."

"He signed the NDA. I checked when I went down to get the water. It was sitting on the reception desk."

"Just because he signed it doesn't mean he'll honor it. If he'd do this to her…"

"Yeah, true. Call Gordon and ask for his discretion. But no one else, Addie. She'll tell the others when she's ready to."

"Okay." Her eyes fill when she glances up at me. "How could he do this to her?"

"I'll never understand how any guy could hurt a woman, especially one he's pretended to care about for months." And that he'd hurt Marlowe, of all people… The kindest, sweetest, most wonderful woman there ever was. She'd do anything for anyone. I've literally seen her give someone she'd never met the shirt off her back.

We were at the beach once, and a homeless woman was shivering in the early evening chill. Marlowe unzipped her sweatshirt and handed it to the woman, who cried from the kindness. If you ask me who Marlowe Sloane is, I always think of that before anything to do with her fame or celebrity. That's who she is to me and the rest of our crew.

If you'd asked me an hour ago if I'd ever admit to anyone, even myself, that my feelings for her go well beyond the bounds of platonic friendship, I would've laughed in your face. I've barely allowed *myself* to entertain those thoughts, as she's so far out of my league as to be in another universe altogether. She's *Marlowe Fucking Sloane*, badass woman, Academy Award-winning actress and the most magnificent human being on the planet.

Sebastian Lowe, formerly of Compton, would have no business whatsoever setting his sights on a woman like her. I've never so much as considered doing anything about my overabundance of admiration for her. She's one of the bosses and one of Hayden's closest friends. The Quantum team puts up with me because I grew up with Hayden like brothers from another mother. But not for one second do I ever think I'm on the same plane with her or Hayden or any of them.

They're among the most accomplished people I've ever known. All I did was have the foresight to make a good friend as a kid and then *listen* to him when he got in my face and told me I was going to end up dead or in prison unless I went to work for him.

I took the job to shut him up—and my mother—and have been with him ever since, as he went from wannabe to Oscar winner. I'm so fucking proud of him and what he and Flynn have built at Quantum. There's nothing I wouldn't do for either of them, and I mean that sincerely. I'd fucking kill for them.

Only for Marlowe would I risk my job and my friendships with them. It's a lot to ask of Addie, who's married to Hayden, to keep this from him. I understand that, but Marlowe is calling the shots, and we have to respect her wishes.

"How do you propose to get her out of here undetected with everyone at the office?"

"I'll take her out tonight, after everyone is gone, and I'll be with her every minute between now and then."

Addie thinks about that. "I guess that'll work." She's obviously still reluctant to go along with my plan. "I'll come by tonight and bring anything you need. Just send me a list."

"I'll do that. Thank you."

She gives me an odd look. "Why're you doing this, Sebastian?"

I realize I need to be very careful here, lest I give away things I've never wanted anyone to know, especially to the always astute and intuitive Addison York Roth. "Because she needs help. I'm the lowest-profile member of our posse. No one would think to look for her at my place. It's really the best place for her to hide out and recover. Don't you agree?"

"Yes, I suppose that's true."

I can tell there's more she wants to say, but Dr. Breslow emerges from the room, closing the door behind her.

I move toward her. "How is she?"

"She's..." That the doctor is upset would be obvious to anyone. Breslow takes a deep breath and seems to summon her professional demeanor. "She gave me permission to update you both on her condition. As far as I can tell, nothing is broken. As I said to her, I can't tell if she has internal injuries without X-rays, but she's adamant about not being transported." Breslow glances at me and then quickly looks away. "I gave her a shot for the pain that'll knock her out for most of the day. She's going to be in pain when she wakes up, so I've written a script for painkillers that'll need to be filled and antibiotic ointment that'll need to be applied to the wounds on her back."

Addie takes the paper from her. "I'll take care of that."

"If there's any sign of blood in her urine or stool or pain that seems excessive, I want you to call 911 immediately. She should be in the hospital."

I answer for both of us. "We agree, but she was insistent."

"Just keep a really close eye on her, and if you sense something is seriously wrong, make that call."

"I will."

"Now, about the person who did this…"

"We're on that. We'll take care of him."

"I assume it'll be handled through proper, *legal* channels?"

"Of course." I tell her what she needs to hear, but I honestly can't promise that our treatment of Rafael Laurent will be entirely proper *or* legal.

"I'm in a difficult spot as a mandatory reporter. I should be calling the police."

"We appreciate your discretion, as always, Dr. Breslow," Addie says.

Breslow glances back at the closed door. "Marlowe Sloane is one of the smartest, toughest women I know. She says she doesn't want the cops involved, for obvious reasons, but no one should get away with what was done to her."

"We couldn't agree more," Addie says with the same fierceness that grips me.

"We'll be consulting with our security personnel about how best to handle this in light of Marlowe's request for privacy." I hope to set the doctor's mind at ease so she'll leave us to tend to Marlowe.

"All right, then. I'll check in with you later."

I shake her hand. "Thank you so much for coming."

"Of course."

While Addie walks her out, I go in to check on Marlowe, who's sleeping peacefully. As I study her beautiful, bruised face, I think about what the doctor said, fearing we're risking Mo's life by not taking her to the hospital for a more thorough examination. What if something terrible happens to her because we didn't do the right thing?

"Stop. Take a breath." I whisper the words to myself any time my lifelong struggle with anxiety threatens to suck me under the way it used to when I was younger and didn't yet know it for what it was. Years of medication and therapy have helped me combat it to the point that it has very little effect on my daily life anymore. However, in stressful situations such as this one, it hovers just below the surface, ready to rear its ugly head to remind me there're times when I'm powerless against its destructiveness.

This cannot be one of those times. Marlowe needs me, and I'm going to be there for her, no matter what it might cost me personally. She and the others at Quantum have done everything for me, and it's time to return the favor.

My hands roll into fists that I want to pound into that arrogant Frenchman's pretty face until he's not so pretty anymore. How *dare* he do this to her? If I wasn't so furious with him, I might feel sorry for him. When the Quantum team seeks retribution for Marlowe, which they will certainly do when they find out about this, the guy's life won't be worth living. That's the very least of what he deserves.

Addie returns from seeing the doctor out. "Is she asleep?"

"Yeah."

"I need to get back upstairs before I'm missed."

"Okay."

"You sure you've got this, Seb?"

I've never been more certain about anything in my life. "Yeah. I've got it covered."

"Call me if you need *anything*. Okay?"

"I will." I glance at her. "You gonna be able to keep it cool upstairs?"

"I'll do my best."

"I know this is hard for you, Addie."

"It's *horrible!*" She chokes on a sob. "How am I supposed to pretend like nothing is wrong when *everything* is? Hayden will take one look at me and know something's up." Swiping furiously at the tears on her cheeks, she makes a visible effort to pull herself together. "She's going to be all right, isn't she?"

"Eventually. We'll make sure of it."

She nods, takes another deep breath and turns on her three-inch heels to head for the stairs. I don't envy her the task of having to pretend everything is all right when it isn't.

I sit next to the bed where Marlowe is sleeping, determined to keep watch over her for as long as she needs me.

CHAPTER 4

Marlowe

Everything still hurts, and I have no idea where I am. My mouth is painfully dry, my eyes feel goopy and I have to pee—urgently. I make the mistake of moving, and the sound that comes out of me resembles that of an injured animal. It all comes back to me in waves of memory, things I'd much sooner forget than have to relive over and over again.

Where in the hell am I? The room is unfamiliar to me. I was in one of the private rooms at Club Quantum. So how did I get to wherever I am now? This room is painted a dark beige, and the quilt on the bed is red-and-tan striped. The sheets bear the fragrance of fabric softener.

A soft knock on the door precedes Sebastian poking his head in. "Thought I heard something."

"You heard me groaning. Where are we?"

"My place."

"How'd we get here?"

"I brought you last night after everyone left the office."

"Wow, I slept right through that."

"Whatever Dr. Breslow gave you knocked you out cold."

"Thank God for that." I try to sit up and nearly pass out from the pain that zips through every inch of me. Groaning, I sag back into the pillows.

"Take it easy, honey."

"I have to pee."

"I'll carry you."

"You don't have to do that."

"I know I don't. Let me help you."

I look up at him gazing down at me with worry in his soulful eyes that are so dark brown as to be almost black. I've always thought his eyes were beautiful, and the thick lashes women would kill for only make them more so. "Okay, thanks." I concede only because I have to go so badly, and I'm not sure I could actually get there on my own.

He's super gentle with me as he slides his arms under my back and legs before lifting me carefully, so carefully I barely feel the twinge of pain that comes from being moved. In the hall bathroom, he puts me down slowly and waits to make sure I'm steady before he lets go. "Will you be all right if I leave you alone?"

"I'll be all right. Thanks for the lift."

"Any time, sweetheart."

He's such a doll to take care of me this way. Some women would be taken aback by the big, burly, muscular body that bears its fair share of scars and tattoos. But anyone who knows him well can attest he's a teddy bear in wolf's packaging, and I adore him. We all do.

"Call me when you're ready for a lift back to bed."

"Will do."

"There's a toothbrush, toothpaste, hairbrush and that fancy face cream that Addie said you can't live without. Let me know if you need anything else."

I smile when I see the effort my friends have gone to in order to make sure I have what I need. Addie knows me so well, and the cream, which is four hundred dollars for three ounces, is at the top of my small list of must-haves. "Thank you."

He smiles and closes the door.

I take the most satisfying pee of my life and then, remembering what Dr. Breslow said, I take a quick glance at my output. I'm relieved not to see any sign of blood. Thank goodness. I know it was a big risk not to be seen at an ER, but that risk was worth taking to protect my privacy.

It's hard to explain to people who aren't famous what it's like to have to guard one's privacy so fiercely that you'd forgo emergency medical care to ensure your business isn't all over the web in a matter of minutes. That's how fast it can happen. I couldn't let Addie and Sebastian call 911.

All it would've taken was one person in the ER waiting room seeing Marlowe Sloane brought in after having been beaten up, and this incident would be catapulted around the world within seconds—perhaps even with photos that would stick to me forever. Every search of my name would yield those photos. *Forever.*

Ah, the joys of the digital age. If this story gets out, it's going to be on my terms and my timeline. No one else's.

I use one of the white washcloths Seb left out for me to wash my bruised face and then slather on the cream that feels like a cool oasis against the painful bruise on my cheek. While I ache all over, I don't feel as bad as I did yesterday, which is good news.

"You okay in there?" Seb asks.

"I'm good." I brush my teeth and hair and feel much more human by the time I open the door to find him leaning back against the wall across the hallway, ink-covered arms bulging with muscles crossed over his broad chest. Only because I know him so well can I immediately see that even though he keeps his expression neutral, he's extremely upset about what happened to me. There's rage in the eyes that usually convey only tenderness to me and the others he cares about.

"I'm okay, Seb. You can stand down."

"You're not okay, and I won't stand down until that son of a bitch is hurting every bit as much as you are. Perhaps more."

A fierce scowl accompanies the fiercely spoken words that make my heart flutter with love and gratitude for my amazing, incomparable friends. Thank God for them. After I lost my mom to cancer, I never expected to feel at home with anyone again. But then I met Flynn, and he made me part of the Godfrey family and, later, the family he and Hayden were building at Quantum. Thanks to them, I've never felt alone in this merciless world in which we live and work.

Because I can see that Sebastian is hurting, too, I take two steps to cross the hall, nudge his arms away and hug him, resting my head against his chest. "Thank you for taking care of me, for keeping my secrets and for wanting revenge on my behalf."

His arms encircle me cautiously, above and below the wounds on my back. "I want him dead. The others will, too."

"I know." And even though no one is going to kill him, I wallow in the knowledge that any of them would kill for me and not think twice about it. They love me that much, which makes me one lucky girl.

"We need to tell them what happened. Before they fire me for keeping this from them and Hayden divorces Addie."

"Neither of those things will ever happen."

"They'd want to be there for you, Mo."

"I know that, too. Give me one more day?"

"Whatever you need. You're the boss." He kisses the top of my head. "Are you hungry?"

"I could definitely eat something."

"Can you walk, or would you prefer a lift?"

"I can walk, but thank you for offering to tote me around."

"It's a pleasure to tote you anywhere you need to go."

He makes me smile when I wouldn't have thought it possible. He reminds me that no matter what happens—good, bad, evil—I'll always have my beloved friends, and there's comfort in knowing they're here for me. I take the arm he offers, and he escorts me, slowly, through the small condo to the open-concept living room, dining room and kitchen that looks down upon the enclave of Malibu and the Pacific Coast.

"This place is great!" I take in the rich leather sectional sofa, the glass tables and lamps made of brass compasses. "Why have I never been here before?"

"Because we hang out at the bigger houses now that there're so many of us."

"True. We have become an unruly mob." I wander to the windows to check out his view, which is fantastic. He's high enough up that he can see all of Malibu and the ocean. "I had no idea how great the view is from up here."

"I love it."

"I can see why."

"It's not as great as your oceanfront palace, but it works for me."

"My oceanfront palace, as you call it, comes with nonstop activity and people around. This is very tranquil."

"It is until the chick next door brings home her flavor of the week and they go at it until all hours."

"No way, really?"

"Uh-huh. Stick around for a couple of days and you'll get treated to her show. She's a screamer."

I laugh and then wince with regret. My body isn't up for laughing quite yet.

"What do you feel like eating? Addie stocked us up with all your favorites— organic eggs, goat cheese, tofu, spinach, Greek yogurt, that birdseed bread you all eat and organic rotisserie chicken."

My mouth waters when I hear my choices. "I'll do a goat-cheese-and-spinach omelet with birdseed toast. I can make it."

"No need. I gotcha covered." He gets busy in the kitchen, and I sit at the bar to watch him, noticing how comfortable he seems as he moves from the fridge to the stove.

His lips quirk with the start of a smile. "Whataya staring at?"

"I had no idea you were such a cook."

"Been taking care of myself for a lotta years." He glances at me. "You want coffee?"

"If it's not too much trouble."

"No trouble. Addie brought soy milk for you." He makes a face that lets me know what he thinks of soy milk and then makes enough coffee for both of us.

When it's finished brewing, he fills a mug for me and puts it on the counter with the soy milk and a spoon. "I don't have any stevia or unsugar."

I smile at his gruff tone. "That's okay. The soy milk is all I need."

"Ick."

"It's good!"

"No, it isn't." He dumps enough half-and-half into his coffee to turn it tan. After taking a sip, he smacks his lips. "Now *that* is how coffee is supposed to taste."

"I'm surprised you can still taste coffee with all that cream."

Scowling playfully at me, he flips the eggs, adds the goat cheese and butters the toast before plating the food and sliding it across the bar to me.

"This looks amazing. Thank you so much."

He leans his elbows on the bar. "I'm glad you feel like eating. You seem a lot better than you were yesterday."

"The drug-induced coma helped," I say between bites of what's quite possibly the best-tasting thing I've ever eaten. Wanting to make it last, I put down my fork and take a sip of coffee.

"I'm not sure if I should tell you that your phone has been going crazy with texts from the piece of shit. It's taken everything I have not to answer him."

That news turns my stomach, but I love the nickname Seb has given *him*. "What's he saying?"

"That what happened wasn't his fault and how is it fair that you kept such a big thing from him. Were you faking it every time you were in bed with him? Among other things."

"If I block him, will he be able tell that he's blocked?"

"Does he also have an iPhone?"

"Yeah."

"The texts he sends to you will change colors on his phone when you block him, so he'll know you're not getting them."

"Do it."

He slides the phone across the counter to me. "Punch in your code."

I push it back to him. "It's five-five-nine-five."

"Blocked." Then he does a double take.

"What?"

"He said he took pictures, and he's not afraid to use them if you're going to be a bitch about this."

"Is that right?" I struggle to remain calm. "He signed the NDA. He wouldn't dare."

"Wouldn't he? I feared he had a dark side, but if you'd asked me two days ago if he'd dare to whip you bloody and leave you in shock and hanging from the ceiling, I would've said no fucking way."

The way he says that—and how he looks at me—does something to me. A profound feeling of well-being overcomes me. "What the fuck are you smiling at?"

"You. You make me feel very safe."

"You are safe now. I won't let him get anywhere near you ever again."

"Why?"

His brows furrow with confusion. "Why what?"

"Why do you care so much?"

"Why do I care? You're my friend, Marlowe. And my boss. And a good person who didn't deserve to have this happen to you."

"It's very sweet of you to care."

"Would you care if someone beat the shit out of me?"

I give him a skeptical look. "As if that would ever happen."

"It's happened."

"*When* has it happened?"

"I used to get beat up a lot when I was younger."

I stare at him in disbelief.

He flashes the grin that I've often thought of as devastating, as in it would be devastating to be on the receiving end of that sexy grin. I was right. It is. "I wasn't always six foot three and two hundred twenty-five pounds of muscle, sweetheart."

It occurs to me that even after spending countless hours in his presence, I don't really *know* Sebastian Lowe that well, and I suspect that's by design on his part. "Who beat you up?"

"Other kids."

"Why?"

"Because I didn't do what they wanted me to."

"What did they want you to do?"

"Hurt people. Steal. That kind of thing."

"They beat you up because you wouldn't hurt people?"

"Something like that."

"And you refused, knowing you'd probably get beaten up for saying no to them?"

"I did."

"Who were these kids?"

"Doesn't matter now, does it? Eat your breakfast."

Clearly, he doesn't want to talk about it, but I do. I want to know who these kids were who would dare to hurt him because he refused to go along with their illegal behavior. And then I recall something I heard once about Hayden rescuing Sebastian from a gang and taking him off on location to get him out of town.

He's lucky they didn't kill him.

I take a bite and force myself to swallow.

The scars. I put down my fork, wipe my mouth with a paper napkin and take a sip of my coffee. I've seen the raised scars on his back and neck, but Hayden told me once that Sebastian doesn't talk about them. Is that what he meant by "beat up"?

"Not hungry?" he asks, brows furrowed.

"I'm getting a little full. Could I wrap up the rest for later?"

"Of course."

He opens a deep drawer full of neatly arranged plastic storage containers in various sizes and shapes.

"Look at you with grown-up storage containers."

"As opposed to what?"

"Mismatched takeout containers with lids that never fit?"

"I know what I'm getting you for your birthday. This was the best thing I ever bought myself."

"You surprise me."

He glances my way, his lips quivering with the start of a smile. "Why? Because I have containers with lids that fit?"

"That and you cook, and your place is really nice."

"You know what I get paid. What were you expecting? A hovel?"

Now I'm afraid I've offended him. "Not at all! I'm actually ashamed to confess that I never gave much thought to where you live or what your place would be like."

"Don't be ashamed. Why would you care about where I live? You're Marlowe Sloane."

He says that the way people always do, as if fame somehow excuses me from common courtesy. "Don't do that," I say softly.

"Don't do what?"

"Don't let me off the hook because people know who I am. We've been friends a long time. I should've visited your home before now."

"Quit being tough on yourself, sweetheart. You're a busy lady. You don't owe me anything."

"That's not true! I owe you the same courtesy you've always given me." Before I have a second to process the swell of emotion that comes from realizing I haven't been a great friend to him, a sob erupts from my throat.

He comes around the counter and wraps his arms around me. "Shhh." His hand rubs a soothing circle on my back, above where I'm cut. "I don't know where you're getting the idea that you haven't been a good friend to me. Where would I be without all of you guys at Quantum? Hayden gets credit for saving my life, but you and the others have given me a purpose and a family."

With my head on his chest, I take a deep breath to calm myself and discover he smells really, *really* good, like soap and laundry detergent and fresh air. He holds me for a long time, but since he doesn't seem to be in any rush to let go, I stay there for as long as he'll have me.

"Why don't we talk about what's really going on?"

It takes me a long time to find the words to articulate my thoughts. "I can't believe I let this happen."

Every muscle in Sebastian's big body goes tense as he pulls back from me, keeping his hands on my shoulders. "What did you say?" His fierce expression all but dares me to blame myself for what happened with Rafe.

"You all tried to tell me."

"That's utter bullshit, and you know it. This is *not* your fault. He's the one who thought it would be a good idea to beat a woman and leave her tied up overnight. In no way are you responsible for that."

"Maybe I am. We dated for months, and I never mentioned the BDSM until I sprang it on him."

"You could've sprung your desire for sex with cows on him, and that wouldn't have given him the right to do what he did to you."

I know he's being dead serious, but I can't stop the titter of nervous laughter that escapes from me.

"It's not funny!"

"Cows? Really?"

"You get the point!" He's fierce and furious and wonderful.

I smile, even though that makes my face hurt. "I get the point."

"Tell me you know this wasn't your fault." His voice is husky, his eyes full of raw emotion. In that fleeting second, I begin to wonder if he feels more for me than platonic friendship, if maybe he's always felt more for me and I didn't see it.

I'm in no condition today to go there, so I give him what he wants. "It wasn't my fault."

"Do you honestly believe that, or are you humoring me?"

"I believe that, even if I also believe that I could've handled things better."

He shakes his head and cradles my wounded face in his big gentle hands. "No qualifications. You did nothing wrong. You were sharing part of yourself with him. He should've been frigging honored to be breathing the same air as you, let alone being allowed into your private life."

As he gazes down at me, I have the strangest suspicion that he'd like to kiss me. I've kissed a lot of men in my time, and I'd like to think I can tell when someone wants to kiss me. I may be wrong, but before I can decide for certain, his hands are gone and he's stepped back to take care of the dishes.

The moment is gone, but I'm left feeling curious. What would it be like to kiss Sebastian Lowe?

CHAPTER 5

Sebastian

I can't believe I almost fucking kissed her. What the hell was I thinking? I wasn't, and that's the problem. Just because I'm providing her with sanctuary for a couple of days doesn't mean I have the right to touch her or kiss her or even *think* about doing either of those things.

Get it together, you asshole. She's *Marlowe Sloane,* for God's sake. And after what she's just been through, the last thing she needs is another guy bothering her.

Is it too early in the day for vodka?

Fuck, yes, it is.

She joins me at the sink with her plate and silverware, giving me a cute little hip check that nearly sends me flying because I wasn't expecting it.

That makes her laugh—hard—and God, if the sound of her trademark guffaw doesn't have me wishing I was a better man, that I was someone who'd be worthy of a fucking goddess like her. I'd willingly sign on for monogamy if I could be monogamous with her. All I can do is smile because that laugh, holy hell, it's amazing. I've always thought so, but being the one to make her laugh that way is the best kind of high.

"Feeling rather pleased with yourself, are you?" I ask when I return to my place by the sink.

"I wasn't expecting to be able to budge you, let alone send you flying." She starts laughing again.

I hope she never stops laughing.

"Didn't see it coming. Next time, you might hurt yourself."

That triggers a low snort and then more laughing.

She can laugh at me all day if she wants. As long as there's no more crying, I'm good with whatever she wants to do. I simply can't bear to see her cry.

"Are you done laughing at me?"

"For now."

I wash and she dries. It's all so domestic and easy, as if we've done this very thing a million times before. What would that be like, I wonder, to have someone like her around every day to call my own? I wouldn't know. I've never had anyone who belonged only to me, and I've liked it that way.

How can one morning with Marlowe have me thinking I might be missing out on something?

When we're done cleaning up, I toss the dirty dish towel in the laundry room that's off my kitchen. "We need to tell the others what happened."

"Not yet."

"It's a lot to ask Addie to lie to Hayden."

Her gaze drops to the floor. "I know, but I'm not ready for all that anger and testosterone."

"They'd want to be here for you." I tuck a stray strand of her glorious red hair behind her ear. "Just like you'd want to be there for them—the way you've always been there for them."

"I'm not ready for them to know yet. I just need another day." She looks up at me with bottomless green eyes. "Please?"

If she looked at me just like that and asked me to capture the sun for her, I swear I'd die trying. "Whatever you want, sweetheart. You're the boss."

"One more day, and then we can tell them. I'll tell them."

"Okay. What do you feel like doing?"

"I'd like to take a shower, if that's okay."

"Of course it is. Addie brought a bag for you last night. She said she thinks she got all the most important lotions and potions, but to let her know if she missed anything."

I'm horrified when her eyes again flood with tears. "What is it?"

"I'm just so lucky," she says softly. "To have such incredible friends."

"We're lucky to have you, too. Works both ways." I kiss her forehead. "Go take your shower. You'll feel better after."

"You think so? You think I'll ever feel good again?"

"You will. I promise." That's a promise I intend to keep, no matter what I have to do. She *will* feel good about herself again. Under no circumstances can we let that dirtbag Rafe win. I actually can't wait to tell Flynn and Hayden about this. I'm dying to see what they're going to do about it. One thing I know for sure is whatever they do will make that son of a bitch sorry he was ever born.

I'm looking forward to that.

Flynn and Hayden will close ranks around Marlowe and make Rafe's life a living hell, the same way they did when Jasper's asshole father tried to blackmail him. Quantum takes care of its own, and Marlowe is ours. With my thirst for vengeance profound, it's painful to keep this from the others, but I have to respect her wishes.

I'll give her one more day, and then I'm calling in the cavalry. I just hope I'll still have a job after they find out what I've kept from them.

After Marlowe showers, we spend the rest of the day on my deck, lounging in the sun. We trade sections of the morning edition of the *LA Times* and then work on the crossword puzzle together.

She's tucked in next to me on a single-sized lounge chair, but I only have the one, so when she crawled in next to me, I raised my arm and made her feel welcome, even if her closeness has me trying not to have a typical male reaction to the nearness of a gorgeous female who smells good enough to eat.

"What's a seven-letter word for vacation?"

I'm glad to see her engaged in something other than self-recriminations. "What else do we know?"

"First letter is a G and the fourth is an A."

"Getaway."

"Yes!" She bites her lip as she fills in the letters, her brows furrowed adorably in concentration. "You're good at this."

"I've been doing crosswords for decades."

"Another thing I never knew about you. What else is there?"

"I'll never tell. I'm an international man of mystery."

She flashes the toothy grin that made her a superstar. "I can't believe I'm saying this the day after I was beaten up, but today has been fun."

"For me, too."

"Don't you have to go to work?"

"The club is closed today, so I'm all yours."

"You don't have to babysit me, Seb. I'm okay."

"I know that, and I'm not babysitting you. I'm allowed to stay home with my friend. Someone else can do the cleaning and inventory this week. That's what employees are for." I texted Quisha, the trans woman I recently hired to help me manage the bar, and asked her to take care of the stuff I normally do, promising to pay her time-and-a-half for the extra hours.

"You like to do that stuff yourself."

I shrug. "Won't kill me to delegate once."

"Are you *sure*?"

"Are you making fun of my anal retentiveness, by any chance?"

"Would I do that?"

"Yes, I think you would."

She laughs, and once again the sound fills me with relief. If she can still laugh, she's going to be okay, and I *need* her to be okay.

I nudge her shoulder gently. "How you holding up?"

"I'm strangely fine, other than some aches and pains. Maybe it's denial or whatever you want to call it, but it happened, it's over, and I'm going to put it behind me where it belongs."

"I'm glad you're feeling okay, but what happened was traumatic and upsetting and painful, and you need to *deal with it* before you move on, or it'll come back to haunt you. Trust me on that."

"Sounds like you've been there, done that."

I shrug again. "Maybe."

"Did you deal with it?"

"Not the way I should have, and it fucked me up for a long time." Sometimes I think I'm still fucked up from shit that happened twenty years ago. I've begun to accept that I'll always be a little fucked up. Some things can never be fixed or forgotten, as much as we might wish that was possible.

"The thing that bothers me the most is that I didn't listen to the people closest to me who expressed serious concerns. Why didn't I listen to you guys?"

"Because you cared about him, Mo. No sense second-guessing it now. If you hadn't been given reason to be afraid of him, why would you be?"

"That's the thing." Her gaze is set on something in the distance. "There were signs that he wasn't what he seemed."

"Like what?"

After a long pause, she begins to speak in a low, soft tone that carries humiliation and regret that only enrages me more than I already am. "This one time, when we were in Paris, we got into a fight about me talking to a guy at a party. Rafe didn't like how much attention I gave him, but he was a young actor asking my advice, and I enjoyed talking to him."

"Nothing wrong with that."

"I didn't think so either, but he didn't see it that way. It got pretty heated, and he said…"

"What did he say?" My teeth are clenched together in an effort not to let her see how upsetting it is to hear that she's been mistreated. I honestly can't bear it, but she doesn't need to know that.

"He said I was an attention whore who could never get enough of the limelight."

All the breath in my body exits in one big whoosh that leaves me lightheaded from the pressing desire to find that son of a bitch and give him a taste of his own medicine. "Which, of course, you know is not true."

"I said as much, but when I tried to leave, he grabbed me by the hair and yanked me hard."

"Marlowe." I want to scream.

"He got right in my face and told me not to walk away from him when he was talking to me."

"What did you do?"

"I punched him hard in the gut."

"That's my girl."

"He wasn't expecting that, and it sent him reeling. I grabbed my purse and phone and got the hell out of there, leaving everything else behind. I went to a hotel and checked in, and made him grovel and beg for three days before I'd even talk to him. He swore to me nothing like that would ever happen again and apologized for what he'd said. He told me that the thought of losing me to some other guy made him crazy." She shakes her head. "I was a fool to go back to him again. I've played that character. Remember Gretchen in *The Other Woman*? I know how the story ends. What the hell is wrong with me, Seb?" She'd gotten an Academy Award nomination for playing a battered wife in the psychological thriller.

"Nothing." I'm so fucking furious that she could even ask that. "Not one thing is wrong with you." I gather her into my embrace and kiss the top of her head, breathing in the fresh, clean scent of her soft hair.

"There must be something wrong if I could let a man treat me like that and then take him back because he says pretty words to me in French and promises it'll never happen again. It *always* happens again. I *know* that."

"It's different when it happens to you. Sometimes you can't see the forest for the trees when you're in the thick of it."

"Or maybe we don't want to see what's right in front of us."

"That, too." I hate to concede that point, but this is one of those times when the truth just hurts. There's no way around it. It pains me to realize she kept this incident from her closest friends because she knew we didn't approve of him for her. Did we endanger her by not supporting her relationship? God, that possibility kills me.

We stay wrapped up in each other for a long time. Every second feels like a year to me because I want to hold her this way forever—and I've never once experienced that particular feeling before now. Usually, I'd be trying to wriggle my way out of something like this rather than holding on tighter. But a team of mules and twenty men couldn't convince me to move. Maybe if the house were on fire I could be compelled to do something else, but short of that, I'm staying put and hoping she won't be able to feel what her closeness, her softness, her sweetness are doing to me.

She can't ever know that I want her this way. I can just imagine how she'd look at me with empathy and pity as she lets me down easily. That'd be worse than wishing for something I can't have. I need to rein this in while I still can.

"Are you hungry?"

"Not really." Her hand makes lazy circles on my chest, inside the shirt I didn't bother to button. Every inch of my skin feels like it's been attacked by fire ants, and that's what finally breaks me.

Out of desperation, I cover her hand with mine to stop it from moving.

She raises her head off my shoulder to look at me. "What's wrong?"

"Nothing." The single word comes out sounding strangled. "Is it time for more pain meds?" I need to get up and get away from her before I do something that can't ever be undone.

"I'm not in pain."

I am… I'm dying a slow death from the drumbeat of desire that's more intense than anything I've felt before. I can't let this happen. "I gotta pee."

She shifts to let me up, and I move quickly, hoping she won't see the thick ridge of flesh making my shorts feel two sizes too small. I go inside and head straight for the bathroom attached to my bedroom, closing the door behind me and leaning back against it for a series of deep breaths intended to calm the storm inside me.

It doesn't work.

I can still smell her and feel her lush curves pressed up against me.

My dick is hard enough to pound nails, and there's only one thing that's going to give me relief at this point. I go to the bedroom door. "Hey, I'm going to grab a shower."

"Okay." She's still on the deck, otherwise known as the scene of the crime.

I return to the bathroom, shut and lock the door and begin tearing clothes off in my haste to find relief. Under the hot water, I turn my face up, wishing I could wash away the thoughts I'm having about my *friend*, my friend who was *beaten up* by her boyfriend and who is taking *sanctuary* with me.

Wrapping my hand around my cock, I give it a tight squeeze, wishing my erection would go the fuck away before it ruins everything. It's not easy to hide a hard ten-inch cock from anyone, let alone someone like Marlowe, who misses nothing. She probably knows what I'm doing in here, a thought that humiliates me, but not enough to stop what I'm about to do.

I squeeze a handful of shampoo into my palm and grasp my cock, stroking hard and fast to get this over with so I can get back to supporting my friend.

My gorgeous, sexy, amazing friend.

A deep groan escapes from my tightly clenched jaw. I'm disgusted with myself for being so weak, especially when I pride myself on always being in control after years spent spinning out of control. But something about her does it for me. She's always done it for me, if I'm being honest.

I've just never once allowed myself to entertain the possibility because she's so far out of my league as to be laughable. It's a joke to even think about anything more than friendship with her.

But as I stand in my shower, one hand propped on the tile wall as I stroke myself to orgasm, it seems I'm doing a lot more than thinking about the impossible.

What would it be like, I wonder, to spend every day like we did today, hanging out together, talking, laughing, fucking…

"*God.*" That's all it takes to send me right over the edge into absolute madness. I come as hard as I ever have, which is saying something when you consider that sex is my favorite hobby. If the thought of fucking Marlowe can give me the most powerful orgasm of my life, what would it be like to actually—

"Stop. Right now. Get yourself together." I need only think about how far I've come from the horrors of the past to know how critically important it is that I get this shit under control before I cross a line that can't ever be uncrossed. I owe everything I have to Hayden and the others at Quantum, who've not only given me a job, but have made me part of their inner circle. Marlowe is beloved by everyone inside that tight circle, and if it came down to a choice between her and me, I'd be on the losing end every time.

I need to remember my place and keep my filthy hands off her.

I use the shampoo for its intended purpose and finish cleaning up, trying not to notice that my dick is still halfway hard. For fuck's sake. Can I get a break here, please? I'm trying to do the right thing, and the least my body can do is fucking cooperate. In my bedroom, I put on clean clothes, and this time, I make sure my chest is covered with a T-shirt before pulling on the loosest cargo shorts I own, hoping they'll hide any random boners that might appear out of nowhere.

I can't even believe this is happening. It's been years since I've had to worry about rogue boners. Maybe I can convince Marlowe to call in the others sooner rather than later. Being alone with her isn't working out well for me.

Fuck you. It's not about you, you selfish son of a bitch.

While I agree with my conscience that it's not about me—me sporting wood around her isn't what she needs. She's had enough of guys who think only of themselves. She needs a friend who can keep it in his pants and not make it about him.

I stare at my reflection in the mirror, disgust warring with yearning. Now that I've let the genie out of the bottle and admitted to myself that I've had a low-burn thing for Marlowe Sloane for years, trying to jam the genie back in the bottle is fucking impossible. Be that as it may, no one else can ever know. Ever.

Get it together and stop being a dick with a hard-on. It's not about you.

I open the bedroom door, determined to carry on like the genie is still in the bottle, even if the little bastard is out and proud and making my life a living hell.

Marlowe has moved inside and is curled into a corner on the sofa. The bruises on her face are a startling reminder of what she's been through and why I need to keep the focus on her. Whatever she needs, whenever she needs it. That's what she'll get.

"Everything okay?" she asks, looking me over with eyes that see far too much. She probably knows exactly what I was doing in there.

"All good. You?"

She nods. "I called Flynn. He's calling the others, and they're coming over. I hope that's okay."

Thank Christ. "Of course it is."

CHAPTER 6

Marlowe

He's different. Whatever happened on the deck has him agitated and off-kilter, and what I think happened on the deck has *me* off-kilter and more than a little agitated myself. I only caught a glimpse as he took off, but I know a hard dick when I see one, and his dick was hard. For me.

Holy. *Shit*. That's all I've been able to think about since he made his getaway. Snort. There's that word again.

Getaway.

And then when he said he was taking a shower, well, damn. I know what that means.

Sebastian was hard for *me*.

Again—holy shit.

He's always been an enigma to me, a man who is respectful, polite, friendly but distant. He doesn't get "involved." I've seen him in action with other women at the club, and again, he's a respectful, professional Dom who takes care of the woman he plays with. He's also incredibly selective, unlike some guys who're less discerning. Seb has never been an "any vagina will do" kind of guy.

So the fact that he's having those thoughts about *me* is nothing short of astonishing.

The man is the literal definition of the term *sex on a stick*.

Tall, dark, handsome in a rough-around-the-edges kind of way with more tattoos than I can count on his arms, chest, back and neck. And... I lick my lips. He's got one of the biggest, most beautiful cocks I've ever seen outside of porn. The thing about belonging to a sex club with your closest friends is that you know things about each other that vanilla people don't know about their friends. It's not like I sit around thinking about the guys' junk, but let me tell you... Sebastian's is memorable.

I've seen it only twice, because he's private about his sex life most of the time. He's done only a couple of public scenes in the club. Both my glances were fleeting, but I've never forgotten the full majesty of aroused Sebastian.

If the talk amongst the subs who frequent the club can be believed, he also knows what to do with his God-given assets.

What the hell am I doing thinking about Sebastian and his God-given assets one day after I was beaten up and hog-tied by the man I thought I was in love with? What's *wrong* with me? Sebastian says there's nothing wrong with me, but there must be something if I'm thinking about his cock when Flynn, Hayden and the others are on their way over here so I can tell them what Rafe did to me.

They'll take one look at my bruised face and want to commit murder on my behalf.

"Seb."

"What, honey?"

Why does him calling me *honey* or *sweetheart* make me want to sigh? Probably because I know there's genuine affection behind the terms of endearment, and now I know there might be desire, too. *Shiver.* Focus! "When the guys see what he did, they're going to want to go after him. You're going to need to block the door."

"Yeah, I got it covered. Don't worry."

"I *am* worried. They're going to want to murder him."

"Right there with them, babe."

"You can't murder him. There're other ways we can ruin him without resorting to violence."

"Yes, there are, but you can't blame me or the others for wanting him to hurt as much as you are—or more so."

"That's not what *I* want. You have to help me make that clear to them."

"I'll do what I can."

"Do not let them out of here. That's an order." I give him my most severe Dominatrix stare, and he stares right back at me without blinking, one Dom to another.

"You're handing out the orders now, are you?" His tone is light and teasing, but his eyes are heated with something I've never seen before from him.

"On this one thing. You know Flynn and Hayden as well as I do, and you know I'm right."

"Yes, I do. I'll keep an eye on them. Try not to worry."

My stomach is in knots as I wait for the cavalry to arrive—and they'll come in hot. I have no doubt about that. I told Flynn only that something happened with Rafe and I'm at Sebastian's. I asked him to let Hayden and the others know. He said, "I'm on my way."

Everyone is in town this week, which means I'll be surrounded by loving, concerned friends.

"What made you call Flynn?"

"I got a text from Addie that Hayden knows she's keeping something big from him, and unless I want to see her in divorce court, I need to let them know what's going on." I look down at my phone when it lights up with a text from Addie.

Thank you. We're on our way.

"What difference does it make if it's today or tomorrow, right?"

"It should be when you want it to be, not when Addie wants it to be."

"It's fine. I know how Hayden can be when he gets something in his head."

"He's like the proverbial dog with a bone when he senses something is up. I can only imagine the pressure Addie must've been under if she actually texted you."

"I know."

He sits next to me and reaches for my hand.

I'm immediately on full alert. Even my nipples tingle with awareness of him.

"You okay?"

"Sure, never better."

"You don't have to pretend with me."

"I don't?"

He shakes his head. "You can keep it real with me. You don't have to be Marlowe Sloane the superstar. You can just be Marlowe Sloane, wonder woman."

It's quite possible that's the sweetest thing any guy has ever said to me. "Thank you." My voice is gruff, infused with emotion. "You have no idea how much it means to me that you've stepped up for me the way you have."

"Please don't thank me for doing what any good friend would do for another."

"I will thank you for sticking your neck out the way you did. I'll be out of your hair soon. I'm sure Addie will want me to come home with her."

"Stay."

My eyes go wide as I stare at his arresting, compelling face. His eyes are dark and gorgeous, his cheekbones prominent and his lips just the right size. He's often mistaken for the actor Jeffrey Dean Morgan, which I can totally see, even if Sebastian says there's no way he looks like him. "Why?" I feel like I did the time I fell off the slide at school and had the wind knocked out of me.

"No one would think to look for you here. If the piece of shit does something he shouldn't, the press will descend on your place, Flynn's, Hayden's, Jasper's, Kristian's. They'd never think to look for you here."

The possibility of Rafe releasing photos or anything else about me has my stomach turning with nausea. He wouldn't dare. Would he? "That's true." It's no picnic being a celebrity these days, no matter how great it might seem from the outside looking in. The internet and social media have made it a nightmare in many ways. "You don't think he'll release the photos, do you?"

"He'd be a fool to do that. It'd be career suicide for one thing. For another thing, revenge porn is illegal in California."

"Obviously, he doesn't care too much about his career in the first place if he'd do what he did to me. He has to know that Quantum will pull its business from his company."

"I suspect that's the least of what Quantum will do."

A pounding sound echoes through the condo.

"Sebastian! Open up!"

"Speaking of Quantum." He smiles. "That'll be Flynn. You ready for this?"

"As ready as I'll ever be."

He kisses my forehead. "If they get to be too much, let me know and I'll kick their asses out."

"I will. Thank you."

"You got it." He opens the door and stops Flynn from charging inside by putting his hand on Flynn's chest. "Take it easy."

Flynn starts to snap back at him, but then takes a look at Sebastian's face, which must be set in that ferocious thing he does when he or someone he loves is threatened. I've seen it before and thought that I wouldn't want to cross him when he's wearing that expression. Apparently, it works on Flynn, too.

"I would like to see Marlowe. Please."

Sebastian steps aside to admit Flynn and his wife, Natalie, who follows him in, moving a little slower than her husband due to her pregnancy.

Flynn gasps when he sees my bruised face. "Mo." He drops to his knees next to me and takes my hand. "Oh my God. I'm going to fucking murder him."

"No, you're not."

"Yes, I really am."

Natalie places a hand on his head and gives a gentle tug of his dark hair. "Stop it."

I love, love, *love* the way she manages him. And I love, love, *love* how much he loves me. I reach for him, and he comes to me, wrapping his arms around me.

"You gotta let me kill him." His voice is thick with unshed tears.

"No."

"Then let me ruin him."

"Please do."

"With pleasure." He pulls back from me, brushes the hair from my face and takes a closer look at my bruises as well as the rope burn on my neck. A nerve in his cheek pulses with tension. "Where else are you hurt?"

"My ribs and back, but I'm okay."

"Did he…"

"No, he didn't."

"When did this happen?"

"Night before last."

"Why didn't you call me?"

"I needed a day to get my head together before I told everyone. Seb has been great. Please don't be angry with him."

"All I care about is that you're all right. That's the only thing that matters."

"I'm pissed off, but I'm all right. I swear."

"I'm glad you're pissed off, because I'm fucking furious. That he would dare to lay a finger on you…"

"Seb said the same thing."

Hayden comes rushing in through the door Seb left propped open. He takes one look at my face and Flynn on his knees next to me and lets out a roar that can probably be heard for miles.

Addie is behind him, out of breath from running to catch up.

Hayden spins around as if to leave, but Addie stands firmly in his way. "I told you not to do exactly what you're doing."

"Addie—"

"Hayden! Stop it. Right now."

"Hayden, come here." I extend my hand to him.

Flynn and Nat move so Hayden can get to me.

He takes my hand, and I give it a yank, bringing him down on the sofa next to me.

"I'm okay."

"He… I can't… I'm going to…"

I smile. "I'm *okay.*"

"Mo…"

"I know." I reach for him and hug him, feeling blessed to have these incredible men as two of my closest friends, the brothers I never had. There's nothing they wouldn't do for me, which they've just proven yet again by the way they reacted to seeing me injured.

"I knew I hated that son of a bitch for a reason," Hayden says.

"She says we're allowed to ruin him, but we can't murder him," Flynn tells his partner.

Hayden scowls fiercely. "He's going to be sorry he ever met us and that he ever fucked with you."

"He texted me to say he has pictures and isn't afraid to use them. I made him sign the NDA, but who knows what he'll do."

"Wait…" Hayden glances at Addie and then back at me. "This happened at the club?"

"Yes. I never should've taken him there. I know that now—"

"Marlowe."

One word from Sebastian shuts me down.

His intense gaze connects with mine. "You did nothing wrong."

I find myself staring at him, drinking in the words and the fierce way he says them.

"You did nothing wrong." He says it more softly the second time, but his eyes give away the torment inside him, making me see how upsetting it is to him that I'd blame myself in any way.

"He's right." Hayden squeezes my hand. "There's only one person to blame here, and we're going to make him pay, Mo. You can count on that."

I lean my head on Hayden's shoulder and release a deep breath. If I can't look away from Sebastian, oh well. Who could blame me?

CHAPTER 7

Sebastian

Jasper, Ellie, Kristian, Aileen, Emmett and Leah arrive over the next half hour, and Marlowe has to go through it again for each couple. I can tell that she's exhausted and emotionally drained, but she continuously assures each of our friends that she's all right. She takes care of them when they should be taking care of her, but they're so upset by what's happened that they can't pretend otherwise.

Leah is in tears as she sits next to Marlowe, holding her hand. The younger woman has fully embraced her position as Marlowe's assistant and has made herself indispensable to Mo.

With Marlowe surrounded by the women, I head for the kitchen, in need of a beer. I'm taking my first sip when I turn to find Hayden has joined me.

"What the hell were you thinking keeping this to yourself for more than a day?"

"I was doing what she asked me to do, the same thing you would've done if you'd been the one to find her bruised, bloody, hog-tied and barely conscious in the dungeon."

"Jesus." Hayden runs his hands through his hair, tugging viciously. "I'm sorry. I don't mean to come at you. It's just…"

"What? You don't think I'm the right one to take care of your precious Marlowe? Here's a newsflash for you, *boss man*. She's precious to me, too. So back the fuck off." He hates when I call him that, and I know it, but I do it anyway because he's pissing me off.

I'm prepared for him to come back at me, because that's what we do—what we've always done—but rather, he tips his head and gives me a weird look.

"What?" I rub my cheek, wondering if there's something on my face.

"What's going on, Seb?"

Fuck. Proceed with caution... "Other than our mutual friend getting beaten up by her asshole boyfriend?"

"Yeah, other than that."

"Nothing is going on."

"Why'd you bring her here? Why not my house? Addie is one of her closest friends."

"She wanted a minute before she had to face you and Flynn and the others. I brought her here so she could have some privacy."

"From *us*? We're her *family*!"

"And I'm not?"

"That's not what I meant!"

"Isn't it?"

Addie comes into the kitchen, loaded for bear. "She can *hear* you two fighting, so maybe you could table this argument and have it another time?"

"Sorry," I mumble. "Your husband is being an asshole."

"He gets like that sometimes."

Hayden scowls furiously at his wife.

"What? You do. This is no time to be questioning why anyone did what they did during a *crisis*."

"I'll deal with you when we get home," Hayden says.

Addie rolls her eyes. "Spare me."

I snort with laughter as Hayden's wife makes him her bitch. She's absolutely perfect for him, and I would've hand-chosen her to tame my ferocious friend.

He glares at me. "Shut the fuck up."

"You shut the fuck up."

"Okay, children." Addie gets between us, holding up her hands. "Make yourselves useful and order some food for this crowd. Hurry up about it." She turns and leaves the room.

Hayden pulls out his phone.

"Whipped," I say under my breath, earning an elbow to the gut from him.

"And proud of it. You oughta try it."

I rub my poor gut. "That'll be the day."

"Tell me the truth," he says without looking up from his phone.

"About what?"

"You got a thing for Marlowe?"

I owe this man my life, and I mean that sincerely. He saved me from myself. In all the years I've worked for him, I've never once lied to his face. Until now. "Shut up, Hayden."

He glances up at me. "That's not a no."

"Aren't you supposed to be ordering food?"

"Already done. I texted Diego's and told them to send us everything, enough for ten, along with margarita stuff and more beer."

"Good call. She'll love that." Marlowe's adoration of Mexican food is well documented, and it's the only thing she's capable of cooking.

"Are you going to answer the question or continue to dodge, which tells me everything I need to know?"

I look him dead in the eyes. "I'm doing for her exactly what she'd do for me, what any of us would do for each other. Don't make it into something it's not."

"I'm not. Are you?"

"I say this with all due respect. *Fuck. Off. Hayden.*"

The bastard cracks up laughing. "I see how it is."

"You don't see anything, and if you don't shut the fuck up, I'm going to throw you out of my house."

"What*ever.*"

He knows I won't actually do it, but he should know that I want to. I take a step closer so I'm right in his face. "Knock it off. I mean it. She's very fragile right now, and the last thing she needs from her closest friends is unnecessary rumors or gossip."

"Easy, killer. I'm not starting rumors. I was merely asking my friend a question."

"Sure, that's all you were doing. Rather than grilling me, why don't you start thinking about what we're going to do about the son of a bitch who hurt her."

"Oh, I'm thinking about that. I'm definitely thinking about that, and I believe we'll start with a call to his boss to let him know we're more than willing to move Quantum's business to another distribution company in France unless they get rid of him immediately."

"That'd be a good place to start. Then what?"

"Then we go after him personally. I'm going to have Gordon investigate the living shit out of the guy."

"Already did that," Flynn says when he joins us.

The two of us stare at him in disbelief.

"You did not." Hayden keeps his voice down so we won't be overheard.

"You bet your ass I did. I knew there was something wrong with that guy. I *knew* it. I asked Gordon to look into him months ago."

"What did you find?" Hayden asks.

"His ex-wife accused him of roughing her up during their divorce."

I'm incensed. "And you never said anything to Marlowe? What the fuck, Flynn?"

"I was afraid she'd be pissed I had him investigated. I blame myself for this. I should've told her."

"It's not your fault, Flynn." Hayden looks at me as he tries to comfort Flynn. "You were looking out for her."

Flynn runs both hands through his hair, frustration coming off him in waves. "I thought the guy was a jackass, but I never thought he'd have the audacity to hurt someone as powerful in the industry as Marlowe is."

I have to acknowledge that I felt the same way. "None of us thought he'd have the balls to mess with Mo."

"She seemed so happy with him. I didn't want to fuck with that. And now look at her." Flynn's voice breaks. "I want to find him and do the same thing to him that he did to her."

"So do I," Hayden says, "but we're not going to do that. Do you hear me?"

Flynn looks down at the floor, every muscle in his body tense.

"Flynn. Do you hear me?"

"Yeah, yeah, I hear you."

"Do you?"

"Yes! I won't do it. But I want to. Very badly."

"We all do, but we can't let him have the upper hand by damaging ourselves in the process of damaging him. There are other ways."

"What kind of photos does he have?" Flynn asks.

I tighten my grip on the countertop behind me. "Of her after he beat her up. He sent her one to make sure she keeps her mouth shut."

Flynn sucks in a sharp deep breath, and I immediately fear he's about to take back his promise not to personally go after Rafe.

"He signed the NDA before she took him in," I add, "but he has the photos and told her he's not afraid to leak them if she decides to come after him. Right after he sent that text, we blocked him."

Flynn crosses his arms and silently seethes. There's no other word for it. I start to worry that he's going to actually blow a gasket. "If he's already left the country, and he probably has, we'll be hard-pressed to enforce that NDA, which, of course, he knows. We need to move fast to ensure that doesn't happen."

Kristian comes into the increasingly crowded kitchen, cell phone in hand. "I want to call Pierre Marchand." He's the president of Cirque, the company Rafe works for.

Hayden nods. "Do it."

I check the time. It's almost five o'clock here. "It's the middle of the night in France."

"Who cares?" Flynn asks. "We need to put a lid on this before he does something with those photos." He looks to Kristian. "Make the call."

As Kristian puts through the call and waits for Pierre to answer, the rest of us coexist in tense silence. From the other room, we hear the others talking to Marlowe. The sound of her distinct laugh calms me somewhat. If she can laugh after what she's endured, then I can calm the fuck down and help do what needs to be done to protect her.

"I know it's the middle of the night," Kristian says, "but we've got a situation that requires your immediate attention." He goes on to tell Pierre about what happened between Rafe and Marlowe, providing chilling details that make me sick all over again. "Yes, we're sure it was him. She said it was him, and don't you dare even suggest that she's lying. He's texted her with photos of her after the assault and threatened to release them to the media, despite the fact that he's under an NDA. What you need to be doing is telling me, *right now*, what *you're* going to do about it—and I encourage you to think before you speak if you'd like to continue working with our company."

Quantum is Pierre's most profitable client, and Kristian's statement has the desired effect. Kristian ends the call with assurances that Pierre will immediately meet with Rafe, who he confirmed is back in France, to terminate his employment and to make clear that if those photos are released, Pierre will see the man prosecuted and his name ruined in the industry. Perhaps that ought to happen anyway, but it would require Marlowe pressing charges, which she's indicated isn't going to happen.

"We need to report this to the authorities here," Kristian says.

"I agree," Hayden replies.

"No." The three of them look at me. "Her privacy is more important to her than seeing him charged, and she has the right to make that call, even if we don't agree."

My comment is met with total silence that puts me immediately on edge. They may be my closest friends, but they're also my bosses. Though they never pull rank on me, I have no idea how they'll react to my line in the sand on Marlowe's behalf.

"He's right," Hayden finally says. "It's not our call. It's hers."

"And she made that call yesterday when she refused to be transported to the hospital or call the cops," I tell them. "We have to respect her wishes."

"What's going on?" Marlowe asks when she comes into the kitchen.

The rest of us have to squeeze closer together to make room for her.

No one says anything.

"Whatever you're planning to do, stop it right now. I'll take care of it."

"We already did one thing," Kris says.

"What?"

"I talked to Pierre and told him the scumbag has photos he's threatening to release."

"That's fine, but nothing else. I want to do this my way."

"You can't let him get away with this, Mo," Flynn says.

"I have no intention of letting him get away with anything, but you have to back off and give me room to breathe and think. I know it's very upsetting for all of you to see me hurt, especially after you tried to warn me about him."

"No one is thinking about that." Hayden sounds as pained as the rest of us feel.

"Why not? I would be if I were you. I didn't listen to you guys when you told me you had a bad feeling about him."

Flynn clears his throat. "We didn't think he was good enough for you."

"Well, you were right, and I'm sorry I didn't listen when you tried to tell me that."

I can't bear to hear her blaming herself for any of this. "You don't have to apologize to anyone. It's not your fault this happened."

"He's right, Mo." Flynn puts an arm carefully around her shoulders and draws her into his embrace. "We didn't like the guy, but we never thought he'd have the balls to fuck with someone who could ruin him in the industry."

She tips her head to lean against his shoulder. "Thank you all for caring so much. It means a lot to me."

"We love you," Hayden says bluntly.

Her eyes fill with tears that gut me. God help that guy if he walked through the door right now. I'd have to be stopped from killing him myself, if for no other reason than he made the indomitable Marlowe Sloane cry.

A knock on the door takes me out of those unsettling thoughts. Murder is the last freaking thing I need to be contemplating. I left behind the desire to maim and kill when Hayden dragged me away from people who were trying to turn me into a ruthless killer. They hadn't succeeded yet, but it would have only been a matter of time when Hayden intervened.

Hayden goes out to get the delivery, with Flynn and Kristian following him. I glance at Marlowe. "Are you okay?"

"Yep. You?"

"I'm good."

"I hate that I've put you all through this. I know how hard it is for everyone else when one of us is hurt."

"It is hard because we love you, and we never want anything bad to happen to you."

"I feel the same way about you guys, but we've all lived long enough to know it's unrealistic to expect that nothing bad will ever happen."

"I still like to hope for the best." Hope was the only thing I had back in the darkest of days when I was trying to decide what kind of man I was going to be. I clung to tiny glimmers of hope like life rafts in a stormy sea, and they got me through the worst of times.

Hayden comes in carrying a box. "Let's eat."

I get plates and silverware, and we set up at my dining room table, which has never had so many people using it at one time. I like the way my family looks there. Only my parents and Aileen's kids are missing. Maybe next time I can get them here, too, and then everyone I care about will be gathered in my home. Wouldn't that be something? Perhaps I can volunteer to host the next holiday get-together.

We eat, we drink the margaritas that Marlowe loves (the virgin variety for Natalie and Ellie), and we laugh—a lot. Everyone makes an effort to keep things as normal as they can for her sake, but underneath the merriment, the tension is ever present.

A little after eight, when Marlowe begins to fight back yawns, Addie puts an arm around her. "Do you want to pack your stuff and come home with us?"

"I, um… Well…" She glances at me. "I think I'll stay here. I've got everything I need, and Seb made a good point that no one would think to look for me here. If the piece of shit releases the photos, at least the media won't be able to find me."

"If he releases those photos, I'll kill him with my bare hands," Hayden says.

"No, you won't," Addie and Marlowe say in stereo and then share a smile.

"What's your plan, Mo?" Flynn's entire being radiates pent-up rage and the same thirst for vengeance we're all feeling.

Marlowe gives herself a minute to collect her thoughts. "When I first started seeing Rafe, Teagan Daily reached out to me by text. She said she wanted to talk to me about him."

"Didn't she date him a couple of years ago?" Jasper asks.

"Yes."

Addie absorbs this info with her usual intensity. "What did she have to say?"

Marlowe looks down at her hands, which are folded in her lap. "I never replied to that text or the one I got from Veronica Jones, who was also with him for a time about five years ago. I didn't want to hear his exes talk shit about him. But now I think it's probably time I got back to them."

Natalie, who's sitting on the other side of Marlowe, puts her hand over Marlowe's in a silent show of support.

"Maybe if I'd replied to them or listened to you guys, none of this would've happened."

"Don't go there, Mo," Ellie says gently. "You cared about him, and he hadn't given you any reason not to."

"There were signs. Here and there. I chose to ignore them, which is the part that pisses me off the most. It's not like this was my first rodeo. I know better than to ignore the signs or to let a handsome, charming man convince me that the signs don't matter." She shakes her head. "I'm mad at myself more than anything."

I can't bear to hear her say that. "I think Marlowe's probably had enough for today. She needs a good night's rest."

Thankfully, everyone takes my not-so-subtle invitation to leave. They quickly clean up the remnants of dinner, fill the dishwasher and stash the leftovers.

"There's enough for dinner tomorrow night," Aileen tells me.

"Thanks."

She squeezes my arm. "If you guys need *anything*…"

I nod. "Will do."

"You sure you don't want to come with us?" Addie asks Marlowe again.

"I'm sure. Sebastian has made me very comfortable in his lovely home."

Hayden gives me one of his famous looks, and I give it right back to him, daring him to say something that'll give me no choice but to punch that smug grin off his face.

Fortunately, Addie gives him a shove toward the door, saving me the trouble of sore knuckles.

Ellie, Aileen, Kristian and Jasper give Marlowe careful hugs on their way out, leaving Emmett, Leah, Flynn and Nat.

Emmett hugs Marlowe. "If you change your mind about pressing charges, let me know."

"Thanks, Em. I will."

Leah, who's teary-eyed again, embraces Marlowe gently. "I'll call in the morning to see what you need."

"Sounds good."

"Call if you need anything," Flynn says. "Day or night. I'll be here as fast as I can."

She leans in to hug him. "I will. I promise."

I close the door behind him and Natalie and turn the dead bolt, which I don't usually bother to do. I want Marlowe to feel safe here, and that lock makes a loud clicking noise that lets her know no one's getting through that door unless we want them to.

"Thanks for calling it a night." Marlowe curls up in a corner of the sofa and then winces.

"I could tell you were getting tired." I sit next to her, careful not to jar her in any way. "What hurts?"

"My back."

"Dr. Breslow prescribed antibiotic ointment to put on the cuts. You want me to do that?"

"In a bit, maybe."

"How about another drink?"

"Maybe a glass of wine. I've had enough tequila."

"Coming right up."

Ellie brought a bottle of the chardonnay they all love. I open that and pour a healthy glass on top of a couple of ice cubes. I grab a beer for myself before returning to the living room.

"Here you go."

"Thank you—for this and everything. You've let me completely overtake your home and your life."

"My home is a lot homier with you here." The words are out of my mouth before I take so much as a second to contemplate the deeper implications of saying such a thing to her. I'm not one to show my cards like that, and she knows it.

She raises a brow. "Is that right?"

"Yep." Too late to turn back now. "I like having you here."

She looks at me with affection that does weird things to my insides. "I like being here."

Now would be a really good time to remind myself she thinks of me as a friend and nothing else. *Nothing else.* Maybe if I say that to myself enough times, my cock will get the message that his services are not needed here.

She sips from her wineglass, seeming a million miles away from me, lost in thought.

"You want to talk about it?" I wish I had the right to brush the strand of red hair back from her face, but I don't have the right to touch her. Not that way. Not any way.

It takes everything I have to keep my hands to myself when all I want to do is touch her, hold her and assure her that I'll always be here for her.

CHAPTER 8

Marlowe

I'm glad it's just me and Seb now. I loved seeing the others, but they're so distraught over what happened, and it upsets me to know I'm the cause of that. Seb is upset, too. I know he is, but he does a better job of keeping it hidden from me than the other guys did, and I appreciate that.

"You can tell me anything," he says. "I hope you know that. It'll never leave this room."

"I do know that." After a pause, I speak somewhat hesitantly, not sure I should make this particular confession. "I was thinking earlier, when everyone was here, about how I got caught up in the outbreak of love going on all around us."

"How so?"

I take another drink of wine, needing all the fortification for this confession that I can get, and place the glass on the table. "The first time Flynn ever brought Natalie to meet me... It was Golden Globe weekend last year, and they stopped by when he was showing her around LA. I could tell the first time I saw them together that he'd found his *one*, you know?"

"Yeah, they were pretty intense from the get-go."

"I was so jealous, Seb." I hate to admit that to even myself, let alone someone else.

"Did you... I mean, with Flynn..."

"No, no. We tried that once, and it was ridiculous. It wasn't that I wanted him. I wanted *them*. I wanted what they had, that undeniable something you can't put into words, but when you see it, you know it. And then it was Hayden and Addie, Jasper and Ellie, Kris and Aileen. Hell, even Leah has found her one with Em, and I'm *eleven years* older than her."

"How's that fair?"

"Right?" I love that he gets it. "Please don't think for one second I'm not happy for all of them."

He puts his big hand over mine, and my skin sizzles from the heat of him that warms the cold places inside me. "I know you are. *They* know you are."

"I hope so."

"They do."

"When Rafe came along, I saw my chance. He was handsome and charming and romantic, whisking me away to his penthouse apartment in Paris for long weekends and to Provence for his best friend's wedding. I got caught up in the fairy tale, and I've *never* been that girl. I became someone else with him, someone I don't even recognize."

"You wanted to make it work, Mo. People do crazy things when they're in love."

I snort with disdain. "I wasn't in love with him."

"No?"

Shaking my head, I turn my palm up and curl my fingers around his, wanting to keep him and the comfort that comes with him close. "I was in love with the *idea* of him, which was shattered when he punched me in the face. Actually, if I'm being truthful, it was shattered long before that, but I chose not to see it. That's the part I'm having the hardest time with. I *knew* he was no good, and I stayed because I wanted the goddamned fairy tale."

"You're no different from anyone else. Hell, I've even felt that way a few times recently, seeing how happy everyone around me is and wondering what's wrong with me that I've never come close to having what they do—or even wanting it."

"There is nothing wrong with you."

He grunts out a laugh. "Yeah, there is."

"No, there isn't. You're the most faithful, loyal, giving friend any of us could ever hope to have, and hello? Do you own a mirror in this place?"

His brow furrows with confusion as he rubs a hand over his jaw. "Why? Did I miss a spot shaving?"

I bust up laughing when I realize he has no idea that I'm trying—and failing—to pay him a compliment. "No, silly. You're ridiculously hot."

He seems momentarily speechless. "You think so?"

I roll my eyes. "*Everyone* thinks so."

I'm stunned to see a flush of color creep up his neck. Is Sebastian Lowe actually *blushing*? "Nuh-uh. Shut up."

"I won't shut up. I see the way women—and men—stare at you at the club."

"They stare at me because they want another drink."

"No, Seb, they stare at you because they want to take you—and your legendary cock—for a ride."

"*Marlowe!*" He actually sputters. "Oh my God!"

I crack up laughing. I laugh so hard that my ribs hurt, but I can't stop. While I'm hysterical with laughter, he just stares at me in disbelief.

And then I see that his legendary cock is hard and the laughter dies on my lips, replaced by something much more elemental.

I'm completely fucked up in the head if I can get beaten up by one guy and a couple of days later feel full-on desire for another, this time one who's been a close friend for years. I won't say that I've never thought of Sebastian that way, because I don't usually lie to myself. Rafe was a notable exception. Of course I've thought about Sebastian that way. But I've never once thought to act on it out of respect for our friendship.

But now...

"Have you ever, you know, thought of me that way?" God, could I be any more awkward?

He stares at me, his dark eyes boring holes in me. "Marlowe." His voice is barely a whisper as he says my name.

"Oh God, I'm sorry. I don't know why I said that. I'm such a fucking mess. Ignore me."

His hand cups the uninjured side of my face, his thumb stroking my cheek and setting off fireworks inside me. "Yeah, I've thought about you that way. I've thought about it a lot."

I lick lips that've gone dry as unbuttered toast. "You... you have?"

He leans in super close to me, until his lips are a fraction of an inch from mine. "Yes."

We stay like that, suspended in time and breathing the same air, for what feels like hours when I know it's only a few seconds. His hand drops from my face, breaking the intense moment.

I want to beg him to come back.

"I can't be your rebound, Marlowe, as much as I'd love to act on what I feel when I'm with you."

Ignoring the rebound part of the equation for right now, I force myself to look at him. "What do you feel when you're with me?"

"Things."

"Care to elaborate?"

"Nope." He taps his finger to my forehead. "You need to get yourself sorted and healed before you do anything else."

I know he's right, but sitting here next to him, discovering he feels "things" for me, I find that I'm as sorted as I've been in a long time.

Sebastian wants me. What else do I need to know?

"What're you grinning like a loon about?" he asks, his tone gruff.

"You *like* me."

He rolls his eyes. "This isn't middle school, Mo."

"Believe me, I know."

"How about we put some of that medicine on your back and get you tucked in for the night?"

I'm oddly disappointed, even though I have no right to be. "Are you letting me down easy?"

His eyes flash with something dangerous and wild, and I feel like I've touched lightning or something equally powerful. "I'm putting you on ice." He bounces his index finger off my nose. "For now. Talk to me on the other side of this crap with the piece of shit, and we'll see what's what. But until you give yourself some time to deal with what happened, you shouldn't be having this conversation with me or anyone else."

Even though he's right, I don't appreciate being told what to do.

"Hey."

"What?"

"Look at me."

I force my gaze to meet his.

"If this hadn't happened with him, I'd be all over it—and you—in a fucking heartbeat. I'd have you in my bed so fast, your gorgeous head would spin. This is *not* a rejection. It's a time-out."

As I look into eyes darker than midnight, I can see the fierce internal battle he's fighting to do the right thing, to be my friend and not take advantage of my fragile emotional state. Except, I'm not feeling particularly fragile. I'm feeling something else, something I can't put into words. Whatever it is, it's powerful and determined and the absolute opposite of fragile.

"We should put some medicine on your back. Dr. Breslow said we need to stay on it to avoid infection."

I don't want anyone touching or even seeing the wounds on my back, but I can't do it myself and he's been nothing but gentle with me since he found me the other morning. "Okay."

He stands and offers a hand to help me up.

I curl my fingers around his large hand and wince when my ribs and abdomen fight back against the movement. A memory of Rafe, out of control and enraged, raining blows down on my body, has me shuddering in revulsion.

"Easy." Sebastian puts his arms around me and holds me until the trembling subsides.

"I'm okay."

"No, you're not, but you will be." When I'm steadier, he leads me into the guest room. "Get comfortable."

I stretch out on the bed, facedown, arms wrapped around a pillow. My entire body is tense in anticipation of pain. Flashes of memory bring back the excruciating lash of the whip, and the harsh words.

"Is this what you like to do to other people? How do you like it? Is this what gets you off, you sick fuck?"

The whip broke my skin, but his words broke something much deeper. In all my years as a practicing Domme, I've never once broken the skin of one of my subs. I'm not about injuring people. No, my kink is all about pleasure and satisfaction, especially that of my partner. But Rafe hadn't given me a chance to explain. No, he'd taken one look at the dungeon and had lost his shit.

The bed dips when Seb sits next to me. "Ready, sweetheart?"

I bite my bottom lip—hard—and nod, hoping I can get through this without falling apart.

Sebastian

It hurts me to hurt her. I can't bear it, but her wounds must be cared for, so I force myself to press on. I raise her T-shirt and carefully remove the gauze that covers the worst of the lash marks. The sight of those angry red cuts on her back makes me want to howl with outrage.

"Here we go." The hands that I've washed thoroughly are shaking from the effort to be gentle, to not cause her any more pain than she's already experienced. "Nice and easy."

She gasps at the first touch of my finger.

I move quickly but carefully, wanting this done so she can relax. I venture a glance at her face, see tears rolling down her cheeks and I'm gutted. Her tears are like a knife to my heart. "Almost done. You're doing great, sweetheart."

"Hurts."

"I know." I want to cry myself, but I need to stay strong for her. When I've covered every inch of the four wounded strips of skin with the antibiotic ointment, I cover the areas with new gauze and tape it back into place. "All done." I draw her T-shirt back down over her back.

She exhales and closes her eyes, breathing through the pain.

I grab a tissue from the box on the bedside table and wipe up the remaining tears on her face, wishing there was more I could do to comfort her. I lean in and kiss her temple. "Get some rest."

"Seb."

"What, honey?"

"Don't go."

Christ have mercy. I'm powerless against those two little words coming from this particular woman. I stand, turn off the light, walk around to the other side of the bed and lie down next to her. "I'm here."

"Talk to me."

"What do you want to talk about?"

"Tell me things I don't know about you."

I grunt out a laugh. "That's stuff you don't need to know."

She turns her head so she can see me in the faint light filtering in from outside. "I want to hear it anyway. Tell me the bad stuff."

"Marlowe…"

Her hand grasps mine, sending a sharp bolt of sensation up my arm that reminds me of the danger she represents. Hayden and Flynn would kill me if they ever knew that Marlowe touching me in the most innocent way possible makes me harder than I've ever been for anyone else. I try to figure out what's different about her touch, but all I know is that when she touches me, I feel it *everywhere*.

"Why do you want to talk about that?"

"I want to know you."

"You do know me."

"I know what you want me to."

She's incredibly insightful. I've always known that, but she proves it again with that telling statement. "You won't like me anymore if I tell you the bad stuff."

"Yes, I will."

"No, you won't."

"I promise I will."

She links her fingers with mine and holds on tighter to my hand.

Desire is like a live wire, crackling and sizzling between us, as if I've opened a door that can never be closed again.

"You know most of it."

"Tell me the rest."

This is the last thing I want to talk about with anyone, let alone her. If I tell her my truth, she'll never look at me the same way again. Ah, who am I kidding anyway? Me with Marlowe Sloane is the biggest pipe dream anyone has ever had. She's a certifiable goddess among women. And me?

You're in a bed with her, holding hands, the hopeful part of me thinks.

The realistic part of me scoffs at that. *You're a reformed thug not worthy of breathing the same air as her.*

That may be true, but I *am* breathing the same air, and she wants to know me. The part of me that's burned for her for as long as I've known her can refuse her nothing. "You know my mom."

"I *love* your mom."

Everyone does. She's the best. "You know she worked for Hayden's dad when we were kids, that we grew up together."

"Right. Brothers from another mother."

"Yeah." Hayden, who grew up as the son of a wealthy, if often self-destructive and ultimately unsuccessful, actor, has never treated me like he thought I was less than him. None of the Quantum principals have ever treated me as anything other than a trusted friend and colleague. But I am less. They're wildly talented and successful, each of them Oscar winners in their own right and as a group. I'm a hanger-on compared to the rest of them, a lackey. "My dad took off when I was six, and that was when my mom had to go to work for Hayden's family. We were lucky she landed such a great job, even if his dad could be a bastard a lot of the time."

"Still can be, from what I hear."

"Yeah, he's a tiger who'll never change his stripes." I haven't thought about this shit in a long time, and if I had my druthers, I'd leave it in the past where it belongs. But Marlowe wants to *know* me, so I press on, despite significant reservations. "I was really messed up after my dad left. I couldn't understand where he'd gone or what I'd done to make him want to leave. My mom was equally heartbroken, so she wasn't much help to me. By the time I hit high school, I was getting into trouble in school. I got suspended for two weeks for fighting."

"What grade were you in?"

"Eleventh." I place my free hand over our joined hands and stroke her soft skin. Now that I've been given permission to touch her, to share secrets in the dark, I can't help but want more. "I was so *angry*. That suspension was actually the start of much bigger trouble. Here I was, pissed off with nowhere to go all day for two whole weeks. My mom was at work, and even though she told me not to leave the house, I did anyway. I went looking for trouble, and I found it. I met an older kid at an arcade who saw the same anger in me that was in him. He introduced me to others, and it sort of took off from there. Before I knew it, I was into all sorts of illegal shit—stealing cars, breaking and entering, assault, arson. You name it, I've done it. I didn't realize it at the time, but they were testing me, making sure I was loyal and trustworthy before they 'promoted' me to bigger and better things."

"I'm almost afraid to ask what bigger and better might entail."

"You really don't want to know, but suffice to say they would've been looking for me to prove that there was literally nothing I wouldn't do to demonstrate my loyalty. Hayden intervened two years later. I was an adult by then and in danger of doing serious time if I got caught."

"What did Hayden do?"

"He called and told me he was in trouble and needed my help. Because it was him, I dropped what I was doing and went running. Apparently, that's what they'd counted on with this plan."

"They?"

"He and my mom were in cahoots. He'd had me followed, realized how bad it was, went to her and ratted me out."

"Ah, I see."

"He had me meet him at his place, where he took me by surprise, overpowered me and handcuffed me to a chair."

Marlowe's low, sexy laugh makes me smile, even though there's nothing funny about this, even all these years later. "What's so funny?"

"I'm trying to picture Hayden overpowering you."

"I wasn't the beast then that I am now. I'd break his neck now. Back then, we were more evenly matched, and he got the better of me."

"What happened after he handcuffed you to the chair?"

"I told him I was going to fucking kill him if he didn't let me go. He sat across from me and said I could rage all I wanted, but neither of us was going anywhere until I agreed to his terms."

"Which were?"

"Join him on a shoot in West Virginia for the summer, or he would call the cops and tell them he had the guy who burned a shop owner in Compton out of his store."

"Did you do that?"

The shame has never really gone away, even if time has tempered it somewhat. "Yeah."

"How'd he know?"

"He'd been having me followed for months and had the footage to prove it."

"Wow. What did you do?"

"I fought with him for twelve hours, during which he wouldn't let me eat or drink or take a leak or do anything but sit in that fucking chair with my arms shackled behind my back while he threatened me with almost certain death if he called the cops. Or, he said, I could get on a plane with him to West Virginia in the morning and start a whole new life. The choice was mine."

"Holy crap. That sounds intense."

"It was. The whole time, I just kept thinking about how I was going to kill the motherfucker the second he let me out of those cuffs. I was going to wrap my hands around his neck and squeeze the life out of him."

"He must've known you'd come at him if he let you go."

"He did, and that's when he brought in the big gun."

"What was the big gun?"

"My mother."

"Ohhhh." Marlowe props her head on an upturned hand and hangs on my every word.

"Mama cried and begged and told me that I'd broken her heart, shattered it into a million pieces that could never be put back together again. She said…" Some things could never be forgotten.

"What?"

Sighing, I tell her the rest. "She said she was disappointed with me, devastated that the child she'd raised had become a lawless, heartless thug. If I didn't go to West Virginia with Hayden, she said I would no longer be welcome in her home, where I still lived." My gut twists with the pain of that memory. "Hayden said he would let me go, but if I walked out the door, I was dead to him, too. 'It's us or them,' he said."

Marlowe sniffles and dabs at her eyes.

"I was infuriated that they'd do this to me, that they'd force me to choose between the two people who'd always been there for me and the people who'd given me a purpose and an outlet for my rage." I can still remember the fury and the fear of that day so clearly, as if it had happened yesterday rather than twenty years ago. "Hayden unlocked the cuffs, and God, my arms hurt like a motherfucker. First thing I did was take the most satisfying piss of my life, and the metaphor of that wasn't lost on me. I wasn't so far gone that I couldn't see that I was pissing my life away and looking at hard time if Hayden made good on his threats to turn the video over to the cops."

"Do you think he really would've done it?"

"I've thought about that a lot, and I've decided that he probably would've, because if he had a choice between me being in jail or dead, he would've picked jail."

"So you went to West Virginia."

"I went to West Virginia and hated every fucking minute of it. I made sure that Hayden regretted bringing me by being a complete pain in the ass for the entire summer."

She lets loose with that legendary laugh of hers. "I would've liked to have seen that."

"I'm glad you didn't. I was such a dick back then. I can't stand to think about the way I behaved toward the man who saved my life." I glance over at her. "That kid I met when I was suspended?"

"What about him?"

"I stayed close to him, and he taught me everything I needed to know about how to get away with just about anything. When I came home from West Virginia, I found out he'd been killed in a shootout with cops. I would've been with him when it went down and probably would've been killed, too."

She squeezes my hand. "I'm so glad you went to West Virginia."

"So am I. Three months away, learning something about making movies—even if I thought it was the stupidest thing I'd ever been part of at the time—and coming home to that news as well as the hopeful look on my mother's face… When Hayden offered me a permanent job, I took it, even though I knew I wasn't qualified to get him coffee, let alone work as an assistant to him after what I'd seen him do in West Virginia. I didn't want my mom to be disappointed in me anymore, and even though I tried to convince myself that I hated Hayden's guts, I didn't. Not really."

"This is why you volunteer at the community center, isn't it?"

I'm shocked that she knows about that. "How do you know that?"

"I hear things. You're there to try to keep other kids from making the same mistakes you did, aren't you?"

"Something like that."

"I want you to know that I admire the way you turned your life around."

I bark out a laugh. "Don't. I never would've done it on my own. I had people who cared and intervened. Otherwise, I'd be either dead or doing life in prison."

"I don't think you give yourself enough credit for getting on that plane when it would've been much easier to stay and keep doing what was familiar by then."

"All the credit goes to Hayden and my mom. They turned things around for me."

"Sebastian." She tugs her hand free of mine and places it on my chest, the heat of her palm working its way through my T-shirt. I break out in goose bumps in reaction to her touch. "They couldn't have done it unless you *allowed* them to. They might've given you the ultimatum, but *you* made the choice. You did that."

"You're giving me way too much credit."

"You don't give yourself enough."

Her hand moves from my chest to my face, her thumb caressing my cheek. "I want to kiss you."

"Marlowe…"

"Sebastian." She sounds amused, and damn if that doesn't do it for me. *She* does it for me.

"Why do you want to kiss me?"

"Because I've always wondered what it would be like to kiss you."

"You have not."

"I have too!"

I can't believe she's saying that when it can't possibly be true.

With her hand on my face, she turns me, forcing me to see her in the faint light coming from the nightlight I put in the room for her. "I have *always* wondered what it would be like to kiss you, among other things."

"You... you're injured and..."

"I'm fine."

I should get up, leave the room, walk away from her while I still can. Except I can't seem to do anything but breathe and wish I was a better man so I would deserve a woman like her. While I'm paralyzed, she's not and moves toward me slowly but intently. I want to tell her to stop, to not do something that can't ever be undone, but she's undeterred by my silence and my paralysis.

Her lips slide over mine, and I feel it everywhere. My scalp tingles, my muscles clench and my dick gets so hard so fast, I wonder if there's any blood left to keep the rest of me alive long enough to enjoy this. I'm kissing Marlowe. I'm kissing Marlowe, and she's... Oh, fuck, that's her tongue sliding along my bottom lip.

Suddenly, I'm not paralyzed anymore. I turn toward her, bury my hand in her thick auburn hair and suck her tongue into my mouth.

The sound of pleasure that comes from her sends sparks down my spine. If you'd asked me yesterday if I could still be surprised by a kiss, I would've said no way. Been there, done that, a million times. I would've been very, very wrong. There's kissing and then there's kissing Marlowe, which is in a whole different league of kissing.

We devour each other, lips and tongues and teeth, nothing is off-limits. With two Doms going at it, we're like a dancing couple in which both people want to lead. I have no idea how long the fierce battle goes on before we pull back from each other, gasping for air. In the faint light drifting in from the hallway, I can see that she looks as stunned as I feel.

I rest my forehead against hers, close my eyes and focus on breathing as all the reasons this is a bad idea cycle through my mind. But with ninety percent of the blood in my body making my dick throb with desire for her, my brain is getting overruled.

"I knew it," she says in a husky whisper that has the hair on the back of my neck standing on end.

"What did you know?"

"That kissing you would be amazing."

"Was it?"

"God, yes. Wasn't it for you?"

"Yeah, it was…" There isn't a word that would do it justice. "Are we fucking with a good thing here, Mo?"

"Or would fucking be a good thing, Seb?"

I sputter with laughter. "Stop. I'm being serious."

"I know." Her deep sigh says it all. "I don't mean to take advantage of your kindness."

"Sure you do. You've got me right where you want me." I use a teasing tone so she'll know I'm trying to keep it light. My intention is to disengage, to get out of there before I do something else that can't be undone. But my intentions disintegrate into dust when she licks her lips and zeroes in on mine.

Before I finish deciding, my lips are back on hers, my mouth is open, my tongue desperate for another taste of her unique flavor. Despite endless temptation back in the day, I've never gone anywhere near hard drugs. From what I've heard, this is what it's like to have one taste change you forever, to fuel an addiction so ferocious, it grabs hold of you and sinks its claws in so deep, it's almost impossible to get them out.

This is the best kind of instant addiction, a natural high that can't be achieved by any drug. I should've listened to my better judgment and kept my hands—and lips—far away from her, because now that I know what it's like to kiss her, to touch her… I'm so totally fucked.

CHAPTER 9

Marlowe

I wake to daylight streaming into the bedroom where Sebastian and I slept last night. Memories come flooding back, of kissing him until I ached from wanting more and him refusing to do anything but kiss, like we were teenagers with a curfew. I have no idea when we fell asleep, but I slept better in his arms than I have in ages.

My lips are sore, actually *sore*, from kissing him. When was the last time that happened? I can't recall.

Dear God, the man can *kiss*.

And his tongue game isn't too shabby either. Just thinking about it has my nipples tingling and my clit throbbing in ways they haven't tingled or throbbed in years, even with Rafe. I shift, looking for a more comfortable position, and bump up against a long, hard ridge of flesh.

He lets out a grunt in the second before his eyes open, his gaze colliding with mine in the bright light of day. "What're you doing in bed with me?"

"Um, I think *you're* in bed with *me*."

His hand moves from my waist down to cup my ass, bringing me in tight against his throbbing length.

He's fucking huge. I've known that for a while now, but until I was up close and personal with all ten inches of him, I didn't fully appreciate the magnificence.

"Tell me we aren't making the biggest mistake of our lives, Marlowe."

I nuzzle my face into the curve of his neck and breathe in the masculine scent of him—deodorant and soap and laundry detergent. "We've both made bigger mistakes than this."

"I have. I doubt you have."

"You're not the only one who's done things they regret, Seb."

"I'm sure your regrets have nothing on mine."

"Don't be so sure." It's all I can do to contain the urge to rub out a quick orgasm.

As if he's a mind reader, he tightens his hold on my ass and pushes that big cock against my pussy, hitting all the right spots and lighting me up like a Christmas tree. "Tell me if anything hurts," he says gruffly.

"Nothing hurts, but there's an ache…"

"Where?"

"Right… *There.*"

Never let it be said that the man can't take direction. He turns onto his back, bringing me with him, handling me carefully so as not to jar any of the places where I'm hurt. Looking up at me with those dark eyes that're now heated with desire, he says, "Take what you want, sweet girl."

With my hands flat against his chest, I push myself up and spread my legs.

His hands on my hips guide me as I begin to move, never breaking the intense eye contact.

What should be awkward, isn't. It's sublime. He plays my body like a maestro, moving beneath me with the exact rhythm I need to get where I want to go. I forget that this is Sebastian, my longtime friend. It's as if I'm looking at someone completely new, someone I just met for the first time.

"Good?" he asks in that same sexy, gruff tone.

"So good."

"Give in and let it happen."

I'm not used to taking. I'm far more accustomed to giving. Naturally, he gets that because he's wired like me.

"Let it all go, sweet girl. I'll catch you when you fall."

Closing my eyes, I let my head fall back and clear my mind of anything that isn't about the pleasure that ripples through me. I've had every kind of sex a person can have, and nothing has ever left me as breathless as dry humping Sebastian does.

He anchors my hips and picks up the pace, pressing into me hard and then retreating, over and over again until I'm out of my mind with the need to come. When he releases my hips and cups my breasts, squeezing my nipples between his fingers, I come hard, writhing on top of him as I ride the wave of pleasure until it passes. Then I collapse on top of him.

His arms come around me, above and below the wounds on my back. Between my legs, his hard cock is a reminder that only one of us achieved satisfaction. I would do something about that, but I can't seem to move after that epic orgasm.

"You're still…"

"I'm fine."

"But…"

"Shhhh. Close your eyes and breathe." He runs his fingers through my hair and caresses my lower back, lulling me deeper into bone-deep relaxation. I actually doze off for a while, awaking to my cell phone ringing.

Sebastian reaches for it and hands it to me.

I take the call from a number I don't recognize.

"Marlowe."

Oh God, it's Rafe.

"I have nothing to say to you."

"Wait… Listen. There're things you don't know about me, and the other night… it was triggering for me."

Was it only a few days ago that his French accent could make me shiver? Now it turns my stomach. "I don't care, Rafe. What you did is unforgivable. Don't call me again."

"You didn't have to get my boss involved. I got *fired* because of you."

"That's the least of what you deserve." My hands are shaking, and my stomach hurts. "And you didn't get fired because of me. It was because of *you*."

"Can't we talk about this?"

"Are you for real? No, we can't talk about you beating and whipping me and leaving me strung up and bleeding for hours."

Sebastian takes the phone from me. "Do not call her again."

"Who the hell is this?"

"Your worst nightmare. Call her again, and you'll find out exactly who I am." He ends the call, shuts off the phone and tosses it aside. "Take it easy, sweetheart. Breathe."

I'm shaking so hard that breathing is all I can do.

"Deep breath in. Hold it." He holds me close, his lips brushing against my face. "Now let it out. That's it. Nice and slow. Do it again."

I focus only on breathing and the sound of his voice guiding me through it.

"You never have to see him again. We'll get you a new phone number so you don't have to hear from him either."

"I've had that number for fifteen years."

"So what? You give the new number to the people who need it and go on with your life. We'll get Leah to take care of that for you today."

He's right. I know it, but I resent having to change my number to get rid of Rafe. However, if it means never having to hear his voice again, I can live with that. "Okay." Suddenly, I realize I've been using him as a mattress while I slipped into a post-orgasmic coma. "I should, um, let you up."

His arms tighten around me. "I'm in no rush."

"I didn't mean to use you and conk out like that."

His low rumble of laughter makes me smile. "Use me any time you'd like."

"How long has it been this way for you?" I ask the question before I take even a second to think about whether I should.

"How long have we known each other?"

Twelve years. I raise my head off his chest so I can see his face and those eyes that look at me with such affection and desire. "How did I not know?"

"I made very sure that you'd never know, that no one would."

"*Why?*"

"Come on, Marlowe. You're *you*, and I'm…"

I narrow my eyes and give him my best sinister look. "Please don't say something that's going to piss me off."

"I'm not trying to piss you off, but it never occurred to me that you might feel the same way or that I'd ever have a shot with you."

Another thought occurs to me, making me gasp from the sheer madness of it. "Is this why you don't get involved with anyone beyond casual hookups and scenes at the club?"

His jaw shifts and his face flushes with… Is he blushing?

"Are you blushing?"

"Fuck no. I don't blush."

"I think maybe you do." I start to laugh, which earns me a scowl from him.

"If you're gonna laugh at me, you can get your ass off me."

"I don't wanna." I plant my elbows on his chest to hold my chin up as I contemplate him keeping such a big secret from me and everyone for twelve freaking years.

"Your elbows digging into my chest feel so good."

"Don't be a baby." I'm emboldened by the knowledge that he has feelings for me, and not just the sexual kind. "Talk to me about this crush you've had on me for all this time."

"I won't talk to you about that, so drop it."

I laugh again. "Like that's going to happen. The genie's out of the bottle, my friend. There's no putting that bitch back in when she gets a taste of freedom, so you may as well admit defeat."

"Not gonna happen."

"You're adorable when you're embarrassed."

"I'm not adorable *or* embarrassed. Those things are for pussies, which I'm most definitely *not*."

I lick my lips and watch his gaze track the movement of my tongue. "No, you're definitely not a pussy, but you are adorable."

"Shut up."

"You shut up and tell me what the fuck you were thinking keeping this a secret for twelve freaking *years*."

"I would rather not do that."

"I'm not moving until you tell me."

"I could move you if I wanted to."

"But you won't, because you'd be afraid of hurting me and you'd never do that."

His eyes glitter with amusement and affection that he's no longer trying to keep hidden. Now that I know, it's as obvious as the nose on his gorgeous face. "You think you're so smart, don't you?"

"I know I'm smart, so start talking if you ever want to leave this bed today."

His hands slide down to squeeze my ass. "*Not* leaving this bed today is hardly a threat."

"My next move is to tell you to keep your hands—and every other part of you—to yourself until you tell me what I want to know."

He squeezes my ass again. "Make me."

I flatten my hands on his chest and look into his eyes. "Please tell me why you kept this to yourself for so long."

His eyes close, and he takes a deep breath, releasing it slowly. "It's going to make you mad."

"I still want to know."

After another long pause, he finally opens his eyes and gives me the truth. "I'm not good enough for you, sweet girl. You need someone who's your equal, not a former thug who's now a club manager only because his best childhood friend threw him a bone."

He's right. I'm pissed. I push myself up and out of his embrace, wincing when my bruised ribs and wounded back protest the sudden movement.

"Where're you going?"

"I think I should go home."

"You asked me to tell you, I told you it would be better if I didn't, and now that I did, you want to leave? How is that fair?"

I turn to him, furious. "You want to talk about fair after you kept something like this from me for *twelve* years?"

"When would've been a good time to tell you? When you were dating Leo maybe, or how about when you were with Sam? Or how about Devyn or Rafe? Would any of those times have been the right time to tell you that I wanted you?"

"Thanks for reminding me of all the losers I've dated. That's helpful."

"I'm merely reminding you that you haven't exactly been available for this information for twelve years. And for much of that time, the info wouldn't have been welcome, and you know it."

I can't deny that's true, so I don't try to. But there is one thing I can deny. "I can't bear to hear you say you aren't good enough for me. You don't get to decide that. I'd take one of you over ten of any of those other guys you named. Leo—an award-winning producer who's also a malignant narcissist. Sam, a multimillionaire businessman who's also a drug addict. Devyn, an award-winning actor, is actually gay, not that there's anything wrong with that, unless you're looking for a man who likes women. And we both know what Rafe is in addition to being a high-ranking executive at a film company."

"A former high-ranking executive."

I wave my hand in acknowledgment. "The point is, on paper, all of them were 'good enough' for me, and yet none of them were good *for* me. So, yes, I'm pissed that you kept this from me and denied me the chance to be with someone who might actually be *good for me!*" It's not my style to yell, but I'm so bloody furious with him for the things he said about himself and for all the time we've wasted. If only he'd been honest with me. If only we'd been honest with each other.

"How come *you* never said anything to *me?*" he asks.

"About what?"

"About how *you've* thought of *me* as more than a friend."

"It never occurred to me that you'd care."

He sits up and then stands, hands on hips. "*What?* Are you insane? I would've *loved* to know that." Crossing his arms, he stares me down. "The way I see it, we're both guilty of keeping secrets."

When he puts it that way, it's hard to stay pissed with him for not telling me how he felt. "I'll give you that, but I'm still pissed that you'd ever think you're not good enough for me. That's utter bullshit, and you know what makes me really mad about that?"

He tips his head and raises a brow. "I can't wait to hear this."

"I thought we were friends."

"We are friends. Of course we are."

"Then you should know how much I hate people acting like I'm something special just because I've had a successful career. That's my *job*. It's not me, and after all the time we've spent together, I'd expect you to know that."

"I do know that."

"If you think I'm better than you, you don't know shit about me."

Before he can respond to me, his phone chimes with a text and then rings with a call. He glances at the phone on the bedside table. "It's Leah. Okay to take it?"

"Sure."

I take the opportunity to go to the bathroom and brush my teeth. The water drowns out the conversation Seb is having with Leah, but I don't care what they're talking about. I'm still processing the conversation I just had with him. What will happen now that we've both put our cards on the table and acted on the attraction we now admit has been simmering between us—albeit on the far back burner—for years?

It's surreal to think that Sebastian—my good friend and colleague—has had feelings for me all this time and I had no idea. I feel stupid that something like that could've been happening right in front of me and I missed it, even as I nursed my own secret thoughts about what it might be like with him.

He comes to the bathroom door, his brow furrowed. "Someone tipped off the media that you were involved in an altercation. They're camped out at your place and the office."

"Son of a bitch. Rafe is the only one who would've done that."

"The question is why would he do it?"

"Because he's pissed that we went to Pierre, and he's looking to exact revenge."

"He's lucky you didn't go to the cops."

"He knew I wouldn't want the publicity of having him charged, and he left the country just in case he was wrong about that, knowing it would take forever to have him extradited. He knows how much I hate being the subject of celebrity gossip, so he went for the jugular." And now he's made it so I can't go home, even if I wanted to, which I don't, knowing Sebastian has feelings for me—and that he can make me come like he did earlier. Sign me up for more of that.

"Listen, Mo…" His expression is tortured. "I'm glad we got a chance to talk before, but…"

I hold my breath, waiting to hear what he will say.

"I think it would be better if we didn't, you know…"

"Fuck?"

He inhales through his nose. "Yeah."

"Ever or just right now?"

Grasping the doorframe, he can't seem to look at me. "Ever."

"Why?"

"I, ah, I just think it could turn out to be really complicated, and that might not be the best idea, you know, because of work and our friends. And everything."

Oh, this is funny. He confesses to having feelings for me, to wanting me, kisses me like he's been starving until he had the chance to gorge on me, and now he's having buyer's remorse? Isn't that rich? "Sure." I speak with nonchalance I don't feel. "If that's what you want. I can go stay with Hayden and Addie. I'll call her to come get me."

"No." He says the single word emphatically. "You can't leave. If they don't find you at your place, they know where else to look for you. They have no way of knowing to look here. It's the best place for you to be for now. Leah said the others talked about it, and they agree you should stay here."

"I don't want to stay here." I give him my fiercest look. "I'm pissed at you."

"Because I was honest with you about this not being a good idea for either of us?"

"Because you showed me what you really want and then you took it back like a coward."

His entire demeanor turns stormy, but I'm not the slightest bit afraid of him. This is not at all what it felt like when Rafe turned on me. With Rafe, I experienced bone-deep fear.

"I'm *not* a coward."

"We'll have to agree to disagree on that." I push him aside as I leave the bathroom and go find my phone in the bedroom. I power it up and send a text to Leah. *I need you to grab a few things from my house and bring them here without being followed. Can you do that?*

Yep. Send me a list of what you need.

I sit on the bed, smiling to myself as I type out the list without an ounce of embarrassment about what I'm asking my assistant to do. I pay her a small fortune to do whatever I need, and at times like this, she earns it.

He thinks this isn't going to happen? We'll see about that.

CHAPTER 10

Sebastian

I'm fucking furious that she called me a coward. That's what I get for trying to do the right thing for her, for me and for the rest of our friends, all of whom would be involved if shit went sideways between Marlowe and me. And how could it not? What will happen when the media that pursue her relentlessly find out that she's with a guy who used to be a gangbanger? They'd have a fucking field day with that and would tear apart both our lives looking for dirt—and they would find it in my past. I blame my confessions on the incredible high of holding Mo and watching her fall apart in my arms. The words were no sooner out of my mouth than the potential implications began to set in, and my better judgment intervened.

Backing off is the right thing to do. We got caught up in a moment. That's all it was. Allowing it to become more than that would be an invitation to disaster for both of us as well as the people we love best. And when it all goes bad, which one of us will be on the outside looking in on the life they once treasured? Not her.

So, yeah, a big part of my decision to back off is centered on self-preservation. I love my job. I love my friends. I love my life. Fucking things up with Marlowe, no matter how amazing it might be until it goes bad, endangers all those things. I made the right decision for both of us. I made the *courageous* decision. Because it sure as hell would've been easier in the short term to say fuck it and take what

I want so badly, I can still taste the sweetness of her lips and feel the heat of her pressed against my cock.

Trying not to actually moan from the memory that will haunt me forever, I go into the kitchen, pour a glass of ice water and down it in three big gulps. I have to get out of here. In my bedroom, I use the bathroom, brush my teeth, splash cold water on my face and then change into a tank top and basketball shorts. There's a gym in the basement of my building where I can expend the energy that has me tied up in knots.

"I'll be back in a bit," I say to Marlowe, who doesn't reply.

So now she's gone silent on me? I hate this shit. I take the elevator down to the basement and put myself through a punishing workout over the next ninety minutes. Sweating profusely and lightheaded from not eating, I stagger outside and walk to the coffee shop on the corner to pick up coffees and breakfast sandwiches for both of us, ignoring the people who give me a wide berth. I'm not sure if it's because I stink, or they can sense the fury that wasn't snuffed out in the gym. Whatever. That's their issue, not mine.

I return to my place, and the first thing I hear is singing. Marlowe is singing in the shower. Like the fool that I am, I go to the bathroom door, trying to hear what song she's singing. I listen intently and hear "coming," "humming," "moaning" and "nonstop loving." It takes a minute for me to remember the song, but it's "Blow" by Beyoncé. Listening to Marlowe's take on the down-and-dirty song has me once again harder than granite and about to blow.

"Fuck," I mutter, turning to walk away while wondering if she chose that song on purpose. I wouldn't put it past her.

Ten minutes later, she emerges from the bathroom wearing a thin silk robe that leaves absolutely nothing to my fertile imagination. Her hair is piled in a messy bun, leaving her bruised but flawless face on display. The rest of the world sees her made up like the movie star she is, but when she's not working, she doesn't wear any makeup. With makeup, she's glamorous and every inch a superstar. Without it, she's simply *stunning,* and I find myself staring at her as she types on her phone, legs curled under her and the front of her robe gaping open to reveal most of a plump breast.

I tear my gaze off that tempting sight and put the coffee and sandwich on the table in front of her.

"Thank you."

"Welcome." Taking my coffee with me, I go into the bathroom to shower, and within seconds of stepping under the water, I've got my hand wrapped around my cock as I try to find relief from the nearly painful need for something I've convinced myself I can't have. After hours on the edge of release, it takes almost nothing to make me blow.

Ugh, there's that word again.

I want her so bad that I burn from the need to touch her, to worship her, to protect her. I'd give her everything I have if I thought she'd want or need what I can give her, which isn't much compared to what she already has.

After washing my hair and body, I stay in the shower until the water starts to run cold. Anything is better than facing the redheaded temptress in my living room. I've never felt like my place was small until she arrived and filled it with her unique brand of magic. I'll never be able to look at my home again and not see her there.

Fuck.

I get out of the shower and take my time getting dressed, trying to get my head together so I can face her without making everything worse than it already is. More than an hour has passed by the time I step out of my room to find that Leah has arrived.

"Hey, Seb," she says.

"How's it going?"

"Pretty good. Liza and her crew are dealing with the media, and Emmett is involved, too."

"That's good."

"Gordon wants to send a few guys over to keep an eye on things here," Leah adds.

Our security director is nothing if not thorough when it comes to protecting the principals. "Is that really necessary? No one knows she's here." And then another thought occurs to me. "You weren't followed, were you?"

"Nope. I was careful when I left Marlowe's so I wouldn't lead them to her."

"Oh, good." I breathe out a sigh of relief. Then I realize Marlowe is taking things out of the bag that Leah brought her—silky things with lace and thin straps and netting. Fuck me to hell and back again. What's she planning to do with that stuff?

"You found Big Johnny!" She withdraws a gigantic dildo from the bag and holds it up for closer inspection before planting a kiss on the tip of the huge cock.

"He was right where you said he would be." Leah hasn't got an ounce of shame, which doesn't surprise me. She's known for being somewhat shameless.

"Gotta have Johnny if I'm going to do without for a while."

Leah laughs. "A girl has her needs."

"Yep. Speaking of needs, how're things with Emmett?"

"So, so great. I can't get enough of him." Leah sits back on the sofa, a dreamy look overtaking her face. "He's amazing in every way, especially in the area of stamina."

Marlowe unleashes the dirty laugh that helped to make her a superstar, and I have to bite my lip to hold in a moan of frustration. "That's a very important quality to have in the man you love."

"That's very true. The man can go all night. I have to beg him to let me sleep, even though that's the last thing I want to do when he's in bed with me."

"Now you're just bragging, you lucky bitch."

"Sorry."

"Don't be sorry." Marlowe pokes Leah's leg with Johnny's broad head. "You're in love. That's the way it should be."

"I'm so in love."

Watching Marlowe handle that fucking dildo has me on the verge of losing my shit all over again, like the orgasm in the shower never happened. "I'll, ah, give you ladies some privacy." I make a quick exit onto the deck and close the door behind me, before I can do something stupid, like drag her into my bed and give her the real thing.

Marlowe

We wait until the sliding door closes before Leah and I dissolve into laughter. "Oh my God, you're so getting a raise."

"I deserve a raise after having to dig through your sex-toy drawer to find Big Johnny."

"That was above and beyond the call of duty, but it had to be done."

"I deserve hazardous duty pay for this mission."

"You shall be richly rewarded. I promise."

"Actually, watching Sebastian try not to lose his mind while you were stroking Big Johnny was a pretty nice payoff."

"I think you missed your calling as an actress."

"Really? You thought I was good?"

"You were *perfect*."

"I just followed directions. I can talk dirty shit about Emmett all day, every day—and all night, too."

I smile at her. "I'm so glad you guys are happy."

"We're *so* happy, but you wanna tell me what the hell is going on here?"

"Well, it's like this. Sebastian told me he's had feelings for me for as long as we've known each other."

Leah's mouth falls open. "Isn't that like ten years?"

"More like twelve."

"Holy shit. What did you say to that?"

"At first, I couldn't believe what I was hearing, and then… Then I was kind of thrilled because I've thought about what it might be like with him."

"So all this time, you've both had a crush going on and no one knew, not even each other?"

"Something like that."

"This is so exciting! So you're gonna, like, go for it while you're here with him?"

"Not exactly. He doesn't think it would be wise to pursue things with me."

"*Why?*"

"Something about how it wouldn't work because he's not good enough for me, and it would be a hot mess for everyone if it doesn't work out."

"That last part is true, but he really said he's not good enough for you?"

"Yep, and that's what led to me bringing you in with some props and an award-winning performance."

"You're going to show him he's good enough for you." She rolls her bottom lip between her teeth, which she does when she's thinking. "Don't take this the wrong way, but…" She shakes her head. "Never mind. It's none of my business."

"Just say whatever you're thinking. Aren't we past the point where you have to worry about what you say to me? You've seen my sex toys, for crying out loud."

Leah laughs. "True. It's just that I was thinking about what happened with the piece of shit and whether it's too soon to be moving on after something like that."

I look down at Big Johnny, which Addie gave me as a joke gift for my thirtieth birthday, and try to find the words to explain how I'm feeling. "I don't want to ever again think about him or what happened."

"I totally understand. I never want to think about him again either. I can't begin to know how you must feel."

"I'd rather stay focused on exacting revenge than gnashing my teeth about another failed relationship, you know?"

"What're you going to do?"

"We've already made sure he lost his job. Kristian told his boss that it was either him or us, and being the smart businessman that he is, the boss chose us."

"He'd be insane not to. Quantum makes his company a shit-ton of money every year."

"Yep, so he's out of a job, and I'm planning to return some of the texts I got from his exes when I first started seeing him. They tried to tell me to watch out. I was too busy ignoring the warnings because I was determined to get my happily ever after, too."

Leah's brows knit with confusion. "Too?"

"Look at what's happened to my friends in the last year. I started to feel desperate about being alone while everyone else was happily in love, which, in hindsight, makes me a little crazy. What's wrong with me to be thinking that way? That stupidity led me to think Rafe was the one for me. I didn't want to entertain the possibility that I was making yet another big mistake when it came to men."

"Give yourself a break, Mo. You liked the guy. Of course you didn't want to think it was possible he wasn't what he seemed. If someone told me Emmett isn't a good guy, I would ignore it, too, because I've seen proof to the contrary. You must've, too, or you never would've stayed with him for months."

"There were good things but also not-so-good things that I ignored because I so wanted to get my happy ending. Stupid, right?"

She takes hold of my hand. "It's never stupid to be hopeful, Marlowe. And it's never stupid to put your faith in someone you care about."

"You're very sweet and maybe just a little naïve about how shitty people can be."

"I'm not as naïve as you think. My mom was an alcoholic. My junior year of high school, she fell down the stairs and broke her neck. I was the one who found her."

"Oh no. Leah… I'm so sorry."

"It was a long time ago, as was the bullying I endured in school, but you know about that."

I do know. One of the girls who'd treated her so viciously released compromising photos of Leah after she came to work for me. "I'm sorry I called you naïve. You're not."

"I am about some things, but shitty people isn't one of them." She glances over her shoulder, presumably to check that Sebastian is still outside. "What's your plan?"

"I was thinking I'd give him a little taste of what he'd be missing if he decides to stick to his ridiculous decision to keep his distance from me."

"Oh, I like it," Leah says on a low, dirty laugh. "He won't stand a chance against you and Big Johnny."

"That's the idea."

"Like you asked, I brought you the sluttiest lingerie I could find in your drawer."

"You did good, kid."

"Aww, thanks! I'll tell you one thing, when I was teaching, my boss never asked me to go get slutty lingerie and sex toys from her house."

I lose it laughing. "I should hope not."

"Tell me something... Have you ever actually used Big Johnny for his intended purpose?"

"Dear God, no. He's freakishly large."

"Oh, thank you, Jesus. I was hoping you'd say that."

"That being said, Sebastian doesn't need to know that Big Johnny and I have never done the deed."

"No, he doesn't."

We're still cracking up when the slider opens to admit Seb. We try to curb our laughter, but Leah is one of the funniest people I've ever met, and the face she makes at me when she hears him coming has me losing it all over again.

"I'm going to go," Leah whispers. "Let me know if you need any other props for your performance."

"You'll be the first to know." I give her a quick hug and send her on her way, thankful as I am every day for Natalie, who suggested I hire Leah as my assistant. Best decision I ever made. That she's become my friend, too, is an added bonus.

Taking Big Johnny and the bag she brought me into my room, I close the door and change into an electric-blue bodysuit that takes some effort to put on properly. There are cutouts that leave more skin showing than covered, with thin strips of fabric slashing across my breasts, concealing only my nipples. I've never worn this before, but I bought it for a trip I was supposed to take with Rafe.

No sense letting it go to waste if it can be put toward a good cause. And Sebastian is definitely a worthwhile cause.

CHAPTER 11

Sebastian

My throat feels weird, like I've got a tie on, and it's tied way too tight around my neck. My skin is hot, the same way it got when I broke out in hives after eating shellfish for the first time when I was nineteen, which is how I found out I'm allergic. Now I'm wondering if there was something in that breakfast sandwich I ate that's giving me similar symptoms.

Or is it Marlowe and Big Johnny and the bag of frilly bits that Leah brought her that has me wondering what the hell she's thinking asking her assistant to bring such things here when I told her earlier that nothing is going to happen.

Why does it seem that she's working five steps ahead of where I am on this thing? Probably because she is. Marlowe is one of the sharpest, smartest women I've ever known, and I've long admired her ability to slice through the bullshit to get to the heart of a matter. Except when she's using those superpowers on me, as I'm sure she's planning to do.

I'm on edge waiting to see what will happen next, and that's so not like me. My anxiety issues don't usually extend to women. At least they never have before. I'm all about having a good time, making sure my partner leaves happy and going on with my life without ever looking back.

With Marlowe, not looking back wouldn't be an option, which is one of many reasons why I told her this shouldn't happen. Not to mention, we're both

Doms, which isn't ideal. I can't picture myself with someone like her—or anyone, for that matter—long-term. I'm a lone wolf. Always have been, even when I was running with gangbangers. I preferred to work alone so I wouldn't have to count on anyone but myself. In my entire life, I've truly trusted a half-dozen people: my mother, Hayden, Flynn, Jasper, Kristian and Marlowe. Emmett too, I suppose.

Period. End of story.

My thoughts are interrupted by loud music coming from my guestroom. "Why Don't We Get Drunk (And Screw)" by Jimmy Buffett. I huff out a laugh. "Subtle." Then my phone chimes with a text from her.

I could use your help.

I've never understood the expression "gallows humor" before now. I feel like a condemned man going to my doom, having no doubt that whatever she needs my help with will be the end of me. I fear that confessing my longtime crush on her will turn out to be the biggest mistake I've ever made—and I've made some doozies.

When I knock on the closed door, she calls out for me to come in.

Hand on the doorknob, I take a deep breath and summon the fortitude I'll need to contend with whatever she's got planned for me. When I open the door, the sight that greets me is one I'll remember in the final moments of my life. It's all I can do not to laugh out loud at her shamelessness, but I don't laugh because with one quick glance at her face, I see vulnerability just beneath the surface of her bravado.

She's wearing an electric-blue… thing. Calling it a bodysuit would be giving it too much credit, especially since it leaves most of her body uncovered. Strips of blue crisscross her chest, covering her nipples but leaving the rest of her full breasts visible to my hungry gaze. Miles of creamy white skin, marred only by bruises here and there, are on full display, and then she turns down the music on her phone and shifts ever so slightly to show me her back.

"I can't reach the snaps. Can you help?"

I can't move or breathe or do anything other than stare at her. I've seen her in the skimpiest of bikinis and managed to control myself, but this… This is for me, and knowing that shatters any semblance of control I normally would have around her.

"Sebastian? Are you all right?"

No, I'm not all right. I'm completely and totally fucked. And the best part? She knows it, judging by the smug little smile she sends my way.

She turns fully onto her belly, showing me her sweet ass. Then she spreads her legs, ever so slightly, but just enough to make me want to howl, and glances at me over her shoulder. "Can you help?"

Three thin strips of fabric hang from each side of her back. The angry-looking lacerations are what finally snap me out of my stupor. "We should tend to those wounds."

"No."

"What?"

"That's not the kind of help I need."

"Marlowe…" My voice is strangled sounding, and I know that if I touch her even once, I'll be lost forever. I can't.

My oversexed neighbor picks that moment to start her moaning and groaning act, and I have to marvel at the way the universe is fucking with me.

Marlowe's eyes glitter with delight. "Must be nice to enjoy it so much. I'm not sure I've ever enjoyed it as much as she does."

Behind me, I grasp the doorframe, still hanging on to the last thread of resistance. Who am I kidding? I'd give her anything and everything, if only I were worthy of her. "You can do so much better than me."

Anger flashes in her gorgeous eyes. "If you ever say anything like that again, I won't be responsible for my actions."

"It's true." My fingers ache from the effort to stay put, to not take the one big step that would take me to her and change everything.

"It's not true."

"You don't know…" I shake my head. "Anything."

"I know everything I need to know. Come here."

"You… you're hurt."

"I'm fine. You saw to that."

"But… the bruises, and your back…" I'm a stuttering, stammering fool. That's what she's done to me.

"Please?"

With one softly spoken word, she decides my fate for me. I can no more resist her than I can stop from taking my next breath. I'm moving toward her before I consciously decide to let go of the doorframe. I sit next to her on the edge of the mattress and lean over her to press gentle kisses above the healing wounds on her back.

She shivers violently, her hands clutching the bottom sheet. "Don't stop."

"We shouldn't do this."

"Yes, we really should."

I drop my forehead to her shoulder and breathe in the fresh, clean scent of her skin. No perfume or lotion or anything that can be bought in a store could properly capture the essence that's so uniquely hers. I've experienced it before, of course, whenever she's hugged me or leaned into me or sat next to me in a car packed with friends. But I've never before had the chance to luxuriate in the scent that's driven me mad more times than I care to count. Until now, when she invites me into her bed and asks me to give her something she needs.

"Is it because I'm here?"

Her head whips around, and again I witness the spectacular flash of anger that seems to come from her very soul. "Do you honestly think I'd risk years of friendship for a cheap fuck?"

"No, but…"

"Stop talking."

"Marlowe—"

"Do you want me, Sebastian?"

My throat closes, making it impossible to speak or breathe or do anything other than stare into her magnificent eyes and nod. I've always wanted her, and I can't lie to her, not now when it seems so important to her that I give her the truth. "Yes."

"Then have me."

"What about after?" I manage to choke out.

"It'll be okay."

"You promise?"

"Yeah, I do." She moves onto her side and reaches up, cupping my face with her soft hand. "I swear this isn't a rebound or a pity fuck or any of the things you're thinking."

"You're sure about that?"

"Very sure."

"I'm afraid if I touch you the way I want to, I'll hurt you."

"You couldn't."

"Yes, I really could." Desire beats through me like a wild animal set free from years in captivity. I'm so hard, I ache. I grit my teeth against the burning need to have her. Right now. In every possible way. But then I remember the wounds on her back, and I find the last remaining semblance of control that I possess. "Your back…"

"Will be fine if we do it this way." She moves so she's again facedown and looking at me over her shoulder. "Unless you don't want me the way I want you."

My teeth are so tightly clenched that my jaw aches. "That's not it." If I wanted her any more than I do, I'd probably have a heart attack from the pressure building in my chest as I try to do the right thing by one of my best friends.

She drops her head onto her folded arms, sighing deeply. "Never mind. I'm not going to beg you."

It's the defeat I hear in her words that spurs me, finally, to action. I cup one luscious ass cheek and squeeze before leaning in to take a little bite, fulfilling a fantasy twelve years in the making.

She gasps and then squirms.

"Don't move." I summon my inner Dom and put my faith in the tenets of the lifestyle we share, hoping that'll guide me through these uncharted waters. "I'm in charge, you got me?"

"Yes," she says softly.

"Yes, who?"

She looks at me over her shoulder and licks her lips. The movement of her tongue sends a surge of need to my cock. "Sir."

Hearing that word from her makes me crazy, knowing it's not something she'd give to just anyone. Her use of that word also tells me she's dead serious about whatever this is that's happening between us. No way would she ever call me that or give me control over her pleasure if she wasn't.

The realizations make me dizzy with lust and desire and something much bigger, something so big, it fills every part of me with longing. For what, I don't know, but it's a feeling I've never had before. I move so I'm fully on the bed, on my knees between her legs with both hands now on her ass.

"What's your safe word?"

"I've never needed one before."

"Now you do."

She thinks about it for a minute before her lips curve into a small smile. "Famous."

Knowing she's had a complicated relationship with fame, I appreciate the irony. "You're not famous here. You're just Marlowe, the most spectacular female to ever grace the face of the earth."

I'm not sure what it is about this new terrain we're traversing that has me spewing my truths to her, but the half of her face I can see expresses shock and then pleasure. "You really think that about me?"

"Hell yes, I do. Everyone who knows you thinks that."

"Not everyone."

The son of a bitch who hurt her has no place in this room or this moment. "The ones who matter."

"You matter, Sebastian. You always have."

"Same goes, sweetheart."

I drop my head to her shoulder and kiss every inch of soft skin, steering clear of the wounded areas as I work my way down. She follows my directive to stay still, except for the trembles that ripple through her. "You're not afraid, are you?"

"Of you? No."

"Of doing this? With anyone after…"

"No," she says emphatically. "I won't give him that."

"That's my girl." I continue to kiss her and caress the soft globes of her ass and the backs of her legs, making sure that some part of me is touching her constantly, hopefully giving her too much to think about in the here and now so the memories of what happened with *him* can't interfere. That wasn't about love or affection, like this is. It's also about care and concern and need and longing and so many things that defy easy explanation.

My feelings for her have always been complicated, and they're becoming more so by the second. Touching her this way is like a dream come true, a dream I never dared allow myself to have before she looked over her shoulder at me and said, "Please." I want to touch her everywhere, but I'm so afraid of causing her pain that I take it easy with her, giving her vanilla when everything in me wants it kinky. Never more so than with her, but not now. Maybe not ever, but definitely not now.

With my hands on her hips, I lift her so she's on her knees and jam two pillows under her belly to keep her where I want her. "Comfortable?"

"Mmm-hmm."

"Words, Mo. Give me words."

"Yes," she says, sounding a little breathless. "I'm comfortable."

"And nothing hurts?"

"No, but that ache is back…"

Vixen. It's all I can do not to laugh. She knows just what to say to make me crazy. I rest two fingers over her core, which is covered by a scrap of warm electric-blue silk. "Here?"

"Mmm, right there."

I remove my fingers. "Good to know."

She releases a frustrated sound.

"Don't try to top me from the bottom."

"I don't know how to be a bottom."

"You need to learn."

She glances at me over her shoulder. "Will I be allowed to top you?"

"No more talking except if you need your safe word." I kiss and caress her while she continues to tremble, sending the desire pulsing through me into the red zone. She's trembling because she wants me, or so I tell myself. I need to believe that, or I can't do this, no matter how much I want to. And I want to—*badly.*

If she hadn't been so recently injured, I'd fuck her until she begged for mercy, and then I'd do it again and again and *again.* I'd do it until neither of us could walk or move or do anything but sleep off the exhaustion. I could unleash the beast with her, because I know she'd handle it the way most women wouldn't be able to. Marlowe isn't most women, and I've always known she could handle me—all of me—in bed.

No one gets all of me. *Ever.* But Marlowe… She might be the exception to the rule. Eventually. If this becomes something more than right now. In the meantime, I'll give her satisfaction like she's never known, just enough to make her want more. I release the snaps between her legs and push the fabric aside. Before she has time to prepare herself, I run my tongue from the dimples at the base of her spine to her clit, which I suck into the heat of my mouth at the same second I push two fingers deep into her pussy.

Fucking hell, she's tight, and her internal muscles clench around my fingers. I want to howl from the need to replace my fingers with my cock that's now leaking copiously. Instead, I give her my fingers and my tongue and coax her into an orgasm that has her screaming from the power of it.

God, I want her. I want this. I want to do everything with her, but the wounds on her back serve as a stark reminder of why I can't have everything. This has to be enough for now. I remove my fingers and use my tongue to clean her up, tending to every part of her until she's trembling hard again. This was supposed to be one and done, but now that I've had a taste of her, I can't stop. I want more, and judging by the tension I feel coming from her, she does, too.

I slide my fingers back inside her, moving them until I find the angle that makes her gasp. I love that sound and will do whatever it takes to hear it again and again. For the longest time, I use only my fingers, moving them in and out, applying pressure to the place that makes her clench, all the while wondering if this is enough for her, if I'm enough.

She rocks in time with my fingers, defying the order to remain still.

I give her a light smack on the ass to remind her she's not supposed to move.

All the air leaves her in a big whoosh as she settles into the mattress, her hands clutching the sheet.

I love knowing this is affecting her the same way it is me, that she feels a little out of control and off her game and that I'm the one doing that to her. I keep up the torture with my fingers, finding patience I didn't know I had. Then I take her by surprise when I remove them and press my wet fingers against the tight entrance to her ass.

Her back bows and her muscles tighten. "No, Seb. Not there."

She knows the rules of this game as well as I do and is aware that only her safe word will stop me. But she doesn't say the one word that will call a halt to this, and in our world, the word *no* means nothing unless it's accompanied by a safe word.

I press harder, demanding entrance.

"*Seb…*"

I tongue her pussy as I continue to press against her ass, waiting for her to yield to allow me in.

"I can't…"

Still not the word I need to hear to change directions. "Yes, you can. Push back against my fingers."

"*No*," she says on a whimper.

I push my way past her initial resistance, gaining entry. "Easy, sweetheart. Nice and easy."

"Seb..."

"I'm here. I'm right here. I've got you." I add my tongue, dipping into her pussy and swirling around her clit, licking and sucking as I push my fingers deeper into her tight channel while thinking about what it might be like to have her there with my cock. I nearly black out from the surge of pure lust that accompanies that thought.

I fucking love anal, but it's not something I do very often due to my size. Most women can't handle me there, but again, Marlowe isn't most women. When she's on her game, there's nothing she can't handle, even a ten-inch dick in her ass. Or so I think...

I keep up the fingers and the tongue action until I can feel her about to explode, and then I stop moving, leaving her right on the edge with my fingers deep inside her and my tongue pressed against her clit but not moving.

The sound that comes out of her is barely human, and it makes me smile, knowing I'm getting to her.

I bend my fingers ever so slightly, and she screams. I know the difference between screams of pain and those that come from pleasure. This is the latter. She's still screaming when I suck her clit, hard, and she explodes, coming so hard around my fingers that I'll probably be bruised.

It's all I can do not to explode right along with her, but somehow, I manage to hang on—just barely. I bring her down slowly with gentle strokes of my tongue until she collapses into the pillows and mattress, breathing hard. The half of her face that I can see is flushed, and her lips are so plump that I wish I could kiss her.

It occurs to me that I've finger-fucked her ass before I played with her nipples. That would make me laugh under normal circumstances, but nothing about these circumstances is normal. I withdraw my fingers slowly and carefully, reveling in the sounds that come from her as she fights the exit every bit as much as she battled the entry.

I kiss the center of her back and get up. "Stay put. I'll be right back."

CHAPTER 12

Marlowe

I'm completely wrecked. I'm shaking profusely, my ass and sex throbbing with violent aftershocks from two intense orgasms. I'm speechless with disbelief over how he completely owned me. He'd probably be stunned to know that I'm an anal virgin. I've pegged guys who wanted it that way, but I've never had it done to me or wanted it. Being a Domme means you get to say what and how, and that's been a hard no for me.

This is the first time since the training I received at the beginning that I've let anyone dominate me, even lightly. I've never trusted any man enough to allow them that kind of power over me, until now.

My emotions are a mixed-up jumble as I wait for him to return to see what will happen next. I hear the water running in the bathroom, and then there's silence for so long that I begin to wonder what he's doing in there.

Is he... *Oh no. No, no, no, he isn't.*

I jump up off the bed, my legs wobbling under me like they're not capable of holding my weight. I cross the hall to the bathroom and throw open the door to find him stroking the most extraordinary cock I've ever laid eyes on. I'm once again stunned by the sheer size and beauty of it.

"What're you doing?" I keep my gaze fixed on the sight of his hand sliding up and down the long, thick shaft.

He shoots me a defiant look. "What does it look like I'm doing?"

"Why?"

"Because if I don't get some relief, I'm going to injure myself."

Getting me off made him this way, and I love knowing he's in pain from wanting me. I go to him, push his hand away and drop to my knees, compelled to give him the same pleasure he gave me.

"Marlowe, don't." He sounds tense, almost angry, but I could never be afraid of him.

With my hand wrapped around the magnificent cock that stretches past his navel, I look up at him. "What's *your* safe word?"

"I don't have one."

I suck one of his balls into my mouth and run my tongue over it. "You might want to get one. You're going to need it." Running my tongue from the base to the wide, wet tip, I revel in the breath he sucks in, the tense way he holds himself and the fist he makes in my hair. "What's that word, Sebastian?"

"Same as yours. It can be ours." His words are choppy and stilted, not at all the confident way he normally speaks. That and the hard cock in my hand tells me everything I need to know about how badly he wants me. Empowered, I suck him into my mouth, taking him all the way back to my throat, but even that only encompasses about half of him. I use my hand on the other half, stroking as my throat closes tight around him.

"*Fuck*. Marlowe..."

I hear the note of warning in the way he says my name, but I don't need to be warned off this man. My body aches from my injuries as much as the desire to have so much more of him now that we've shattered the walls we'd erected to protect our friendship. With everything on the line, there's no need to hold back. I use my free hand to cup his balls and squeeze, gently but insistently, as I rub the area behind them with my index finger.

His body jerks in the second before he comes in a hot rush down my throat.

I stroke and suck him until he sags against the pedestal sink, his cock almost as hard as it was before he came. I let him down slowly, sliding my lips and tongue over the long shaft, making him shudder from the sensations as the head leaves my mouth with a pop.

I look up to find him staring down at me with fire in his eyes.

"No solo missions, you hear me?"

"Yeah."

"Yeah, who?"

He straightens ever so slightly out of the slouch he'd fallen into. "Yes, ma'am."

I flash a satisfied grin and receive one in return. "Well, that was fun. What's next on our agenda?"

"Food."

I frown. "I want more of this." I kiss his cock, and he flinches before releasing the tight grip he has on my hair.

"That's enough for now."

"No, it isn't."

"Yes, it is. Two days ago, you sustained painful injuries. The last thing we need to do now is aggravate them."

"Is that an excuse to quit while we're ahead?"

His fierce scowl doesn't do a thing for me. "It's not an excuse."

"I'm fine. I want more." I kiss the base of his cock. "I want this. Inside me." Even as I say that, I wonder how it will feel. He'll be the biggest guy I've ever been with.

"Marlowe…" With his hands on my head, he arranges me so he can slide out of my clutches.

"Are you saying no?"

"I'm most definitely not saying no. I'm saying let's take our time. Let's build up to that."

"You had your fingers up my ass twenty minutes ago. I'd say we've already built up to whatever we want next."

He starts to speak, but the words die on his lips as he shakes his head. "This is why two Doms shouldn't be together. Everyone wants to be in charge."

"We'll take turns."

"You just had your turn. Now it's mine, and I say we eat."

"I'm not hungry for food." I eye his cock in case he's still wondering what I'm hungry for.

"Too bad. You're not in charge. I am, and we're going to eat." He helps me up from the floor and surprises me when he wraps an arm tight around my waist and tips my chin up to receive a soft, sweet kiss. My lips are a little sore from the effort to accommodate that beast in his pants, but I don't want to stop kissing him, even after he pulls back. "Easy, sweet girl. We have all the time in the world to figure this out. It doesn't all have to happen now."

While I agree with him, part of me is afraid that if it doesn't happen now, it never will. I already know I'd be missing out on something extraordinary if it never happens. Wrapped up in his comfortable embrace, with his cock hard and insistent between us, I resolve to have my way with him when it's my turn to be in charge again.

***

After Sebastian leaves for work later that afternoon, I get out my phone, turn it on and find numerous new messages from Rafe, who's contacting me on borrowed phones.

I send a text to Leah. *Get me a new phone with a new number ASAP, will you?*

On it. Will bring it over later on.

Tomorrow is fine.

She responds with a thumbs-up.

Next, I do a search in my messages for the one I received a couple of months ago from Teagan Daily, another high-profile actress known for her role in an ongoing superhero franchise.

Got your number from Tenley, she wrote, referring to our stylist. *Heard you're seeing Rafe. We should talk. Kinda 911. Call me any time.*

Her message was followed a week later by one from Veronica Jones, a model and actress I worked with on a film years ago. *Marlowe*, she'd written, *please call me about Rafe. Stuff you should know.*

I put through the call to Teagan and get her voicemail.

"Hey, it's Marlowe Sloane. Give me a call when you can. Thanks."

She calls me back five minutes later. "Hey, stranger, nice to hear from you. How are you?"

"I've been better."

"Uh-oh."

"Yeah."

"Marlowe..."

"I'm sorry I didn't respond when you reached out. I was still in the rose-colored-glasses stage."

"I assume that stage has ended?"

"In rather dramatic fashion, actually."

"Are you hurt?"

"Nothing that won't heal. Eventually."

"I'm so, so sorry that happened to you."

"I take it I'm not the first to experience the charming Frenchman's dark side."

"Oh, hell no. Twelve that I know about so far, many of them B-listers with too much to lose by going public."

I'm shocked to hear that. "What's being done?"

"Well, to be honest, nothing as long as you were with him. No one wanted to do that to you if you were happy, and a few were concerned about him flexing his muscles in Hollywood to ruin them with overseas distributors."

"I feel sick. I don't know what came over me with him. I ignored the concerns of my closest friends."

"Don't beat yourself up for that. Everyone has the same story of being sucked in, bowled over by his charm and the romance of it all. Until he showed his true colors a couple of months later when they would feel they were the crazy ones. Because how could this man who has been everything they ever wanted in a partner actually be a monster. Sound familiar?"

"God, yes. All too familiar. I'm not with him anymore, and my business partners let his company know that if they wish to continue doing business with Quantum, they'll end their association with him immediately. I hear that's already happened."

"That's excellent news. You should know that others have reached out to Pierre about him, but their concerns have been ignored. Someone of your stature and that of Quantum can make a big difference."

That infuriates me. "I want to go public with this."

"Are you sure?"

"Fuck yes, I'm sure. I don't want him to do to anyone else what he's done to me and you and the others. It's time to end this guy."

"I'm so happy to hear you say that."

"Let me get with our publicist, Liza, and make a plan. If you want to let the others know to reach out to me if they want in, that's fine with me. Best to do it by email as I'll be getting a new phone." I give her my email address. "Pass it on to anyone who should have it."

"I will. You have no idea how much it'll mean to everyone else to have your support."

"It means a lot to me to have theirs, to know I'm not alone in this."

"You're not alone. Not at all. If you need to talk about it, call me any time. I've been right where you are, and I know how difficult it is."

"That's very kind of you to offer. I'm more okay than I should be in light of everything. I've been surrounded by great friends and support."

"Glad to hear it. Let me know how you wish to proceed. I'm more than happy to follow your lead, and I'm sure the others will be, too."

"I'll get back to you in the next day or two."

"I'll look forward to hearing from you, and in case I don't get the chance, best of luck at the Oscars. I voted for you."

"Thanks so much." The reminder that the Oscars are right around the corner has me wondering about the timing of my plan to go public with accusations about Rafe. I'd hate to do anything to harm the campaign being waged to elevate *Insidious*. We pay Liza to know that stuff, so I'll turn it over to her to worry about the timing.

"You and Flynn were awesome in *Insidious*. I hope you all win big. Everyone is talking about Quantum repeating."

"Wouldn't that be something?"

"Indeed, it would. I'll talk to you soon."

"Yes, you will." I end the call feeling pissed and empowered to use my platform to bring down a serial predator. After finding Liza's number in my contacts, I put through the call.

Liza answers on the second ring. "Hey, Marlowe. I was going to call you tomorrow to talk about Oscar interviews."

"I have something more pressing I need your help with."

"Of course. What's up?"

"You know I was seeing Rafael Laurent, right?"

"Was, as in past tense?"

"Yes."

"I'm sorry to hear that."

"Don't be. He beat the crap out of me and left me tied up for hours until someone found me."

Her sharp gasp echoes through the phone. "My God. Marlowe... Are you all right?"

"I will be, but it's been brought to my attention that I'm not the first to be treated this way by him. In fact, there're a dozen or so women prepared to join me in going public with our accusations against him, and that's where you come in."

"Wow, well… I'm so sorry for what you've been through."

"Thank you. Tell me you'll help us ruin him."

"You bet I will. But, Marlowe…"

She's quiet for so long that I have to make the next move. "Speak freely, Liza. That's what we pay you to do."

"I just want you to be prepared for the emotional toll that speaking up will take on you and the others. I'd hate to see you or any of the other women revictimized. Social media will be brutal, the coverage will be brutal, every aspect of your life will be open to scrutiny. It could get really ugly, and I know how fiercely you protect your privacy."

"We can't let him continue to get away with this."

"Have you been in touch with the police?"

"No."

"Maybe you should be?"

"What good will that do? He's in France, where our police have no jurisdiction."

"It would help our cause to have the details recorded in a police report before we go public."

Ugh, I so don't want to do that.

"Doesn't Kristian have a contact with the LAPD?"

"Yeah." The three-decade-old murder of Kristian's mother was finally solved last year by the son of the detective who'd been on the case from the beginning.

"Can you come into the office tomorrow? I can ask Kris to call his guy, and I think Emmett should be there, too. You're going to want legal counsel on this."

Because Rafe won't take this lying down, is what she means. "I can do that. Set it up, and let me know what time to be there."

"Will do."

"Tell me I'm doing the right thing, Liza."

"With twelve other women who can attest to similar treatment, you're absolutely doing the right thing lending your celebrity and your huge platform to making sure this guy is stopped."

"And will it hurt anything we're doing for *Insidious*?"

"I can't see how it would. It may even help. People will be furious to know you were assaulted by a man you were involved with."

"I'm not doing it to advance my chances with the Academy."

"Of course you aren't. I'm sure your sincerity will be apparent in how you tell your story. I wouldn't worry about the Academy."

"Thank you. Text me the time of the meeting. I'll be there."

"Will do."

She ends the call, and I sit for a long time, thinking about what she said and wondering whether I'm prepared to open my heart and soul for the scrutiny that'll come my way once this goes public. It's been a long time—almost two decades, in fact—since I burst onto the scene and became a target for the paparazzi. They still follow me, but it's not like it was in the beginning when I couldn't go anywhere without being pursued.

This will restart that madness, and I have to be aware of that before it happens.

I shiver in revulsion, thinking about those early days of being famous and how bizarre it was to suddenly be recognized everywhere I went. People think being famous is the ultimate until they realize the loss of privacy can leave a deep wound on one's psyche that never really heals. I ended up on anxiety meds and was cruising toward a drinking problem until I took control and doubled my focus on the work rather than obsessing about the bullshit that went along with it.

Flynn helped me so much during those heady days when we were both dealing with newfound fame. Having come from Hollywood royalty, he had perspective I badly needed. He took me home to Beverly Hills to meet Max Godfrey and Stella Flynn, who wrapped their arms around me and took me into their family, where I've remained ever since. I never would've survived those early years without the three of them.

So it seems only natural now to reach out to Flynn, the brother of my heart, as I'm about to enter the maelstrom once again.

He answers right away. "Mo. You okay?"

I smile because I knew that would be his first question. "I'm okay."

His slow exhale is audible. "I'm glad to hear that. Been worried about you."

"I'm sorry you've been worried. I wanted to tell you I spoke to Teagan Daily tonight."

"What's up with her?"

"She used to date Rafe. She, um, she reached out to me when I started seeing him, said we should talk, but I never got around to returning her text. I called her tonight and found out there're twelve others, Flynn. He's done this to at least twelve other women." My eyes fill, and my throat tightens around a knot of emotion.

"Son of a bitch," Flynn mutters. "What're you going to do about it?"

I love that he knows me so well. "I'm going public."

"That's my girl."

"My hands are shaking and my stomach hurts, but I'm doing it. Teagan said the others decided to stay quiet because I was seeing him, and they didn't want to hurt me. The least I can do is step up for them and make it so he can't do this to anyone else."

"That's right, sweetheart. You're doing the right thing."

"I'm scared." I can say that to him and know there'll never be any judgment. I don't have to be a badass with my best friend.

"We'll all be right there with you. You know that."

"Yeah, I do, and that helps so much. The timing sucks with the Oscars coming up."

"Fuck the Oscars."

"I don't want to take the spotlight off *Insidious*."

"Don't worry about that. The film will get its moment."

"You think Hayden will feel the same way?" He pours everything he has into every film he directs, and *Insidious* was no exception. Flynn played a drug addict at rock bottom, and I was his counselor. We're both up for Oscars, and the film is up for best picture. In addition, Hayden was nominated for directing and Jasper for cinematography. To say we have a lot at stake as a company is putting it mildly.

"I'd bet my life on it. Hayden would tell you to do whatever you need to and not to worry about us."

"I'm not sure what I ever did to deserve friends like you guys."

"We feel the same way about you. Don't ever doubt that. Addie told me she had to physically sit on Hayden to keep him from flying to France to hunt down Rafe and murder him after he saw what that guy did to you."

"That's so sweet of him, although I doubt he minded having Addie sit on him."

Flynn snorts out a laugh. "Don't put those thoughts in my head." He's incredibly protective of his assistant. He refers to her as his fourth sister. "And just for the record, we all want to kill him."

"Don't do that. It won't help anything. And besides, your complexion would totally wash out in prison orange."

"True," he says on a low chuckle.

"And you have a baby on the way who will need his or her daddy."

"Her."

"It's a *girl?*"

"Yep."

"Ah, Flynn…" I close my eyes to contain a rush of tears. "I'm so happy for you and Nat."

"Thank you, Auntie Mo. We're pretty thrilled for us, too."

Auntie Mo. I like the sound of that. "I'm going to spoil her rotten."

"I wouldn't expect anything less. We love you. You know that, don't you?"

"Of course I do. Love you right back."

"I gotta tell you something."

"What's that?"

"When you first started seeing him, I had him investigated."

"Flynn! What the fuck? You did not!"

"I did, and Gordon… He found out that Rafe's ex-wife accused him of knocking her around during their divorce."

My brain goes completely blank with shock.

"I'm so sorry, Mo. If I'd told you that, none of this would've happened. I was so afraid you'd be pissed at me for investigating him in the first place."

"I would've been."

"Still, I should've told you."

"Guess what?"

"What?"

"He told me he'd never been married, and I believed him."

Flynn gasps. "Seriously? He *lied* about being married?"

"Yep, and I was so caught up in the myth that it never occurred to me to check."

"That son of a bitch. We're going to get you through this so we can focus on all the good stuff that's coming. Don't worry about anything."

"Best friend ever."

"You still think so after I told you I had him investigated and didn't tell you what I found out?"

"I'll always think that."

"Right back atcha."

"There's probably going to be a press conference about this tomorrow—"

"I'll be there. We'll all be there."

"Thank you."

"Try to get some sleep, and remember, this too shall pass. It'll be a blip."

We both know it'll be way more than a blip, but I appreciate him trying to downplay it. "I'll see you tomorrow."

"Yes, you will. Call me if you need anything—any time. Night or day."

"I will. Thanks."

"Love you, kid."

"Love you, too."

Talking to him always makes me feel better about whatever is weighing on me. I'm not at all surprised that he took the extra step of having Rafe investigated or that he kept the worst of the findings from me out of respect for the fact that I seemed so happy with him. From the first time we met on the set of a cheesy B movie, Flynn and I have been the best of friends. We tried dating for about a week, but when we couldn't get naked without laughing, we realized we'd be better as friends than lovers. He's been the brother I never had ever since, and through him, I added my other "brothers"—Hayden, Kristian, Jasper and Emmett. Along with the Godfreys, they're the only family I have, and I'd truly be lost without them.

It occurs to me that I didn't include Sebastian on my list of "brothers." I've never put him into that category, a realization that has me sitting up straighter on his sofa. Sebastian has always been separate from the other guys in my mind, and it's never occurred to me to wonder why. I refused to allow myself to go "there" because I didn't think he'd ever be interested in more than friendship with me. After all, the man doesn't do commitment of any kind, so why would I think he'd want something with me?

Now that I know how he really feels, it's like I'm allowed to officially recategorize him, moving him from the friend column to the lover column.

A shiver of anticipation runs through me as I glance at the clock and wonder what time he'll be home.

When he gets here, I'll be ready.

CHAPTER 13

Sebastian

I'm off my game tonight, distracted, irritated, out of sorts. Usually, I love my job, even dealing with stupid people who have to be reminded repeatedly of our rules. They usually don't bother me, but tonight, they're on my last nerve. For the first time since the Quantum team put me in charge of their LA nightclub, I don't want to be here.

Quisha raises a brow in my direction after I snap at one of the security guys who wants my help with something that ought to be his problem.

"You cranky tonight, boss man." As always, Quisha is in full hair and makeup. Her brown skin fairly shimmers with the sparkly crap that ends up all over me when we work together.

"I get sick of people needing my help with everything."

"That's your own fault. You make them all codependent by being willing to help with whatever they need."

"I don't do that."

"Ah, yeah, you do."

Most of the time, I like how she has no fear of speaking her mind to her new boss. This is not one of those times. "We need more Ketel One and Maker's Mark." I hope that ends the psychoanalysis.

"I'm on it." Teetering on four-inch heels, she heads for the storeroom to replenish.

I don't know how she can stand those heels for five and six hours at a time. When I suggested she might want to wear more comfortable shoes to work, the look she gave me made my balls shrivel. So I mind my own business.

While she's in the back room, I fill a couple of drink orders and wipe down the bar. I keep a close eye on what's happening on the floor. Multiple scenes are playing out, mostly naked bodies writhe with pleasure and discomfort, but I couldn't be less interested if I tried. Usually, I like to watch the various scenes, as I often learn something new from the other Doms. Tonight, I don't care.

All I want is to be home with Marlowe. After the taste I had earlier, I want to gorge. I've been partially hard all afternoon and evening, which is probably why I'm so bitchy tonight.

The clock inches closer to ten, and when Quisha returns with the liquor replenishments, I decide to leave early—another thing I never, ever do. I take my responsibilities as well as the faith the Quantum principals have placed in me seriously, but Quisha is right. I'm in a mood and no good to anyone here.

"I'm going to punch out early. You got the bar?"

If she's surprised, she hides it well. "I've got the bar. I'll put the drawer on your desk."

"No exceptions on the two-drink limit."

"Right."

"I mean it, Quisha. That's our line in the sand. Anyone who plays in our club does so with a clear mind. Liquid courage has no place here."

"Understood. Go on home, boss man. We gotcha covered."

I hesitate, but only for a second before nodding and heading for my office to grab the keys off my desk. Before I go, I look for Stu, the security guy I just reamed, and find him on the far side of the room, watching the floor. "Sorry for being a dick."

"No worries."

"I'm going to take off. Call if you need anything."

He nods, while making a piss-poor attempt to hide his shock at me leaving early. "Make sure Quisha and the others get to their cars before you leave." I never leave until everyone else is safely on their way.

"Will do."

"Thank you." I get the fuck out of there before something can come up that requires my attention. I'm in my truck and headed home two minutes later, with the window open to let in the warm, fresh air that washes over me as I drive faster than I should to get to her. What happened earlier has set off a fever in my blood that only more of her can cure.

I always knew it would be this way if I ever crossed the line with her, which is why I stayed firmly on my side of that line. And now that we've stepped over, we can never go back to who we were to each other only this morning. Which is just fine with me. Now that I've had a taste, I'm determined to do whatever it takes to make her mine. To fuck with the consequences.

The thirty-minute ride to Malibu is made longer by an accident that snarls traffic. Forty-five minutes after I left the club, I finally pull into my driveway and cut the engine. As I go inside, I realize my foul mood is gone. I'm elated to know that I'll see her in a matter of seconds—if she's still awake.

I walk inside to find candles all over my living room, soft music playing on the sound system and a goddess asleep on my sofa. She's wearing a silky black thing that clings to all her curves, and her hair is like spun gold that's been set on fire against a white pillow.

I drop my jacket on a chair and go to her, sitting on the coffee table and taking a full minute just to stare at her before I drag my fingertip lightly over her arm. The bruises that mar her otherwise perfect skin enrage me. If I ever see that guy again, I'll end him.

She's lying on her side, and her full, lush breasts nearly spill out of the scraps of silk that pass for a nightgown. I love that she set this scene with candles Leah must've brought, knowing I'd come home to find her this way. As a fellow Dom, I understand the importance of setting a scene.

I continue to run my finger up and down her arm until she stirs, her eyes fluttering open and lighting up with pleasure when she sees me there. "You're home."

Those two little words inspire a wild yearning in me for a home that includes her, which is something I've never once wanted with any woman. I bring her hand to my lips. "I'm home. I see you kept busy while I was at work."

She smiles. "I was once told I look my best in candlelight."

"You look your best in any light."

Her smile broadens to encompass her eyes, which twinkle with mischief and delight. "Are you home early?"

"Maybe. Are you going to tell my bosses?"

"Depends."

"On?"

"Whether you're nice to me."

"Baby, I'll always be nice to you." I slide my arms under her, pick her up and bring her into my embrace. Though she's fierce and fiery on the outside, her bones are small and fragile, and the thought of that guy hurting her makes me crazy. I hold her close, breathing in the distinctive scent of her that reminds me of an aromatherapy candle my mother has. Marlowe's scent reminds me of home, a realization that has my heart doing backflips in my chest.

Her arms curl around my neck, and she looks up at me expectantly.

I'm dying to kiss her, but I hold off, wanting to draw out the suspense. I can't recall the last time I was dying to kiss anyone. Everything feels new again with her, like it's the first time for all the important things, when, in fact, I'm more than twenty years removed from my first time with a woman. "I missed you while I was at work. How's that possible?"

"Not sure, but I missed you, too."

"The staff said I was cranky tonight."

"I hope you fired them," she says with a teasing smile.

"Couldn't really fire them when it was true."

"And why were you cranky?"

"Because I didn't want to be there."

"But you love that job."

"I know, but there was something else I wanted to be doing."

"And what was that?"

"You."

She fans her face dramatically. "Why, Sebastian, I never knew you were such a romantic."

"Neither did I until the hottest babe in the history of hot babes was staying at my house and wearing these little scraps of fabric that barely count as clothes."

"This old thing?"

"You're a vixen and a very naughty girl. You've got me thinking about you when I should be focused on work. What do you suppose we ought to do about that?"

"I suppose I need to be punished."

I wasn't expecting her to say that, and the shock of it has me rock hard in seconds. "Is that what you want?"

"It might be what I need."

When she looks up at me, I see vulnerability. In all the years I've known her, I've never seen that from her before. Not like this anyway, and I'm unnerved to realize she's giving me something so rare and precious.

"But I have concerns."

"Talk to me." I sit back in the chair, grab a blanket to cover her so she won't get cold and snuggle her into my chest. There's no way she can miss that I'm hard for her, so I don't bother to try to hide it.

"Something has changed for me recently."

"How do you mean?"

"The dominance... The thrill is gone. I've been bored by it, and I think that's why I was excited to share it with Rafe."

"How so?"

"I thought if I could make it part of our relationship, maybe I could get back my mojo. We all know how that worked out."

"He was the wrong guy to help you rediscover your mojo. That's on him, not you."

"I know, but I was wrong in more ways than one." She looks up at me. "I'm so tired, Seb."

"Of what, honey?"

"Everything. It's been a long twenty years."

"How so?"

"You know how my mom and I basically ran away from my dad, who wouldn't allow me to pursue acting, right?"

"I've heard the story from others but never from you."

She takes a minute to gather her thoughts while I continue to stroke her silky skin. "My mom was amazing. She's the one who believed I could be a star, and she's the reason I've had this incredible career. My dad was forever telling her to get her head out of the clouds and stop filling me with foolish dreams that would never come true. But she believed. Oh how she believed, and when he refused to let her take me to LA to meet with agents and casting directors, we took off one day while he was at work, and we never looked back. Did you know we lived in our car for the first year?"

"Yeah, I've read about that." The story is now a thing of legend in this town.

"We had a membership to a YMCA where we showered and they let us park in their lot overnight, too. We were giving it six more months when I got cast as Daisy in *Tell Me Your Name*. Ironic that I played a homeless girl in the film that made me when I was technically homeless myself, right?"

"I think it's amazing." I think *she* is amazing.

"The first thing we did when I got paid was rent a furnished one-bedroom apartment. We shared a bed because we were too afraid to spend more than the bare minimum. What if the movie bombed or the critics hated me or I was a one-hit wonder?"

"Of course they loved you. How could they not?"

"It was so crazy what happened after the premiere. Nothing was ever the same again, and it's been a wild ride ever since."

She got her first Oscar, for supporting actress, for the role of Daisy in the film that made her a star.

"It felt like I'd been shot out of a cannon. I went from nothing to everything practically overnight. And then… Then my mom got sick with advanced cancer and was gone four weeks later. I was so lost without her, and everyone wanted a piece of me. I got swept up in the madness. I made a lot of mistakes during that time."

"You were just a kid, Mo. Everyone makes mistakes."

"Not everyone makes mistakes with the whole world watching."

"You mean Demers." She'd had a well-publicized affair with the director of her second film, who was twenty years her senior.

"Yeah. He promised me the world, and all he did was get me pregnant."

"*What?*" I've never heard that before.

"We managed to keep that part out of the press."

"It was on him. He was older and should've known better."

"It wasn't entirely his fault. I was hurting so bad after losing my mom, and he wanted to take care of me."

"He took advantage of a young, grieving girl who was on the way up while he was on his way out."

"My eyes were wide open to who and what he was, Seb. Don't let me off the hook."

"You'll never convince me that he wasn't the one who should've known better."

"Maybe, but I was easily led at that time in my life."

"What happened to the baby?"

"I miscarried at three months. Ended up in the hospital for a week because I lost a lot of blood. I was so sad. I was going to have it and keep it. Somehow. Hard to believe he or she would be in high school now."

"Did you ever tell anyone?"

"Flynn knows. I met him a month after I lost the baby, when we did *Stardust* together. We hit it off instantly. In many ways, I credit him for saving me. He took me under his wing and brought me into the Godfrey family. Max and Stella… They taught me how to do fame in a way that didn't require me to sell my soul to the devil. I'm thankful every day for Flynn, his parents, his sisters and everyone at Quantum. You all are my family since I lost my mom."

"You've had one hell of a ride in this town."

"I don't want you to think I'm not thankful for every bit of it. After the crap with Demers, I never let myself get caught up in something like that again. I was much more discerning about who I let into my life, which is another reason why the thing with Rafe was so out of character for me."

She runs her hand absently up and down my arm as she talks. Her touch drives me mad, but I bite my tongue and let her touch me because I want to hear what she has to say.

"Flynn introduced me to the BDSM lifestyle after Hayden brought him in on it. I loved it from the beginning. It felt so good to have control over one area of my life when everything else felt so out of control, you know?"

"I can totally see how that would be freeing."

"It was just what I needed, but now…"

I run my fingers through her long hair. "What?"

"I'd like to let someone else worry about the details."

"So what you're saying…"

"I'm tired, Seb. I want someone else to take care of me for a while."

"How long is a while?"

"I don't know."

"I want to be the one to take care of you, Marlowe. God knows, I want to be the one. But I don't know if I can do a fling with you."

"Oh, well… Okay."

When she moves to get up, I tighten my hold on her to keep her with me. "You're misunderstanding me, sweetheart. I'm not saying no to *you*. I'm saying no to a *fling*."

"So you want this to be… more?"

I nod. "More than a fling. Beyond that, I don't know."

"I'm still trying to believe you want me that way and never said anything."

"I wish now that I had. I could've saved you from what you went through with *him*."

"Maybe I was meant to go through that so it could lead me to you."

"Wouldn't that be something?"

Smiling, she nods and reaches for me, bringing me in for a kiss. "I've wondered, for years, what it might be like to kiss you."

God, I wish I'd known that. "And now that you have?"

"I wish I'd done it ages ago."

"Come to bed with me. Let me take care of you the way I've wanted to for so long."

"You and I both know this isn't as simple as we're trying to make it."

I know what she means. We're both dominants, and at some point, we'll need to address that dynamic and how it'll work for us. But that doesn't have to happen tonight. "We'll figure it out."

"What if we can't?"

"We will." With her in my arms, I stand and then put her down so we can gather the candles and bring them with us to my room. Normally, I couldn't be bothered with shit like candles and romance, but I want her to have it all. She deserves nothing less than full romance, and I want to be the one to give it to her. "About that punishment you have coming..."

"What about it?"

"How do you think we should handle that?"

She links her index fingers and looks at me expectantly. "I have no idea. You're in charge. I'd think that would be up to you."

I go to her, put my hands on her hips and kiss her forehead, the tip of her nose and then her lips. "Have you ever been a sub?"

"Not in years. I used to switch, but I could never find a Dom who did it for me, so eventually, I stopped trying."

Her words are like gas on my fire. "And that's what you want now? You want me to dominate you, to take control of your pleasure?"

"I want to try." She looks up at me with courage and determination and trust.

Knowing she trusts me is the ultimate pleasure. "Remind me of your safe word." I love that I don't need to explain the rules to her the way I would with a new sub. "And I want a promise. But first the safe word."

"Famous."

I love that she chose that word.

"What do you want me to promise?"

"That when you feel up for it, you'll return the favor."

Her expressive eyes widen. "You want *me* to dominate *you*?"

I nod, keeping my gaze fixed on hers.

"You're not a switch."

"No, I'm not, but you *are* a Domme. If you try to deny who you really are— indefinitely—you'll be unfulfilled. I want you fulfilled and happy and content. I need you to promise me that, when the time is right, you'll take the lead."

Although she still seems unconvinced that it'd be possible to dominate me, she nods. "Okay, I promise."

"And I promise to let you."

A spark of fire lights up her eyes. "I won't go easy on you."

"I wouldn't expect you to."

"Does that mean…" She swallows hard. "You won't go easy on me either?"

"Do you want me to?"

"Hell no."

I would've bet my life on that answer, and she doesn't disappoint.

"Don't you dare go easy on me. I can take whatever you're handing out."

I sincerely doubt that, but I know better than to say so. "Hard limits?"

Her chin goes up in defiance. "None."

"Marlowe… Don't be ridiculous. Of course you have hard limits."

"I don't."

"So I can bring a goat in to pee on you or—"

She pinches my lips together and then releases them. "No animals, no pee."

"See, you do have hard limits. What else?"

"Are we being honest here?"

"Always."

Her bottom lip disappears between her teeth as she seems to contemplate how honest she wants to be. "I was lightly dominated while in training. So I've never really…"

I'm stunned and wildly aroused. "Had done to you what you've done to others?"

"Something like that."

"Why do I suddenly feel like a kid in a candy store?"

"Go easy, Candy Man. You need to break me in slowly."

"Oh, I'll break you in, baby. I'll break you in so good, you'll be begging your Candy Man for more."

"Give it your best shot."

"I want you naked on your hands and knees in the middle of my bed. And hurry up about it."

As she removes the nightgown, I notice a slight tremble in her hands. It thrills me to know she's excited and nervous. There's nothing I love better than a sub who's a little afraid of what's coming. The fear exacerbates the pleasure. And a sub who's actually a Domme stepping outside her comfort zone? Even better.

When she's in position, I study her for a long time, planning my approach and making a mental list of what I'll need while trying to ignore the intense desire that makes my cock ache from wanting her. *Not yet. But soon…*

"Don't move."

She tosses a saucy look over her shoulder. "Where would I go?"

"Talking back to your Dom, sub? Never a good idea, especially from someone who should know the rules by now. Let me refresh your memory. You're not to speak unless your Dom asks you a direct question or unless you require your safe word. Understood?"

"Yes."

I swear she's doing this on purpose. "Yes, who?"

"Sir. Yes, sir."

"Much better. Now don't move." I leave the bedroom and go into my office where I keep a locked cabinet with items intended to provide the ultimate pleasure. When I have what I need, I return to the bedroom.

Marlowe is right where I left her. Upon closer inspection, I note a slight tremble in her thighs that thrills me. I can't wait to make her tremble everywhere.

If I make her scream, too? Even better.

CHAPTER 14

Marlowe

He's drawing this out to torture me, and it's definitely working. I'm impatient by nature, which is why I'm better suited to being in charge rather than being the one left waiting for the Dom to get on with it already. But I know better than to mouth off, so I voice my frustrations internally when I'd prefer to air them out.

I can't believe I'm actually doing this or how relieved I am to know that I don't have to do any of the thinking. I'm just along for the ride. I've seen Sebastian in Dom mode, so I have an idea of what to expect. He's intense, focused and driven, three qualities I admire in others. But I've never yet had a lover who was all three of those things. Usually, they're one of the three, but never all.

His intensity makes me nervous even as my arousal spikes to previously unmatched levels. Every part of me is on full alert. My nipples tingle, my clit throbs and my muscles quiver in anticipation.

In my effort to put the nightmare with Rafe behind me, I've found something new in a longtime friend, and it's just what I need. Being with someone who truly cares about me the way Sebastian does, someone I can trust implicitly, allows me to relax in a way I usually can't with other men. I'm always questioning their motives and wondering if they're with me for me or for what I can do for them and their careers.

None of that is a concern with Sebastian, who was a true friend long before we ever changed the rules between us. He wants this to be more than a fling, and now that I know how he feels, I can picture us together in a way I couldn't have only a week ago. Funny how things can change when people are honest with each other.

That said, I'm well aware of his issues in the area of commitment, so while I feel comfortable with him in this context, it would do me well to guard my heart where he's concerned. I already care about him so much. Enough that he could probably break my heart if I let him.

The bed dips behind me, and then he's there, his hands on my ass, squeezing and shaping, his hard cock hot against my most sensitive flesh. The coarse hair on his legs brushing against the backs of my legs gives me goose bumps.

I have to give him credit—he's barely touched me, and I'm more aroused than I can recall being in, well, ever.

"You've been a very naughty girl, haven't you?"

"Yes, sir." My voice sounds weird. I wonder if he notices it, too.

"Are you scared, Marlowe?"

"No." I clear my throat. "No, sir." I'm not at all afraid of him.

"What do you think your punishment should be?"

"I leave that up to you, sir. You know what's best for me."

The sound that comes from him is a cross between a groan and a growl. "I believe a spanking is in order."

"I-if you say so, sir."

"I do." He cups and squeezes my ass cheeks. "I say so. How many spanks do you think you deserve?"

"Ah, three?"

"That's nowhere near enough. We need three for you talking back to your Dom and at least five more for you blaming yourself for things that aren't your fault. And then there're the secrets you've been keeping from me."

"What secrets?"

I hear the smack of his hand against my ass before I feel the burn that spreads like an out-of-control wildfire from my backside to my sex in a matter of seconds. I've been spanked before, but it never did much for me. I should've known it would be different with him.

He rubs the spot where his hand connected with my flesh. "Are you recalling the secrets you kept from me yet?"

"No, sir."

His hand connects with the other cheek, and my reaction is even more pronounced the second time. "Mmmm, someone likes being spanked."

I do like it. I like that I can turn over my pleasure to him and not have to think about anything other than what he decides I should think about. My brain is tired, and as Sebastian administers my "punishment," I feel myself shutting down, checking out and focusing completely on the pleasure that's so overwhelming, there's no room for anything else. Nothing else matters but him and me and what's happening right here and now.

One little thought keeps entering my mind, however.

All this time…

He was right here. Capable of *this*.

The next thing I'm aware of is his tongue between my legs, his fingers inside me and the orgasm that seems to come from nowhere, flinging me up and then dropping me into a free fall that makes me scream.

"Ready for more?" His voice is gruff and sexy, letting me know I'm not the only one being swept up in this.

"Yes, sir."

"Do we need birth control? Condoms?"

"I'm protected and safe, if you are."

"I got tested two weeks ago and haven't been with anyone since."

"We don't need condoms, then."

He pushes his cock into me, and I cry out again. The struggle to accommodate him is epic, and before he's halfway in, I've already come again. This can't be real.

These things don't happen to me. I became a Domme because I'd rarely encountered a man who could make me feel anything special when it came to sex. Rather than be continuously disappointed, I'd taken matters into my own hands and doled out the pleasure while rarely taking any for myself.

Rafe had been an exception. I enjoyed sex with him, but I could never let go entirely, probably because I knew instinctively that I couldn't really trust him.

But this... Sebastian still hasn't given me all of him, and I already know he's the best I've ever had.

His hand comes down again on my right cheek. "Let me in."

I force myself to relax, to breathe, to surrender to him.

"Yes. Like that. Just like that."

I'm stretched to my absolute limit and having one orgasm after another. Every nerve ending is on high alert for what comes next.

Grasping my hips, he pulls out and then slams back in.

My eyes roll back in my head, and my mouth opens on a silent scream.

Sebastian

I knew it would be good with her, but this is something else altogether. I have to remind myself to go easy on her, that she was badly injured only a few days ago. Despite her claims to the contrary, she's not ready for any of this, but damn if I could bring myself to say no to her after she told me what she wanted.

Her skin is so soft, her pussy tight, wet and hot. She's a dream come true, a dream I never allowed myself to have. And now that she's here in my home and my bed and my arms, I hope she plans to stick around, because I don't think I could stand to let her go.

I hate to think that we owe that son of a bitch Rafe a debt of gratitude, but this wouldn't be happening if he hadn't done what he did to her. It's an awful thought, but it's the truth no matter how much we both might wish otherwise.

I want to see her face, that gorgeous, one-in-a-million face that millions of men the world over have fallen in love with. I withdraw from her, and she gasps from the impact of my departure. Next to her, I stretch out on my back. "Get on top."

It takes her a second to get herself together and follow my direction.

I'm satisfied to note that her brain seems somewhat scrambled. Excellent. If she's scrambled, she's not blaming herself for what happened with *him* or worrying about going public with what *he* did or focused on anything other than pleasure. That's all I want her thinking about while we're together. She's got enough to think about the rest of the time. In here, it's all about her.

She's still trying to get herself situated, so I decide to move things along, lifting her by the hips and bringing her down on top of me, cautious not to do anything to further injure her. The marks and bruises on her skin infuriate me. She may have my handprints on her ass tomorrow, but she asked for that. She certainly didn't ask for the bruises that mar the flawless skin on her face, ribs, arms and legs or the healing lash marks on her back.

I grasp my cock around the base. "Take me."

Her gaze crashes into mine when she raises herself to follow my order.

I don't do eye contact during sex. It's too personal, but I can't look away from her. I want her to know exactly who she's doing this with.

She comes down on my cock, her eyes widening and her mouth forming an O.

Not every woman can handle me, but I always knew she could. She's a badass. There's nothing she can't handle, even a ten-inch cock. But it takes some time for her to accept all of me, which is fine. I've got nowhere to be until late tomorrow afternoon. I can wait all night for her to work her way onto me, one torturous inch at a time.

I slide my hands from her hips to her luscious, full breasts, cupping them and teasing her nipples. Part of me can't believe that Marlowe Sloane is naked in my bed and riding me with such abandon. I want to ask if she's okay, if anything hurts, but I don't want to take her out of the moment by asking about injuries that *he* gave her. No, I want her thinking only of me and us and this.

"I… I don't think I can do it." She's taken half of me.

"Yes, you can."

She shakes her head.

"Do you need your safe word?"

"No."

"You sure?"

"No."

I laugh as I raise my hips to give her some more of what she thinks she's already got enough of. "Nice and easy, sugar. You got this."

"You got too much."

"Shhhh, no talking. Just feel."

"I feel like I'm being split in half."

I let her get away with the chatter because submitting is new to her, but we're going to have a conversation about topping from the bottom after this. I decide to cut her a break and sit up, wrapping my arms around her lower back where there's no chance of brushing up against the wounds. The new position sends me deeper into her.

"Jesus," she mutters.

"No, it's Sebastian. Hasn't anyone ever told you it's poor form to use another man's name when you're in bed with someone?"

"Very funny." Her teeth are gritted, her fingers dig into my shoulders, and I can feel her having one small orgasm after another.

Despite her protests, she's enjoying this, which is all that matters. I cup her ass, spread her cheeks and lift her, bringing her nipples close enough to my mouth that I can lick and suck and bite them.

She fists my hair and pulls so hard I see stars, but I don't let up, and when I release her many minutes later, she slides down the full length of me and explodes. Her orgasm is so intense that I can't hold back my own. I anchor her hips and power into her, giving in to the desire that seems to come from my very soul.

She comes down on top of me, breathing hard as her pussy continues to contract around my dick, a feeling I could very easily become addicted to. She's a feeling I could very easily become addicted to.

"Are you okay?" I need to know that we didn't make anything worse.

"Mmmmm." She sounds blissed out, which is how I want her.

"Anything hurt?"

"Not at the moment, but I'm going to feel that later."

I run my fingers through her hair with one hand and caress her sweet ass with the other. "I like that you're going to feel me when I'm gone."

"I'll feel you for days."

"Then my work here is finished."

She raises her head to give me a defiant look. "And here I thought your work was just getting started."

"You're right. It is. I've only begun to scratch the surface of my Marlowe-related fantasies."

Her head returns to my chest, and the silk of her hair against my skin fires me up all over again, as if I didn't just come so hard, I nearly blacked out.

"I'm sorry." Her softly spoken words put me on alert.

"For what?"

"That I never once allowed myself to consider this possibility because we were such good friends, which I now realize was seriously stupid on my part. Friendship is a great place to start."

"No need to apologize, babe. I thought of you this way many times but never said anything. We were both a little stupid."

"Will you promise me something?"

"Right about now, you could ask me for anything, and I'd give it to you if I could."

"I only want one thing."

"Name it."

"No matter what happens between us, promise we'll still be friends."

"Always."

"You promise?"

"I will if you will."

"I promise."

We exist in peaceful silence for a long while until she speaks up again. "There's something else I want."

"Tell me."

"If you're doing this with me, you're not doing it with anyone else. That's nonnegotiable for me. I don't share."

I can't help the laughter that spills out of me, even though I know she's dead serious.

Her head comes up off my chest, her brows narrowed and her fabulous green eyes shooting daggers at me. "Why're you laughing?"

"Because if I have the gorgeous, sexy, brilliant, *incredible* Marlowe Sloane in my bed, I have absolutely no need for anyone else. You don't have to worry about me looking for side jobs."

"Even when you want someone who's completely submissive to you?"

"Even then."

"Even when you're surrounded by sexy, willing women every night at work?"

"*Especially* then. You know how rarely I partake of the offers I receive at work." I give her hair a gentle tug, compelling her to look at me. "I've had a lot of fun with a lot of different women—and a few men."

"Is that right?"

"Uh-huh. Does that shock you?"

"Not really. I knew you were adventuresome, even if you kept most of your adventures private."

"I never have gotten into the public aspects of our lifestyle. Once in a while, but not as a rule."

"I don't mind being public when I'm in charge, but I'm not into being the vulnerable one on public display. People would enjoy that too much."

"Because of who you are."

She nods. "I don't really have the luxury of letting it all hang out in public, even if I have faith in the NDAs. It's too easy, especially these days, for people to post something online in a matter of seconds. I've walked a fine line between participating in the lifestyle and doing it in a way that would never leave me open to exploitation. If the public were to see me tricked out like a Domme, I could say it was research for a role. If they saw some guy dominating me, I'd be hard-pressed to explain that, you know?"

"I get it." I've never thought about that from her perspective, but it does make sense when she explains it to me. "If you were outed as a Domme, it would only add to your badass reputation."

She laughs. "That's true."

Something else occurs to me, something so big and wild that I'm not sure if I should go there with her, even in this moment of intimate honesty.

"Why did your whole body just go tense?"

"I... I'm not sure if I should say it."

"Why would you hold back now?"

Why indeed? "It's just that I wondered..."

"About?"

"Are you really a Domme, or have you been hiding behind the whip?"

The question makes her uncomfortable. I can see that in the way her brows furrow and her lips pucker into a thoughtful expression. "I'm really a Domme. I like to be in charge."

"But do you like to be in charge because you truly get off on it, or is it because no one has ever gotten *you* off properly?"

"I don't actually get off on being in charge."

I hold her chin so she has to look at me. "Wait. *What?*"

She licks her lips and then rolls her bottom lip between her teeth.

I stare into her eyes. "Spill it."

She shakes her head and closes her eyes.

"Marlowe… It's me. You can tell me anything, and it'll never be repeated. Tell me you know that."

"I do. It's just that I've never told anyone…"

I'm desperate to know what she's never told anyone. I run a hand from her shoulder down her arm and link our fingers, waiting her out even as my heartbeat slows and I barely breathe as I hope she'll confide in me. I *need* her to confide in me.

After a long pause, she speaks softly. "Being a Domme has never been about satisfaction for me. I don't… It doesn't… It doesn't do anything for me."

"Marlowe." I exhale the deep breath I was holding as I drop to the mattress, shocked and dismayed by her confession. "What *does* do it for you?"

"You did just now."

"Before me, before this?"

"Rafe and I had pretty good sex. It was fun, and he tried really hard, but…"

"He never made you come?"

"No, but he doesn't know that. I…"

"Oh my God! You *faked* it with him?"

"I didn't want to! I wanted him to be different. You have no idea how much I wanted that, but I can never really let go with guys because…" Her voice catches, and a sob comes from deep inside her.

I move quickly to embrace her, to offer comfort—whatever she needs. I can't bear to see her cry. "Shhh. It's okay, baby."

"It's not okay. I'm a fucking fraud. I dominate guys so I won't have to deal with my inadequacies."

"There's *nothing* inadequate about you." The idea that she could think that is mind-boggling to me. "When I look at you, I see perfection. A woman in charge of her own life and her own hugely successful career. I see beauty and resilience and fortitude. I see authenticity."

She shakes her head. "I'm not authentic."

"Yes, you are." I brush the hair back from her face, sweeping away tears at the same time. "You're true to yourself and the people you love. You're fiercely loyal and steadfast and so heartbreakingly beautiful. And you know what makes you beautiful? The fact that you don't even know you are."

It doesn't matter to me if I sound like a man in love as I go on about her many positive qualities. Whatever it takes to convince her that she's in no way inadequate. That she could even think such a thing breaks something inside me.

"You're a very good friend to say such nice things about me."

"I'm not just saying nice things to make you feel better. Everything I said is true." I continue to stroke her hair and caress her back. "Tell me how this happened."

"How what happened?"

"How did you become a Domme who doesn't really want to be a Domme?"

"It's not that I don't want to be a Domme. It's more that it's never about me. It's always about the sub of the moment."

"It should be about both of you."

She shrugs. "That's not how it's been for me."

"Tell me why. Start at the beginning."

CHAPTER 15

Marlowe

It's been a long time since I've thought about how I became involved in the scene that's been so much a part of my life.

"You know that Flynn and I were briefly involved way back when. It didn't take long for us to realize we were far better as friends than anything romantic. He took me to a BDSM club for the first time, and I was instantly captivated by it, especially the communication. I'd never had a conversation with a lover about what was going to happen before we had sex. I couldn't believe the way everything was discussed ahead of time, down to the smallest detail."

"That's actually one of my favorite aspects, too. That conversation can be the best kind of foreplay."

"Yes, exactly. I met a guy at that first club, and he trained me. He immediately identified me as a switch, but that was right around the time my career started to take off. I wasn't comfortable submitting. It made me feel too vulnerable."

"That's totally understandable."

"So I put my focus on the domination side of the equation and never looked back. I had a few relationships here and there, but I never included the lifestyle in them. I would take a break from it when I was involved with someone. Rafe was the first one I tried to bring into it, and we all know how that went."

"He didn't deserve the trust you put in him."

"No, he didn't, but what does it say about me that I wanted so badly to have what my friends have with their partners that I was willing to risk so much for a guy who'd already shown me who he was?"

"It says that you still want to think the best of people. You shouldn't let him diminish your optimism."

"I'm trying not to. I know you hate when I blame myself for what happened with him, but I put myself in that situation, and I have to own that part of it."

"Fair enough, but you getting assaulted? That's a hundred percent on him."

"Yes, it is. Teagan, Veronica and I are going public with what he did to us at a press conference tomorrow."

"Is that right?"

"Uh-huh." Now that I'm allowed to touch Sebastian any way I want to, I slide my fingertips over the contours of his arresting face. "Do you think I'm doing the right thing?"

A beat of tension appears in his cheek. "Definitely."

"Am I doing the right thing going public while my face is still bruised?"

"Absolutely. People need to see what he did to you. Between you and the others, you'll ensure that he'll never again get the opportunity to hurt a woman. He'll be lucky to get a date after you ladies are done with him."

"That's the goal."

"You know what else?"

"What?"

"All the women out there who're living in abusive relationships will see that it happened to Marlowe Sloane, and not only did she survive, but she's out for retribution for herself and all the other women that guy hurt. You might give them the courage to find a way out of their own situations."

"That'd be pretty cool."

"You're an icon, babe. It'll be huge for you to come out in support of abused women this way."

"I don't want anyone to think I'm a victim."

"No one will ever think that of you. You're a badass, and the whole freaking world knows it."

"You're very good for my ego."

"This… you and me… It feels good to me, and things like this never feel good to me."

The comment earns him a big smile. "Really?"

He twirls a length of my hair around his finger. "Really." His gaze flips up to meet mine. "You want to go steady?"

I laugh. "Maybe."

"What'll it take to convince you?"

I wrap my hand around his magnificent cock and give it a gentle tug. "Some more of this?"

"Baby, you can have that any time and any way you want it."

***

The next morning, I'm in the Quantum conference room with Liza, Emmett, Teagan and Veronica. I met with Sgt. Markel, Kristian's contact with the LAPD, first thing and filed a report detailing the assault. Emmett and Sebastian were right by my side, assuring me it was the right thing to do. The photos Dr. Breslow took will be included with the report. I'm glad now that I let her take them. If Rafe ever makes the mistake of returning to the US, he'll find a warrant for his arrest waiting for him.

As I listen to the other women share their stories about Rafe, I experience a sinking feeling inside. If only I'd returned their texts months ago, none of this would've happened. I no sooner have that thought than I dismiss it. Things happen for a reason. That was one of my mother's favorite sayings. She used to tell me that sometimes it takes a while to see the reason, but it's always there. I've experienced that truth many times in my own life. If, like Sebastian suggested last night, my going public helps even one other woman escape from a dangerous situation, then it will have been worth it. That'll be my reason.

And maybe Sebastian will be my reason. Without what happened with Rafe, I wouldn't be getting into something significant with Sebastian, something that feels better than anything ever has.

"I want you to hire a female attorney to appear with you at the press conference," Emmett says.

I can tell just by looking at him that he's been deeply affected by the stories the women shared. As a man who respects women, it's hard for him to hear what we've been through.

I shake my head at his suggestion. "I want it to be you, Em. You're the one I trust, and getting someone else will take time. If we want to do this while the bruises are still fresh, we have to do it now."

Emmett thinks about that. "I'm happy to represent you all, but I don't think I should be up there with you. The three of you are more than capable of handling this on your own, if you're comfortable with that."

I look to Teagan and Veronica. "I am if you guys are." Butterflies swirl in my belly, but I don't let them get the better of me. Yes, I'm nervous about going public with my story, but I won't be deterred by nerves or anything else. Rafe is about to get exactly what he deserves.

"I've asked the media to be here for a noon press conference," Liza says. "We'll meet with them in the screening room."

"Do they know the reason they're coming?" I ask.

"Only that Marlowe and two of her friends would like to make a statement." Liza glances at me and the other women. "Have you prepared what you plan to say?"

I've got most of it hammered out. "I need to finish mine."

"We're set," Teagan says for herself and Veronica. "We also have the blessings of six other women to include them in the statement."

My stomach turns with disgust, directed toward Rafe, and disappointment in myself. Despite what Sebastian believes, I have to take my share of the blame for opening the door that let an abuser into my life. Another of my mother's favorite sayings was "live and learn." All we can do, she would say, is learn from our mistakes and try not to make them again. Ignoring the concerns of my friends and allowing him back into my life after the incident in Paris were huge mistakes that I won't make again.

I stand. "I need to finish my remarks. I'll meet you in the theater. Help yourself to the refreshments." I asked Leah to get some food and drinks for my guests, and she came through with sandwiches, salad and cookies, as well as an array of beverages.

In my office, I power up my laptop and read through my statement for the third time, tweaking the draft that poured out of me earlier. I've delivered my share of speeches, memorized countless monologues and recited thousands of lines of dialogue. But nothing I ever do will matter as much as the comments I've put together for this press conference.

I review them repeatedly, the way I do when memorizing lines, and say the words out loud three times, which is enough to ensure that when the lights are on and people are watching, I'll remember what I planned to say. I keep the emotion out of it and treat this like any other script I'm required to learn. That's all this is to me. Another performance. If I keep it in that category, I'll be able to get through it without breaking.

I refuse to break.

I refuse to give him the satisfaction of knowing he got to me.

I won't give him that.

I've already given him everything he's ever going to get from me.

I'm fierce and determined.

He thought he broke me, but he didn't.

I will *destroy* him.

I recite these vows over and over and over again, until I'm as prepared as I can possibly be to perform the role of my lifetime. This time, I'll play myself, the most important person in my life. Today, I'll get retribution for Marlowe and, in so doing, get retribution for the other women he hurt.

Thirty minutes later, I leave my office with a printout of my remarks in hand and go straight to the viewing room on the third floor, which is a theater we had built to host screenings of our films for the in-house team.

The room is jammed with people and cameras when I walk in.

A few people I recognize from the Hollywood press call out to me, but I ignore them.

I keep my head down, my hair hiding the bruises on my face until I'm ready to reveal them. I'm wearing tan dress pants, a cream-colored blouse and a brown blazer. I once had my colors done and was told I should wear earth tones exclusively. That's been my go-to palette ever since. Leah got the clothes I needed from my place and delivered them to the office this morning.

I walk up the three stairs to the stage, where I hug Teagan and Veronica.

Seeming to sense something is happening, the people gathered in the room go quiet. Liza had offered to make introductory remarks for us, but I declined, preferring to handle that myself.

"Are we ready?" I ask the other women.

Both of them nod.

Teagan squeezes my arm in a show of support that I appreciate more than she'll ever know.

I step up to the dais and push the hair back from my face.

The audience gasps at the sight of my bruises.

"I met Rafael Laurent more than a year ago in Paris. Until recently, he was an executive with Cirque, the company that distributes Quantum films in France. He's well-known throughout the film community and worked between his offices in Paris and Los Angeles. We began a friendship that consisted at first of texts and drinks whenever he was in Los Angeles or I was in Paris. Over time, our friendship evolved into romance. When our relationship first went public, I received texts from both Teagan and Veronica, women who'd dated him in the past. Both of them urged me to get in touch with them, but I didn't return those texts. They were his exes—what could they possibly have to say that would interest me?

"It turns out they were trying to warn me that he was dangerous. The other night, I made the decision to share something deeply personal with Rafe. For most of my adult life, I've participated in and enjoyed an alternative lifestyle that supports dominant and submissive relationships between consenting partners. I wanted to share my love of this practice with the man I thought I loved. The injuries you see on my face resulted from that evening, during which Rafe tied me up and whipped my back until it bled. When he was finished, he left me bound and bleeding for hours until I was found by a friend."

Gasps of shock ripple through the gathered crowd.

"In the days since the attack, he has repeatedly threatened to release photos of me naked, bound and beaten."

When I look up from my prepared remarks, I'm staggered to see Sebastian, Flynn, Natalie, Hayden, Addie, Emmett, Leah, Kristian, Aileen, Ellie and Jasper lining the back wall of the room.

Seb nods and gives me a thumbs-up, his fierce gaze encouraging me to keep going.

I swallow the lump in my throat that formed when I noticed my closest friends, the family I chose for myself, lined up in support of me. I love them so much in that moment, more than I ever have before.

I shift my gaze to Flynn and then Hayden as I continue. "My closest friends despised him. They tolerated him only out of respect for me. They tried to tell me they didn't trust him, that I could do better. I ignored their concerns. That's on me. But what he did to me—and what he did to many other women? That's on *him*. I've come to learn he's a serial abuser who's preyed on women his entire adult life. That stops right now. If you meet this man…" I gesture to the screen, where a massive image of his face appears. "Steer clear of him. His charming good looks are a front for a monster. It's my hope that by going public with my story, I might save someone else from being abused by this man. You might ask why I haven't reported him to the police before now. I didn't want my personal business broadcast to the world. I still would prefer to keep this and my personal life private.

But after talking to Teagan and Veronica and learning what happened to them and the other women he's hurt, remaining silent was no longer an option. I filed a police report with the LAPD this morning, and they've issued a warrant for his arrest. We believe he's currently in France, but if he should return to the US, the authorities will be waiting for him.

"To all the women out there who're living in abusive relationships, I want you to know you're not alone. No one is immune from abuse. We've made a list of resources where you can go for help that we'll distribute at the close of this press conference. We'd appreciate your support in putting that list out to the public. And now I'll turn it over to Teagan."

Immediately, the reporters start calling my name and shouting questions.

Liza intervenes. "After all three women have spoken, they'll take your questions."

I listen to Teagan and Veronica bravely share their stories of fairy-tale romances with Rafe that turned abusive over time.

My heart aches for both of them as well as the six other women they refer to by name who can tell similar stories.

"This is a dangerous man who hates women," Veronica concludes with her trademark bluntness. "Please don't think you're going to be the one to save him or fix what's broken inside him. Stay away from him. That concludes our prepared remarks. We'll take your questions."

I'm not surprised that most of them are for me, in light of the BDSM bombshell I dropped, along with my bruises.

"Are you a Domme, Marlowe?"

I meet Sebastian's intense gaze. "I'm actually a switch, which means I can be both dominant and submissive."

"What is it about the lifestyle that attracted you?"

"I appreciate the open communication most of all."

One of the women reporters asks the next question. "As someone who has spent most of your adult life in the spotlight, how did you keep something like this a secret for so long?"

"I kept my private life private. It's not always easy to maintain a personal life under the glare of the Hollywood spotlight, but I've managed to keep my public and private lives very separate. I want to be clear on one important point. I'm not in any way ashamed of my participation in the BDSM lifestyle. Those who'd consider it deviant lack an understanding of the basic tenets of the lifestyle, which promote safe, sane and consensual interactions between adults. There's nothing illegal or immoral about two or more people agreeing to engage in consensual activity. Anyone who would try to make it into something dirty or deviant would be showing their ignorance to the world."

In the back of the room, Flynn raises a fist that he points in my direction, which is his way of saying, *You go, girl.* I probably should've warned my partners that I planned to disclose my involvement in the lifestyle, but I wasn't a hundred percent sure I was going say that part until the words were coming out of my mouth. I wanted to take away all the weapons Rafe might've tried to use against me.

A few reporters have questions about Rafe. They ask for the proper spelling of his name, the spelling of the company he worked for and other things about his background.

I'm glad to know that at least a few of them will be focused on the main reason we called this press conference.

After an hour of answering questions, Liza informs them that we're done and any other questions can be directed to her office.

I'm stunned and touched when the room explodes into spontaneous applause and further astounded to see Teagan and Veronica applauding, too.

I hug them both. "I couldn't have done this without you both."

Teagan pulls back from our hug. "Yes, you could have. You were incredible. I think it's pretty safe to say that the women of the world will be avoiding *him* from now on."

"And for *him,*" Veronica adds, "that'll be a worse punishment than jail would ever be."

It's true. Rafe needs sex the way other people need air.

"I bet he won't even be able to pay for it after this," Teagan adds.

The three of us share a laugh and another hug. I note they're both careful not to touch my back, which I appreciate. This experience has bonded us for life, and I'm thankful to have made two new good friends as a result of one of the most difficult things to ever happen to me.

My Quantum family is waiting for me when I come off the stage, each of them hugging me gently and telling me how proud they are of me.

Flynn and Hayden dodge reporters who want to take advantage of the fact that they're in the room with two of Hollywood's top players.

"Mr. Godfrey and Mr. Roth are not available for media inquiries," Liza tells them. "Move along."

They do what they're told so they won't fall out of favor with the hottest team in town.

"I'm so fucking proud of you, Mo," Flynn whispers when he embraces me. "You handed that son of a bitch his ass and totally owned your truth up there."

"Thank you." Having his support means everything to me. "Thank you all for being here for me."

"We wouldn't have missed it," Ellie says.

Sebastian is the last of the group to hug me, and he holds on for a good long time, making yet another public statement on my behalf, this one in front of our mutual friends. He all but confirms that things have taken a turn between us in the last few days. "You were great up there, but I never had any doubt you'd kill it."

"I'm glad one of us was confident."

He drops his head to my shoulder and takes a deep breath. That's when I realize he was nervous for me. I hold on tighter to him, aware that everyone close to us is watching. And I don't care one bit.

"Let's go home," he whispers gruffly.

"You dispatched the living fuck out of that son of a bitch," Hayden says. "This calls for a party."

"Not today." With his arm around me, Sebastian heads for the door.

"Wait a minute," Hayden says.

Sebastian keeps moving.

Realizing he wants to be alone with me and doesn't care who knows it is the most exciting thing to happen in, well, ever.

"Let them go," Addie tells her husband. "We'll celebrate tomorrow."

I hear Hayden start to object, but I'm far enough away from them now that I don't hear what he says.

"Such a pain in the ass," Sebastian mutters.

I laugh as we emerge into the bright late-afternoon sunshine. A weight has been lifted from my shoulders. I shared my story and "came out" as a participant in the lifestyle on my own terms. I give zero fucks what anyone thinks of me or my choices. I'm way past the point where I need to worry about those choices affecting my career. When you're a partner in one of the top production companies in Hollywood, there's much less to worry about career-wise. If I'm shunned by other producers, what do I care? I've gotten to the point in recent years where I accept very few roles outside of Quantum anyway.

As we walk toward Seb's truck, a photographer pops out from behind another vehicle and takes a picture of us.

Sebastian growls at the guy, who wisely backs off. Seb opens the passenger door of the truck and waits for me to get settled before he closes it and stalks around to the driver's side, having words with the photog that I can't hear from inside.

He's fuming when he gets into the truck, slamming his door closed. His jaw is clenched so tightly that his cheek twitches. His rage on my behalf is a huge turn-on. If the parking lot wasn't crawling with press, I might've crawled into his lap to show my appreciation. But I've given the public enough of me today. They're not getting that, too.

CHAPTER 16

Marlowe

Seb floors the accelerator, and we roar out of the parking lot, heading for the sanctuary of his home in Malibu. I wonder when I'll be able to get back to my house at the beach. I miss the sound of the ocean and the smell of the sand.

"You okay?" he asks after a long silence.

"Yep. You?"

"Better now that it's done."

"Thank you for the support. It means a lot to me."

He reaches for my hand. "You mean a lot to all of us. We hate to see you suffer the way you have the last few days."

"It hasn't been all bad."

When he glances my way, I see fire in his dark eyes and a hint of a smile on his sinfully sexy lips. The twitch in his cheek is gone, and he seems to have relaxed somewhat now that we've made our escape.

"We aren't being followed, are we?"

"Nope. I've been watching."

"Oh good." I exhale a sigh of relief. "That's good."

"I won't let them find you, babe. Don't worry."

When other guys have called me babe, it's rankled me. When he calls me that, it makes me feel warm and fuzzy and adored. The realization is something I chew on as we ride in comfortable silence until we meet the coast and head north toward home. Why is a term of endearment that always turned me off different coming from him? Is it because we were friends for years before we became something else? Probably because I know it's coming from a place of affection and respect with him, which hasn't always been the case with other guys.

That foundation of friendship makes everything different with Seb. Other than Flynn, I've never been in a relationship with a guy I was friends with first—and my "relationship" with Flynn, such as it was, didn't last long. I wonder if what I've started with Seb will follow a similar path. Will we discover we're better as friends than lovers? I really hope not, because last night was incredible, and I want more of everything with him.

We arrive back at his place an hour before he has to leave for work. I hope that's enough time to show him how much his support has meant to me. We're no sooner inside than he pulls out his phone and fires off a text.

"Everything all right?"

"Uh-huh. I was just telling Quisha she's in charge at the club tonight."

My heart leaps with excitement at hearing he's taking the night off. He so rarely takes time off. In fact, I've heard Kristian, the managing partner, order him to take a vacation because we can't continue to roll over months of leave every year. Sebastian always says there's nothing he'd rather do than work, and if he loses the vacation time, so be it.

He's our most loyal and dedicated employee, and to see him changing his routine to spend more time with me makes me hot. I go to him, reach up to wrap my arms around his neck and press my body against his. "Have you found something you like to do better than work, by any chance?"

His hands slide down my back to cup my ass. He lifts me right off my feet. "Oh hell yes, I have."

I wrap my legs around his waist and fall into a deep, passionate kiss that has fireworks going off inside me. My breasts are pressed to his chest, and my soft center is tight against the hard column of his erection as he wrecks me with sweeping strokes of his tongue. Dear God… All this time, he was right there waiting for me to see him this way, and now that I have… I can't get enough of how I feel when he touches me.

A few days with Seb, and it's plainly obvious to me that *everything* was wrong with Rafe long before he beat me and left me. I never felt as *consumed* by him as I do with Seb. He walks us into the bedroom and puts me on the bed, gazing down at me with so much emotion in his fathomless dark eyes.

"Has this always been there between us, waiting for us to find it?" I ask him.

"It's always been there for me, but I never allowed myself to believe it could happen."

"*Why?*"

His lips curl into a small smile that doesn't reach his eyes. "You're a queen, and I'm a peasant in comparison."

"That's not true. You're kind and loyal and hardworking and dedicated to the people you love. What more could anyone want from a friend or lover than someone with those qualities? Do you know how *rare* those things are? Especially in this town." I reach up to unbuckle his belt and release the button on well-worn, faded jeans that hug him in all the right places. "I came from nothing, Sebastian. Less than nothing. At home, we were always one disaster away from the lights being shut off or ending up on food stamps. My mother was so ashamed of being poor. After all she did for me, I wanted so badly to give her something better."

He strokes my face with his fingertips, sending goose bumps skittering down my arms and back. "She'd be so incredibly proud of who you turned out to be."

"I hope so." I look up at him. "We're more alike than you think. I didn't always have what I do now, and I try not to let the success I've had define me. At the end of the day, I'm just a girl from Tulsa, Oklahoma, who got very, very lucky."

"It was more than luck. Do you have any idea how talented you are? I was blown away by you in *Insidious*. Just when I think I've seen the full range of your gift you go and top yourself."

That ranks as one of the finest compliments I've ever received. "Thank you."

"You're so going to win the Oscar."

"Shhh. Flynn would kill you for saying that."

"Fuck him and his superstitions. If you don't win, it'll be a crime."

I've already won the Golden Globe, as did Flynn and Hayden, and the film won for best drama, so our chances are good for the Oscars. That said, we take nothing for granted. And besides, I already have a couple of Oscars. If I don't win, I'll survive. But I really want to win.

I unzip him carefully, working around the huge bulge, and exclaim with surprise when his bare cock falls into my waiting hand. I glance up at him. "Commando?"

"Most of the time. I don't like being constricted."

"You think you know someone…"

His bark of laughter pleases me so much. It takes a lot to get a laugh out of the always-serious Sebastian Lowe. The laughter turns to a groan when I stroke him and suck the wide tip of his cock into my mouth. He tangles his fingers into my hair and holds on as I toss in some tongue action. I take him in as much as I can and know a moment of pure satisfaction when I feel the head bump against my throat.

"Marlowe."

I hear the warning in the gruff way he says my name, but I ignore it and cup his balls, which are tight and hard. I press on, determined to bring him as much pleasure as I possibly can even as he's trying to get me to stop. I don't stop. I double down, and within seconds, he's coming hard, scalding my throat with his release.

"*Jesus.*" Though his tone is harsh, his eyes are tender as he gazes down at me, seeming to make sure I'm okay. "You made me your bitch."

I smile up at him. "I know."

"You're rather pleased with yourself, aren't you?"

"Rather."

His phone rings, but we ignore it. When it goes off again, he exhales with exasperation and pulls it out of his pocket. Only because I'm watching him so closely do I notice the shock that registers when he sees who is calling him. He declines the call, puts the phone back in his pocket and reaches out to help me up.

"Who was that?"

"No one."

I know instinctively that he's lying. Whoever called has left him upset, stressed, unsettled.

"My mom invited me to dinner tomorrow night. Want to come?" He asks the question casually, like it's no big deal for him to take me home to his mom. I've met her many times but never as his plus one.

"She won't mind?"

"Of course not. She always makes enough to feed an army."

"Are you going to tell her you're bringing me?"

"I'd much rather surprise her." The boyish grin does wondrous things to his demeanor.

"I'll trade you. Dinner with Mom for a date to the Oscars."

I love the way his eyes go wide with shock. "Seriously?"

"Very seriously."

"You want to take me to the Oscars as your date."

Laughing, I nod. "That's right."

"Wow."

"Is that a yes?"

"I, ah... Are you sure?"

"Yes, I'm sure. Unless you don't want to go."

"I do. I mean... That'd be amazing, but..."

"What?"

"I'm not the type of guy your fans would expect to see you with."

I'm intrigued by his thought process. "What sort of guy do you think they expect for me?"

He scowls. "Someone like the Frenchman."

"And look at how that worked out." I place my hand on his face and compel him to look at me. "I wouldn't be happy if you were to get it in your head that you're not good enough for me, Sebastian. Just because I got lucky and had some success in a business that made me famous doesn't make me better than you or anyone else. We both know a lot of shitty famous people."

"True," he says with a huff of laughter.

"But if you aren't up for going, I would totally understand."

"I'd be honored to go with you."

"Really?"

"Really." He draws me into a soft, sexy kiss that makes me want to purr with the pleasure of being close to him this way.

"I can't believe you were right here all this time..."

"Believe it, baby. I'd watch you in action at the club and have to go in the office to rub one out so I wouldn't embarrass myself by sporting wood all night."

"You did not!"

"I did it all the time. When you're in Dominatrix mode..." His low growl finishes the sentence for him.

"But you're a Dom who's not a switch. It shouldn't make you hot to see me dominating guys."

"And yet..." He takes hold of my hand and brings it down to his hard cock. "This is what *thinking* about watching you does to me."

"This is very intriguing to me."

"The thing I like best about our lifestyle is that no two people or couples navigate it exactly the same way. It's all about what works for *us*, and if taking turns being in charge works for us, then so be it."

I smooth a hand over his well-defined pecs, both of which are covered in ink. "This, with you... It feels good." It feels better than anything ever has, but I'm not ready to admit that to myself or him. A week ago, I was in a full-fledged relationship with a man I thought I was in love with. My judgment hasn't been trustworthy lately, so I'm trying not to get too far ahead of myself with Sebastian. Whether this is the start of something new or a fling that'll burn out before it can go anywhere remains to be seen. However, the more time I spend with him, the more I begin to suspect the former rather than the latter.

"It feels good for me, too. In fact, it feels better than good. It feels extraordinary."

It feels so good, in fact, that we go deep underground for the next five days after he decides to take more time off to spend with me. Kristian is thrilled that he's using some vacation time. By all accounts, the whole world has gone *mad* over my revelation about my affection for the BDSM lifestyle. With everyone wanting more of that story, it's a good time for me to be off the radar.

Other than the night we have dinner with his mother—and she cries with joy when she realizes we're together—we go nowhere, we talk to no one but each other and we gorge on sensual pleasure the likes of which I've never experienced before. It'd be perfectly fine with me if we never left his bed again, I decide the morning of the sixth day as we relax after having wake-up sex.

I've lost track of how many orgasms I've had. What does it matter when they're so plentiful?

We snuggle for such a long time that I have no idea what time it is, nor do I care. I have nowhere to be today, and wrapped up in his arms is the best place I've been in a long time. I wake up quite a bit later to realize I fell asleep.

"Welcome back."

I'm addicted to the sound of his gruff voice. Hell, I'm addicted to everything about him. "Sorry."

"Don't be. Did you know you talk in your sleep?"

"I do not."

"Yes, you do."

"What'd I say?"

"It was hard to tell, but something like, 'Fuck me harder, Sebastian.'"

I crack up and smack his rock-hard shoulder. "That's not true!"

"Next time, I'll record it."

"You do that." I love the way he makes me laugh. I love the way he touches me and dominates me and makes me feel worshipped. Everything about this is different from how it was with Rafe, and after spending this time with Sebastian, I wonder how I ever could've mistaken that for love. This... *This* is love. Though neither of us has said the words, the feeling I get from being with him this way is as close as I've ever been to being truly in love.

The feeling is fragile, like a newborn bird that's still learning to spread its wings. I want to protect and guard it so nothing can harm it.

I stretch out the kinks and note the ever-present twinge of soreness between my legs. That's what I get for tangling with that monster cock of his nonstop for days. "I'm going to take a shower. Want to join me?"

"In a minute. My phone's been ringing. I gotta figure out who's blowing me up."

"Okay." I kiss him and get up, aware of his gaze on my bare ass as I walk into the bathroom. I hope he won't keep me waiting too long.

CHAPTER 17

Sebastian

The second I hear the shower go on, I get up, pull on a pair of boxers and take the phone out to the deck, closing the slider so there's no chance Marlowe will overhear this conversation. I return the calls that've been coming a few a day since the press conference.

"What the fuck do you want?" I ask when he answers.

"Sebastian Lowe. Is that any way to talk to an old friend?"

"We're *not* friends, Turk. We were never friends." The sound of his voice strikes fear in my heart, which isn't easy to do. I'm a long way from the young, foolish, naïve idiot I once was. Back then, the sound of Turk Santos's voice could make my knees quiver. "What do you want?"

"Saw something online that got my attention. You're moving up in the world, hanging with Marlowe Sloane."

Hearing her name from him makes me crazy. "If you come anywhere near her, I'll kill you."

Turk lets out a big laugh. "As if you'd be so stupid. You'd be dead before you took your next breath, but of course, you know that."

"What do you want?"

"Remember way back when your good buddy Hayden came to fetch you and I let you go with the caveat that you owed me one?"

"I have no idea what you're talking about." I know exactly what he's talking about. My chest feels tight, like it would if I were having a cardiac incident. Maybe I am.

"Okay, if you want to play it that way. Here's how this is gonna go. I gotta niece named Ariel. She's a triple threat—sings, dances, acts—and she's gorgeous. She wants to be a star. Your lady is gonna make her a star, or I'm gonna make trouble for you. We clear on that?"

The thought of asking such a thing of Marlowe makes me feel so sick that I fear I might actually vomit. "That's not happening."

"It's happening or else. We had a deal, you and me. You might wanna pretend you don't remember it, but I know you do. And you're well aware that no one gets to just 'quit' our life without making some significant concessions. I let you go way back when, but you owe me, and you know it."

"I don't owe you dick. Don't call me again." I end the call and block the number, hating the way my hands shake ever so subtly as I open the slider to go back inside.

This cannot be happening. I'm so far removed from Turk Santos and the crowd I ran with back when I was too stupid to know better. I take a series of deep breaths, trying to get my heart rate to return to normal before I join Marlowe in the shower. My head is spinning, my blood boiling and my heart aching at the thought of putting her in danger. That can't happen, especially after what she's just been through.

I knew it was too much to hope that we could be something. In the span of a few minutes, I've gone from elated to devastated. After having even a tiny taste of what it might be like with her, how will I bear to walk away from her? It'll hurt like the devil, worse than anything ever has, but I'll do it to protect her. The likes of Turk Santos won't get anywhere near her.

"Seb," she calls from the shower. "Are you coming?"

I'm drawn to her so powerfully that it takes all my willpower to ignore her, to back up onto the deck, to sit on the lounge chair that faces the ocean and stay the fuck away from her. She's beautiful and perfect and everything

I'm not and will never be. It was a pipe dream, a lovely pipe dream, but a pipe dream nonetheless.

I grip the arms of the chair to keep from giving in to the yearning to be with her, to touch her, to lose myself in her. It's painful to stay away, but I do it for her.

Marlowe

Something happened while I was in the shower. Everything is different. He won't look at me as he throws clothes into a duffel bag on his bed.

"I have to go out of town for a few days."

"What's going on?"

"An old friend is in trouble and called asking for help."

"Anyone I know?"

"Nah, he's one of the guys from my old neighborhood."

"Where does he live now?"

"Uh... Outside of San Jose."

"So you're driving up there?"

"Yeah, that's the plan. You're welcome to stay here as long as you need to. I put keys on the counter in the kitchen."

I cross my arms, feeling the need to protect myself from whatever this is. "Okay."

He zips his bag, hoists it to his shoulder and walks toward the door, seeming to stop himself when he realizes he can't just leave without giving me something. For Christ's sake, he was inside me an hour ago. "Sorry about this," he says gruffly as he comes back to kiss my forehead before leaving the room.

Long after I hear the front door close, I can't move because I'm so filled with shock, despair and confusion. Everything was fine until it wasn't, so what the fuck just happened? I have no idea how long I stand there trying to process his hasty departure before I snap out of it. There's no way I'm staying in his home without him.

Still trying to wrap my head around the fact that he's gone, I glance at the rumpled bed where we found such intense pleasure together. Was it too much for him? Is that what happened? I don't know, and the not knowing is going to make me crazy. I quickly make the bed and go into the room where my things are to get dressed.

Then I call Leah.

She answers right away. "Hey, how's it going today?"

"Can you please come get me?"

"Oh, um, sure."

"Can you come soon?"

"I'll leave the office right now and be there as fast as I can. I'll text you to give you an ETA."

"Thank you." I end the call, appreciating that she didn't ask why I want a ride or where I'm going. And where exactly am I going? I can't go home, because my house will be surrounded by reporters. Flynn's and Hayden's homes are probably under siege, too. But Flynn's has a gate to keep them out. I put through a call to him.

"I was just going to call you."

"I need a favor."

"Anything."

"Can I stay with you guys for a few days?"

"Of course you can, but I thought you were hanging with Seb."

"I was. I'm not anymore, and I can't go home." I hate that I can't go home. I want my own bed and my things and my glorious view of the Pacific. I'm usually left alone there, but I won't have any privacy with the whole world wanting a piece of me. And the possibility of Rafe showing up at my place, if he's brazen enough to return to LA, is enough to keep me away.

"Are you okay?"

"Yep." I refuse to let Sebastian's rejection break me. We had fun. It's over. He's gone, and I'm moving on.

"You need a ride?"

"No, Leah's coming to get me."

"I'll let Nat know you're coming. Our home is your home. You know that."

"Thanks." My voice breaks, and I cover it with a cough. I've gotten through much worse than what's happened to me recently, and I'll survive the way I always do.

More than anything, I'm disappointed. The last few days with Sebastian were magical and unexpected and delightful. I thought he was enjoying it as much as I was. Apparently, I thought wrong. I throw clothes into my bag without a care as to whether they'll be a wrinkled mess on the other end. What do I care about wrinkles? I just want to get the hell out of here.

Leah texts a few minutes later to say she's fifteen minutes out.

I grab my bag, do a quick sweep of the bathroom, living room and kitchen to make sure I have everything, noticing the keys he left on the counter for me. I quickly divert my gaze and stay focused on my escape plan, even if my heart aches as I leave the place where I was so happy at a time when I should've been devastated.

Sebastian made me feel happy and safe and secure—until he pulled the rug out from under me and sent me reeling once again. It's a wonder I don't have whiplash from the way things have unfolded. Not that long ago, I thought I was happy with Rafe, and now I'm heartbroken over Sebastian?

I need an intervention.

After making sure the door is locked behind me, I leave Sebastian's condo and take the stairs down to the lobby to wait for Leah. Thankfully, no one is around to see or bother me in the five minutes I'm there before her little red Bug pulls up to the curb. She's got the top down, so I find an elastic in my bag and put up my hair before rolling my suitcase out to the curb, where she's waiting to load it into the trunk.

When we're both in the car and belted in, she turns to me. "Where to?"

"Flynn's."

"Everything okay?"

"Yep." I don't want to talk about it with her or anyone. I want to forget Rafe and Sebastian and everything that's happened, which will be easier said than done, especially the part with Sebastian, which was the best time I ever spent with anyone. I'll do what I always do when life kicks me in the balls. I'll keep my chin up and power through, even if I ache inside.

"I thought you were hanging with Sebastian."

"I was. I'm not now."

She says nothing to that, which I appreciate. "Sorry that I have to stop for gas. I meant to get it before work."

"No worries. You didn't know you were coming out to Malibu today."

A couple of miles later, she pulls into a gas station. "I'll be quick."

I find a ball cap in my bag and put it on, pulling it down over my face in the hope that no one will notice me. I wish I could stop thinking about Sebastian or what happened to make him run away. My mind cycles through every minute of the last few hours and days, but nothing stands out as worrisome or strange, except for the fact that someone was blowing up his phone. As far as I'm concerned, one minute, everything was fine. The next, it wasn't.

"Marlowe Sloane."

Startled, I look up to see a man's face staring back at me. With one look at his cold, dark eyes, I know this isn't someone friendly.

He moves his jacket aside and shows me the firearm he's carrying. "You're going to need to come with me."

"What do you want?"

"Get out of the car and start moving, or your little friend is going to get hurt. Do you want her to get hurt?"

A couple of months ago, Leah was injured in a car accident that nearly killed her. The last thing in the world I want is for anything to happen to her because of me. I get out of the car, feeling strangely removed from whatever this is. I'm not scared or even alarmed. Perhaps I'm numb after the few weeks I've had, but whatever is wrong with me, it's keeping me from hysteria as he pushes me into the backseat of a Charger, where Leah is huddled in the corner.

He shuts the door and signals to some other guy, who drives off with Leah's car.

The whole thing happens in a matter of seconds. It's so smoothly done that no one even notices. I wonder how long it will be before someone notices we're missing. Hopefully, not long.

"What do you want?" I ask when the man gets in the car.

"Hand over your phones, shut up and stay that way until you're spoken to."

We give him our phones, and he powers them down.

I reach for Leah's hand and give her a reassuring squeeze. Her eyes are huge with fright. Whatever this is, it certainly doesn't involve her. I'll do whatever it takes to keep her safe. I try to pay attention to where we're going, but he makes so many turns that I lose track. We end up near a pier that's not familiar to me. He presses a button on a garage-door opener attached to the visor and drives into a massive building. The door closes behind us with a clatter, enveloping us in darkness.

Leah is trembling as we're roughly pulled from the car, marched down a long hallway and pushed into a concrete space that's more of a cell than a room. The door closes with a loud crash that makes us both jump.

When we're alone, Leah turns to me. "What the hell?"

"I have no idea what this is."

"*What're we going to do?*" Her voice is tinged with hysteria.

"We're going to stay calm and do whatever it takes to stay alive."

"Is this about Rafe?"

"I don't think so. He lacks the imagination to pull off something like this."

"Emmett will be looking for me if I don't go back to the office or return his texts."

"That's a good thing. He'll sound the alarm." I put my arm around her and keep her close to me when we sink to the floor to sit and wait. I pray that Leah is right about Emmett and that he'll be looking for her before too long, and that Flynn and Nat will sound the alarm sooner rather than later when I don't show up at their house.

CHAPTER 18

Sebastian

I think about going to my mom's house, but she'll take one look at me and know that something's terribly wrong. After the night we recently spent having dinner with Marlowe, she was happier than I've ever seen her. I don't have the heart to take that from her. So I go to the club, the one place where everything makes sense. I turn off my phone and bury myself in work—invoices, timecards, inventory, cleaning. Hours go by before I stick my head up to figure out what time it is.

Almost two. The club opens at eight. I have time to hit the gym, where I have a change of clothes in my locker. I'm glad I won't have to go home. If I stay away from Marlowe and am never seen with her again in a romantic context, I can keep her safe—or so I hope. That's all that matters to me.

I work out until my muscles are trembling and my body is so exhausted, I'm stumbling by the time I leave the gym and drive back to the club to open. Inside the lobby of the Quantum building, I run into Hayden.

"Jesus Christ, Seb. Where the fuck have you been?"

I'm stunned by the question as much as the heated way he asks it. No one ever questions my comings or goings. I get the job done. They don't care how. "Huh?"

"We haven't been able to get in touch with you, Marlowe or Leah all day. People are going insane, especially Emmett. We're about to call the police."

Since I'm still in a stupor from the gym, it takes a minute for his words to register. "Marlowe's at my place."

"No, she isn't. We were there two hours ago. There's no sign of either of them."

"Did you check Marlowe's?"

"We've been everywhere they might be. We can't find them. I'm going to check Rafe's condo. I swear to God, if he has them…"

"It's not him." I go cold all over with the realization that it's not Rafe who's endangered Marlowe and Leah. It's me.

Hayden's brows furrow into a glare. "What do you know?"

I'm disgusted, ashamed and deeply afraid.

"Sebastian! *What do you know?*"

"Turk Santos called me earlier."

The color leaches from Hayden's face. "What the fuck did he want?"

"He wanted to collect on the favor I owe him for letting me go back in the day. He… He wanted Marlowe to make his niece a star. I told him to go fuck himself. I called it off with her and left, planning to stay gone so he'd leave her alone." Every part of me hurts when I think about that pig getting anywhere near Marlowe—or Leah. Dear God, Emmett will murder me with his bare hands, and I'll let him. That'd be the least of what I deserve. "I never should've gone near her." I'm so freaked out that it doesn't even register with me that I'm basically telling Hayden the truth about me and Marlowe. Although I'm sure they figured it out for themselves when we basically disappeared for most of a week.

"Fuck that. This isn't your fault."

"Whose fault is it? I'm the one who has an outstanding debt to one of the nastiest gangbangers in LA, and he's come to collect. How is this not my fault?"

"You're not the one who took them or put them in danger."

"I put them in danger the first time I touched Marlowe! I should've known he'd do something like this. I made the mistake of assuming he'd forgotten about me."

"We just need to think. Come on." He grabs me by the arm and half drags me to the elevator that goes to the offices upstairs.

We ride in silence and emerge into chaos in the reception area. Everyone is there and in the conference room.

Emmett paces like a hungry tiger about to pounce on fresh meat. His stress and fear are palpable.

Gordon and his team are positioned around the conference room table, all of them working laptops.

"We've got surveillance footage from Sebastian's building," Gordon announces.

The rest of the group falls silent.

"Leah picked up Marlowe just after noon, and they headed north. We're going to try to pick them up on other cameras."

"What about their phones?" Flynn asks. "Any luck finding them?"

Gordon shakes his head. "They're off. Either they don't want to be found or someone has them."

Emmett makes a sound that's barely human.

I feel sick with guilt over what he and the others are going through because of me.

Hayden glances at me, as if to ask, *Are you going to tell them or am I?*

"I know who has them."

All eyes shift to me. I've never been more ashamed of my past than I am in that moment. "I recently heard from someone I knew a long time ago. He... He saw me with Marlowe after the press conference, and he wanted something from me, or, I should say, he wanted something from *her*."

"What?" Flynn's exasperation is obvious.

"He wants her to make his niece a star."

"So what? We get that shit all the time from people we barely know."

"He's a gangbanger," Hayden says. "He's the one who let Seb go back in the day, and now he's come back to collect on the 'favor' he thinks Sebastian owes him."

The entire group stares at me in disbelief.

"What did you say?" Flynn asks.

"I told him to fuck off."

Emmett lets out a roar and comes at me so fast, I don't have time to react before we're both on the floor. Before he can punch or strangle me, the other guys are on him, pulling him off.

"Stop!" Hayden's cry stops Emmett in his tracks. "This isn't going to help anything."

"*Where are they?*" Emmett's scream is primal and strikes the part of me where my deepest insecurities have lived for all the time I pretended to be one of them. I'm not one of them. I was never one of them.

"I don't know. It's been years since I had anything to do with him or his organization."

"What's his name?" Gordon asks.

"Turk Santos."

Judging by the way Gordon's eyes bug, he knows of Santos and his reputation as a ruthless killer. "We need the LAPD."

"No."

Again, they all look to me.

"If you bring in cops, he'll kill them." That's the only thing I know for certain. "He must've had eyes on my place before he called me. He knew I'd leave her before I'd subject her to him." I did exactly what he expected me to do, and I'm terribly afraid I'm going to vomit in front of the people I've thought of as my family. After this, they won't be my family anymore. After this, they'll never speak to me again, and I won't blame them.

"Gordon, please tell me there's something you can do." Emmett's plea is so full of heartbreak, it brings tears to my eyes.

If anything happens to either of them, I'll never forgive myself. The thought of Marlowe and Leah afraid for their lives because of me... This is a hell of a time to realize for certain that I'm in love with Marlowe, that I have been for years, and if I lose her now, I'll die.

***

It's the longest night of my life. Hours go by without any news or clues or ideas or anything. I feel like I haven't seen Marlowe in years. I'm wavering in my certainty that calling the cops would be a mistake. Surely that would be better than this purgatory. In between bouts of tears, Addie takes care of getting everyone fed with the help of Aileen, Kristian, Natalie, Jasper and Ellie. Max and Stella are here, as are Hayden's mom, Jan, and Addie's dad, Simon, who've been spending time together lately.

They prop us up throughout the long night, offering assurances that we badly need. I cling to Max's certainty that Marlowe and Leah are savvy and clever and endlessly capable, that if anyone can get through this, they can.

Hayden must've called my mom because she shows up at daybreak with doughnuts and coffee for everyone. After putting the food and beverages on the conference room table, she comes to me and wraps her arms around me. Her familiar scent surrounds and comforts me.

"Stop blaming yourself, *hijo*. You had no way to know this would happen."

"If it wasn't for me, they'd both be here where they belong and not God knows where going through God knows what." My voice catches on a sob. I can't remember the last time I cried. Wait, yes, I can. It was when my dad left. I was six. My dad came back on the scene when I was in my early twenties, and he and my mom have reconciled to the point where they hang out but don't live together. I'm not really sure what you'd call their relationship these days. I've made my peace with the past, but I'll never be particularly close to him, like I am to my mom.

In this moment of great despair, her love and compassion nearly break me. I manage to hold it together, but just barely.

Ellie gasps, grabs her midsection, looks down at the floor and then up at us. "I think my water just broke."

Jasper lets out a shout and scoops her up into his arms, rushing for the elevator. Max and Stella follow them as everyone else wishes them good luck. I watch them go with a surreal feeling of disconnection from them and the others, as if my excommunication has already occurred, and I'm just biding my time until Leah and Marlowe are found.

Please, God, let them be found.

I haven't asked God for anything in forever. I really hope he can still hear me, because I'd give anything, anything at all, if he would bring them back to us unharmed.

"Pray with me." My always intuitive mother takes me by the hand and recites the Lord's Prayer in Spanish.

I close my eyes and say the words along with her from memory, clinging to the faith that was hammered into me as a child. I bargain with God. *If You bring them back to us safe and sound, I'll go back to church. I'll do whatever I have to.* I'd walk through the flames of hell for Marlowe and for Leah, who has come to mean so much to all of us.

I open my eyes to find that Natalie is crying while Flynn tries to comfort her. Leah is her best friend from New York, and Marlowe has become a close friend since Natalie moved out here. Poor Nat has already been through enough. This is the last thing she needs, especially so late in her pregnancy.

Over Natalie's shoulder, Flynn's intense gaze connects with mine.

He's angry. I don't blame him. Everyone is upset because of me, because of things I did before I knew better and debts that're being collected in the most painful way possible.

"We've got something." Gordon's announcement gets everyone's attention. "Santos's organization has headquarters near the Port of Los Angeles, and apparently, he has an apartment in the same building. We're waiting for confirmation of the address, and then we'll figure out our next step."

At least it's something.

"Let's get over there." Emmett is like a nuclear reactor about to melt down. Energy rolls off him in palpable waves. He waited all his life to find true love with Leah. This is excruciating for him, and for me, knowing I put him in this awful hell.

"We're not going over there until we have a fully fleshed-out plan." Gordon's tone is stern and uncompromising.

Hayden stops Emmett from leaving the conference room with a hand on his chest. "Don't, Em. We've got to do this right. They're counting on us."

"I can't bear the waiting."

"I know."

"No, you don't." Emmett pulls free of Hayden's grasp. "Your wife is right here. You know where she is. There's no possible way you understand how this feels."

"You're right. I don't."

Emmett breaks down into sobs, each of them a knife through my heart.

"I'll go." I'm standing and speaking before I take the time to contemplate what I'm saying. "I'll go after them. I'm the one he wants, and if I go, maybe he'll release them."

Marlowe

We're in that room a really long time before anyone comes for us. We're hungry and thirsty, and we both need to pee. And we're scared, which I suspect was their plan when they left us there for so long—to make sure we're good and afraid so we'd do whatever they ask of us.

The guy who took us is the one who returns, his gaze fixed on me. "Come with me."

"I'm not going anywhere without Leah."

"You're not calling the shots here, superstar."

"Clearly, we're here because you want something from me."

"You assume correctly. Your boyfriend could've made this easier on all of us if he'd only cooperated with my simple request."

I realize two things in that moment. One, Sebastian left because this man threatened me. And two, he loves me enough to do whatever it takes, even leave me, to keep me safe. I'm filled with warmth and strength on the heels of these realizations. Sebastian's love gives me the strength I need to face off with this man, to figure out what he wants and to get us the hell out of here as soon as possible. We both have amazing men to get home to, and I'm determined to get out of here so I can tell Sebastian I love him, too. I think maybe I always have, a thought that makes me want to giggle at the worst possible time.

I look our kidnapper dead in the eyes. "You won't get anything from me if Leah can't come with me wherever we're going."

He tips his head, gives me an assessing look. "Fine, bring your little friend."

I grab Leah's hand and hold on tight as we follow him through a winding set of corridors and into the cavernous warehouse space where men are working on several high-end cars. Flynn would know the exact makes and models, whereas I'm basically clueless. *A chop shop*, or so it seems. My heart sinks when I notice Leah's car on the far side of the vast space. The other men completely ignore us as we go up a set of metal stairs. I'm surprised when we step into a stylishly appointed living space.

"Do you want something to drink?"

"We would love some water and a bathroom."

"Through there," he says, gesturing at a doorway.

Leah bolts for the bathroom.

He hands me ice water in a heavy crystal glass.

I drink half of it in one big gulp.

"You're far more beautiful in person than you are on screen."

Does he expect me to feel complimented by that? "Thank you."

"A queen such as yourself should be with a king, not a peasant."

I wonder if he's the one who convinced Seb that he's nothing more than a peasant. If so, that's another reason for me to despise this man.

As he speaks, he touches my face.

I turn away from his touch.

"You don't need a loser like Lowe."

It takes effort to hide any noticeable reaction to his insult of Sebastian. I want to spit in his face, but I won't give him the satisfaction.

"I could give you everything."

"I already have everything I'll ever need." I never blink as I stare into cold dark eyes. His eyes are every bit as dark as Sebastian's, but with none of the warmth that Seb's have when he looks at me. That silly man, walking away in a misguided attempt to keep me safe. Doesn't he know that I'd do anything it takes to keep *him* safe? "You never said what you want with me."

"Have a seat."

Leah comes out of the bathroom, her relief obvious.

"I'm going to use the restroom."

Leah gives me a fearful look, as if to say, *Please don't leave me with him.*

I don't want to, but I'm about to wet my pants. I hand her the glass of water and move quickly toward the bathroom, anxious to get back to her as fast as possible. I've never been so happy to pee in my life. I return to the room, and Leah is visibly relieved to have me back.

I sit next to her and take her hand. "How about you tell me what you want so we can go home?"

He turns on the television, picks up a remote and points it at the unit. "Watch this."

A blonde girl of about fifteen or sixteen comes on the screen, introduces herself as Ariel and proceeds to put on a polished performance that includes singing, dancing and acting. I'm actually quite impressed by the girl's raw talent, not that I'll tell him that.

When the video ends, he turns off the TV. "What do you think?"

"She's a lovely girl." That much is true.

"And very talented, wouldn't you say?"

"She has potential."

He doesn't like that response. "What does that mean?"

"Just that she's young, and with a little polish, she might be able to turn her potential into something."

"You're going to make my niece a star."

I laugh. "If only it was that easy."

He pulls out the handgun he flashed earlier, cocks it and points it at Leah. "Let me simplify things for you—make her a star or your little friend here is dead. Are we clear?"

Leah begins to cry.

I struggle to keep my composure with a gun pointed at the young, adorable assistant I've come to love like a little sister. "It's not as if I can wave a magic wand and make her a star. It doesn't work that way."

Stepping closer to us, he presses the gun to Leah's head.

She trembles violently from the effort to remain still.

"I'll meet with her and see what I can do."

"And then you'll make her a star."

"I'll do everything I can for her."

He drops the gun from Leah's head. "Now, was that so difficult?"

Leah sobs uncontrollably in my arms. I hold on tight to her while wondering what happens now that I've agreed to give him what he wants.

CHAPTER 19

Sebastian

I'm tackled by Hayden and Flynn, who drop me like a felled oak even though I outweigh them both by at least twenty pounds of muscle. But I'm no match for the two of them together, especially in my current state of despair. I let out a cry that's full of rage and fear and frustration. I know where she is and they won't let me go to her?

I lose all pretense of pride and break down into helpless sobs. "Please let me go. I'll get them back."

"You're not going anywhere." Flynn tightens his grip on me. "We're going to do this the right way and let the experts do their jobs."

When they realize they've succeeded in subduing me, they leave me to sit on the floor with tears rolling down my face as I stare off into space, trying not to think about what Marlowe and Leah might be going through at the hands of one of the most ruthless people I've ever met. I once saw him gun down another guy's mother because she wouldn't tell him where her son was.

I've always known he'd come back for me at some point. I got lazy and let down my guard, and now the person I love most in the world is in mortal danger, along with someone who is an innocent bystander.

I should've stayed the fuck away from her. None of this would be happening if only I'd kept my hands off her. I cross my arms against my knees and put my head down as the memories of the kind of happiness and contentment I only dreamed about before her come flooding back to remind me of what's at stake.

Much later, I pull myself off the floor and go into the men's room to splash cold water on my face. I use a paper towel to dry my skin, open my eyes and find Emmett standing behind me.

"Is he going to kill them?" His voice is strained, his face tight with tension and his eyes… They're full of heartache.

"I hope not."

"I'll die without her."

"I'm so sorry to have done this to them and to you."

"I don't blame you."

My laugh is harsh. "I sure as fuck do." The choices I made years ago are ruining the lives of the people I love. How is that not my fault?

"You'd never subject any of us to something like this. We know how much you love us all, and we love you just as much. No one blames you."

I nearly break down again. "I refuse to think about myself while they're in danger."

He gives me an oddly curious look. "Are you in love with Marlowe?"

The question takes me by surprise. In light of everything that's happened, I find I can't lie to him. "Yes."

Emmett nods. "I wondered."

Now I'm even more shocked than I was before. "When?"

"Always."

I'm stunned to hear that, because I didn't let myself go there until recently, so I was under the impression that no one else knows how I feel about her. I suppose I shouldn't be surprised that the sharp-as-fuck Emmett Burke figured it out before I did.

We leave the men's room together and return to the conference room, where Gordon is briefing the others on the plan he and his team have put together. As I listen to what they're saying, a sinking feeling comes over me.

"Any questions?" Gordon asks.

"If you go forward with this plan, you and your men will be dead before you know what's hit you. The whole place is probably booby-trapped. You'd be walking into a massacre." I take a deep breath and let it out slowly. "As much as it pains me to say it, you need cops to pull this off."

Kristian pulls out his phone. "I'll make the call."

***

Twenty minutes later, we're subjected to the wrath of Sgt. Markel, Kristian's contact at the LAPD. "What the *hell* were you all thinking, sitting on this *overnight*?"

Flynn's not having it. "Let's move past that and focus on how we're going to get them out of there."

Markel glares at him. "I'll call in the gang unit and SWAT. This is officially an LAPD operation now. The rest of you are to stay right here and let us do our jobs."

"We have info you'll need," Gordon says, "so how about we work together rather than engaging in a pissing match over who's got the bigger dick?"

I want to scream at them to stop wasting time and just do *something*. *Anything*.

Markel begrudgingly agrees to coordinate with Gordon and his team, and before long, the office is overrun with cops. Then they're all gone, and we're left with nothing but prayers and hope that they'll bring back Marlowe and Leah.

I can't even think about what I'll do if this goes bad.

Flynn

I'm as stressed as I've been in a very long time. The last time I felt this wound up was the night Natalie's past came to light after she was seen with me at the Golden Globes. Between waiting to hear something about Marlowe and Leah and receiving regular updates from my parents, who're at the hospital with Ellie and Jasper, my head is about to explode.

At least Ellie is doing well, uncomfortable but making progress.

If only we knew something about how Marlowe and Leah are holding up.

I go looking for Natalie, who's taken this situation hard. I know she loves them both, but pregnancy hormones were wreaking havoc on her before two of her closest friends went missing. She hasn't slept or eaten since we discovered they were gone, and I'm worried about her and the baby.

I find her in my office, curled up on the sofa, and pause to make sure she's not asleep before I approach her. When I see tears in her eyes, my heart breaks. I can't bear to see her sad or upset, and right now, she's both.

I sit with her and link my fingers with hers.

"Any news?"

"Nothing new. Markel said it would take some time to get all the players into place."

"How about from the hospital?"

"Mom says Ellie is doing great and making progress."

"At least that's some good news. I can't wait to find out what they're having."

"I know. How can they stand the suspense?" We debated finding out the sex of our baby. I was dying to know, and she wanted to wait. I drove her nuts with my speculating until she finally gave in and decided to find out that our baby is a girl. Can you imagine me with a little girl? She'll make me her bitch the day she's born and will run roughshod over me for the rest of my life. I can't wait.

"No idea, but they're about to find out."

I wrap a strand of her long dark hair around my finger. "Are you okay, sweetheart?"

"I'm trying to be, but the waiting and the worrying is killing me. What'll we do if something happens to them?"

"They're going to be fine. This is Marlowe we're talking about. She's one of the smartest, toughest people I know, and Leah… She'll have them wishing they never messed with her."

Natalie starts to laugh, but her laughter quickly turns to sobs.

"Aww, baby, you know I can't take it when you cry."

"I'm s-sorry. I'm just so afraid for them."

"I know. I am, too."

I stretch out next to her and wrap my arms around her, wishing there was more I could do to comfort her. I worry about her incessantly since she became pregnant, even if I try to keep my worries hidden from her. She doesn't need to know that I obsess over everything that could go wrong when the baby arrives. I waited my whole life to find her, and now that I have her in my life, the thought of living even one day without her is unfathomable. I've glommed on to delivery disaster stories online, to the point that I've had to force myself to stop reading them or go mad imagining the worst-case scenarios.

"What're you thinking about?" she asks after a long period of silence.

"How much I love you."

"You were thinking about that right when I asked?"

"I think about that all the time. I think about how lucky I am that Fluff attacked me in the park that day."

"She didn't *attack* you."

"She bit me and drew blood. What would you call that?"

"She *claimed* you."

That makes me laugh. "Right. Is that why she snarled and snapped at me for weeks after we first met?"

"She was testing you to make sure you were worthy of us."

"That must've been what she was thinking when she bit me on the ass."

Natalie rocks with silent laughter, which I much prefer to the tears.

I poke her side. "It's not funny. She almost unmanned me."

"It is funny, and she never came close to unmanning you."

"She was in the neighborhood of my manhood."

"Stop," she says, laughing helplessly. "You're such a baby."

"Is she behaving for Leslie?" We have the nicest pet sitter who comes to stay with Fluff any time we have to be away. Fortunately, she was available to get over to the house when Marlowe and Leah went missing.

"My Fluff-o-Nutter is a perfect angel, as always."

I snort with laughter that I attempt to cover with a cough, but my wife is wise to me.

Natalie looks up with fathomless green eyes that see me the way no one else ever has. "They're going to be all right, aren't they?"

"Absolutely. I have full faith that Marlowe is probably making them sorry they ever screwed with her."

"If she isn't, Leah certainly is."

That makes us both laugh.

"For sure. They're tough and smart, and they're going to be fine. I know it." God, please let them be fine. "Did you hear any more from the girls?" We're looking forward to having her sisters with us this coming summer. Olivia is going to do some modeling work, while Candace interns in Ellie's department at Quantum. Nat doesn't know it yet, but the girls are also coming out for spring break to help us celebrate Natalie's twenty-fifth birthday. I can't wait to surprise her with everything I've got planned—and to keep surprising her for the rest of our lives.

"They're counting the days until they can come to LA."

"I can't wait to have them with us." I've cleared my acting schedule into the fall so I can spend the next few months with Nat, the baby and her sisters. In September, we begin production on *Captivated*, which will tell the story of how Natalie put her life back together after being attacked and raped as a teenager, and it'll tell our story—hers and mine.

The baby picks that moment to deliver a swift kick that I feel against my belly. "Whoa. She's wound up in there!"

"She's kicking all the time lately. Dr. Breslow says that's a good thing. We want her to be busy and active, even if she's roughing me up."

"What're we going to name this little angel of ours?"

"I've been thinking a lot about that, and I think I finally have a name that I really love."

"Lay it on me."

"Cecilia Estelle."

That she included my mom in the baby's name brings tears to my eyes.

"I was thinking we could call her Cece for short."

"Cecelia Estelle Godfrey. Cece. I like that. My mom will be thrilled."

"I hope so."

"I know so. She adores her daughter-in-law, almost as much as I do."

"I feel guilty being so excited about the baby when Marlowe and Leah are going through such an awful ordeal."

"They wouldn't want you to be anything other than excited about the baby, no matter what." I smooth a hand down the silky length of her hair. "Close your eyes for a few minutes and try to rest. I'm right here, and everything is going to be fine. I promise."

She takes a deep breath and relaxes into my embrace.

As I hold her close to me, I can only hope that's a promise I'll be able to keep.

CHAPTER 20

Hayden

I can't find Addie. I realize I haven't seen her since the cops left. "Where's Addie?" I ask the others after I've checked my office and hers without success.

"I saw her heading for the restroom a while ago," Aileen replies.

I head for the ladies' room we share with the company that leases space from us. Under normal circumstances, I wouldn't be caught dead in there, but nothing about these circumstances is normal. I bust into the room and don't see her.

I'm about to leave when I hear sniffling coming from the handicapped stall. I turn the lock on the main door and go find my love.

She's sitting on the closed toilet with her head in her hands, her body shaking with sobs.

"Baby."

Surprised by my sudden appearance, she looks up at me, her face red and ravaged. I move toward her and lift her right off the john and into my arms before taking a seat.

She resists me, which never happens. "Don't."

"Why not?"

"I just… I can't."

"What can't you do?"

"I can't talk about it."

"Okay, then we won't talk. I'll just hold you for as long as you need me to."

To my complete horror, that makes her cry harder.

She shakes her head and continues to fight me.

I just hold on tighter. "Addison, stop. Just stop. I'm right here, and I'm never letting you go."

"Hayden."

The helpless way she says my name does me in. "What, baby?"

"I can't lose Marlowe. I won't survive it."

"You're not going to lose her."

"You don't know that!"

"I believe it. Marlowe and Leah are scrappy. If anyone can get through this, they can."

"I'm so scared. Aren't you?"

"Yeah, of course I am, but I believe in them. And that guy Turk would be crazy to harm one of America's biggest stars."

"He was crazy to kidnap her in the first place. Does he honestly think he's going to get away with that?"

I'm encouraged to hear her talking like her usual fearless self. "He won't get away with it. We won't let him."

My assurances seem to console her. After a while, the tears dry up—thank fuck for that—and she settles somewhat.

"Hayden?"

"Hmm?"

"I want to have a baby."

Her words are like an arrow that hits me square in the heart, stealing the breath from my lungs. "Like, right now?"

She laughs. "Maybe not right this minute, but soon. Would that be okay?"

"Whatever you want."

"That's a pretty broad statement."

"If you're wondering how much I love you..."

"I never wonder about that. I knew you loved me before you did, remember?"

"Are you ever going to let me forget that?"

"Never."

"That's fine." I breathe in the fragrance that always clings to her hair and skin, the scent of the woman I love. "That means you have to stay with me forever so you can never let me forget what a jackass I was before you showed me the error of my ways."

"You were a jackass. That's for sure. And of course I'm staying with you forever. Where else would I go?"

"Nowhere." I hug her tighter, so tightly I'm probably hurting her, but she doesn't complain. She's proven she can take whatever I'm dishing out. "You can't go anywhere, because I can't live without you."

"Before all this happened with Marlowe and Leah, I was going to tell you that I think I've found our house on the coast with the big yard for parties. It has a pool, too."

"What town?"

"It's in Calabasas, a mile from Kris and Aileen's place."

"When can we see it?"

"We have an appointment tomorrow, but..."

What she doesn't say is that it depends on whether we're successful in bringing Marlowe and Leah home. If we aren't... I can't think about that. I simply can't.

"Let me see the house." I need to keep her thinking about something positive while we wait to hear from the cops.

She pulls her phone from her pocket and calls up the listing before handing the phone to me.

I take one look and know this is the dream house she described to me when we were first together, when she was telling me about the life she envisioned for us, the life I wanted so badly but was afraid to claim for myself. My beautiful, sweet, determined Addison wasn't having that. She claimed it for both of us, and thank goodness for that. I've never known the kind of happiness I've found with her. I didn't even know it existed until she showed me the way.

"Do you like it?"

"I love it." It's huge—way bigger than we need—but if it's what she wants, whatever. "I can see some epic parties in that yard."

"See that window right there?"

"Uh-huh."

"That's where we'll put the fifteen-foot Christmas tree."

"And who's going to haul a fifteen-foot Christmas tree into the house?"

"Duh. You are."

"How did I know you were going to say that?"

"Don't worry." She pats my face like I'm a naughty child. "Flynn and the guys will help if it's too much for you."

I give her a filthy look. "I don't need their help."

She laughs, and my heart gives a happy jolt.

"You knew I'd say that, didn't you, you little minx."

"You're a bit predictable when your manhood is questioned."

"When do I *ever* give you reason to question my manhood?"

"Never." She pats my face again. "Never ever."

"You feel a little better?"

"Yeah. Thanks for coming to find me."

"I'll always come find you, so how about you make it easier on both of us and don't run away from me? Come find *me* when you're feeling down."

"I will."

"They're going to be okay."

"I really hope so."

Kristian

Waiting is hell. I've learned that lesson in excruciating detail every three months since I've been with Aileen and have had to wait for results from her cancer checkups. We were already mired in that hell before Marlowe and Leah went missing, and their disappearance sent my anxiety soaring. I go looking for Aileen, who's on the phone in Addie's office.

She's facing away from me, so she doesn't see me there.

"Are you sure?"

I die a thousand deaths in the pause that follows her question.

"Okay, I'll make another appointment and see you then."

Oh my God. Is the cancer back? I can't hear that. I just can't. She and her children—our children—have changed my life so completely. There's no way I can bear to think about losing her after the joy she's brought to my life. I didn't even know what joy was until she showed me, and now...

I can't.

I back out of Addie's office and go into mine, closing the door. I wish I could leave and go to my place in town. It's on the market, but hasn't sold yet. I want to hide out, the way I used to before I had Aileen. I eye the closet in my office where I keep a change of clothes and my gym bag. It's small, but it'll do the trick. I step inside the dark, cramped space and close the door before sinking to the floor and wrapping my arms around my knees.

I feel like a coward for hiding out this way, but it's been my coping mechanism since childhood, when I would hide from the men my mother brought home to have sex with so she could pay for her drug habit. I watched her be murdered by one of them from inside a closet. Despite that, I still find comfort in the dark, where nothing bad can happen. The darkness is my friend.

I'm there a long time, so long I'm nearly asleep when the door opens.

The blast of light is blinding after being in the dark.

"Kristian."

The sound of her voice is like a balm on the wounds I carry with me. I long ago accepted they'll never completely heal, but with her by my side, the pain is a dull ache rather than the sharp agony it once was.

"What're you doing in there?"

"I needed a break."

She squeezes into the tight space and sits next to me. There's just enough room for both of us. I'm instantly bolstered by the heat of her body against mine. That's all it takes to make everything better. I'm continuously amazed that she can do that for me just by existing. She takes my hand and cradles it between both of hers, making me feel loved and protected the way only she can do. She loves me so much, so perfectly. How would I ever live without her after having had this?

"I know you're so worried about Marlowe and Leah. We all are."

"It's a helpless feeling to know that people you love are in trouble and there's nothing you can do to fix it."

"That has to be so hard for you as the family 'fixer,' the one who makes things better for all of us."

"It's the worst."

"I hate that you're suffering."

"I heard you on the phone in Addie's office. Is it back?"

She gives me a puzzled look. "Is what back?"

How can she not know what I mean? "The cancer, Aileen. Is it back?"

"No," she says on a long exhale. "Everything is normal."

I was so certain that I almost can't process that I was wrong. Gratitude and relief flood my system. My throat closes around a tight lump of emotion as tears fill my eyes. Thank God.

"I'm so sorry you thought that. What did you hear me say that made you think it was back?"

"You said, 'Are you sure,' and then you said you'd make another appointment."

"Oh God, Kris. I'm so sorry you thought that. The bloodwork didn't show cancer, but it did show that I'm pregnant."

For a second, I'm too stunned to react. "You... you're..."

Her face lights up with the incandescent joy that was the first thing I ever noticed about her at Flynn and Nat's wedding. Even in the throes of cancer treatment, she was the most joyful person I'd ever met. "I'm pregnant. We're going to have a baby."

I was so prepared for disaster that it takes a minute for her words to fully register, and when they finally do, my heart swells to a size that has to be unhealthy. We weren't sure she'd be able to have more children after her treatment, so we haven't been careful about preventing pregnancy.

"Are you happy?" The hesitant way she asks that tells me I'm doing a shit job of reacting to the biggest news anyone has ever given me.

I kiss the back of her hand and then her sweet lips. "You really have to ask?"

"Just making sure this is good news for both of us."

"It's the best news I've ever gotten. We'll get married right away."

"We don't have to."

"We do have to. You're going to have the biggest, most beautiful wedding anyone ever had."

"I don't need that. I just need you and the kids and our friends at home."

"Whatever you want. I'd give you everything."

"You already have." She leans her head on my shoulder. "Tell me Leah and Marlowe are going to be okay."

"They're going to be fine. They're tough and resourceful, and they have each other. I'm actually almost more worried about Sebastian. He's never going to forgive himself for this."

Jasper

Watching my darling Ellie suffer is killing me. Surely there has to be an easier way to bring a new life into the world without writhing in unbearable pain for hours.

But Ellie… She doesn't seem bothered by it at all. The more it hurts, the more determined she becomes. How is she able to do that? Of course, I've always admired her strength and the way she'd rather learn how to do something herself than pay someone else to do it. This, however, is on a whole other level.

She squeezes my hand so hard during another contraction that I fear I'll have broken bones by the time our child is born. When the contraction passes, she sags into the pillows, breathing with her eyes closed.

I bathe her face with a cool cloth, feeling impotent and useless. I wish there was something I could do to make this easier for her, but she doesn't need me. She's in her zone, and I'm basically extraneous at the moment.

"Any word on Marlowe and Leah?" she asks when she can speak again.

"Nothing yet."

Ellie's mom comes in, bringing the fitting scent of Joy with her. Stella Flynn is joy personified. "How're we doing?"

"Your daughter is amazing."

Stella sweeps the sweaty hair back from Ellie's forehead. "Of course, we already knew that long before today."

"Are you guys done talking about me?" Ellie's eyes open, and she offers a wan smile.

I can see how exhausted she is, and the hardest part is still to come.

"Do you want some more ice chips?" I ask her.

She shakes her head. "I really want a burger."

They won't let her eat anything in case she ends up having a C-section. I really hope that doesn't happen. It was important to her to try to have a vaginal birth. We went through all the classes and watched the videos and read the books, but nothing can fully prepare you for the reality of this moment.

Dr. Breslow comes in to check on Ellie and, after examining her, proclaims her ready to push. Things start to happen fast after that. The room is transformed for delivery, and additional nurses are brought in to assist the doctor. There are so many people that I get momentarily pushed aside.

"I need my husband."

Will I ever get used to hearing myself described as the husband of the magnificent Estelle Godfrey Junior? No, never. I find my way back to her. I will *always* find my way back to her. "I'm here, love."

"Your *husband*?" Stella's brow is raised as she looks from Ellie to me and then back to Ellie.

"We, um… We got married at the courthouse last week. We were going to tell you guys." She's like a teenager confessing to her mother that she snuck out after curfew. "You aren't mad, are you? I didn't care about having a wedding. I just wanted to be married to Jasper."

"Sweetheart… Of course I'm not mad. I'm delighted." She reaches across the bed for my hand, which I willingly give her. I adore my new mother-in-law. "Welcome to our family, Jasper, although it seems silly to welcome you when you've been one of us for years now."

"Thank you, Stella. I love being a member of the Godfrey family."

Ellie gasps when another contraction seizes her.

"Breathe through this one," Breslow tells her. "On the next one, we're going to push."

The next hour passes in a blur of emotion and pain and love. So much love. I've never admired anyone more than I do my ferocious wife, who's indomitable as she brings our child into the world, squalling and outraged.

"Congratulations." Dr. Breslow smiles widely. "You have a son."

Tears roll unchecked down my face as I cut the cord and take in the scrunched, red, beautiful face of my son. I once thought I'd never have children, and now I have a *son*.

The nurse lays him on his mother's chest, and the look of blissful amazement on Ellie's face is something I'll cherish for the rest of my life. She wanted so badly to be a mother that she'd been prepared to use a sperm bank to make it happen. I'll always be thankful I followed her outside that morning in Mexico when she confessed her fondest desire to me, and I offered to help make her dream come true.

And in the process, she made all my dreams come true—dreams I never dared to have for myself because of the obligations to my family that were placed upon me at birth. Ellie gave me the courage to face off with my father, who put us through unspeakable hell before agreeing to allow my sister to inherit his business. When he passes, I'll become the tenth Duke of Weathersby. My wife has just given birth to the eleventh duke.

Everything will be different for my son. He'll be encouraged to chase his own dreams while honoring his family's heritage. I'll give him everything my father failed to give me.

"We did it," Ellie says, beaming up at me.

Her joy feeds mine. "Yes, we did, love. He sure is a handsome chap."

"How could he be anything but handsome with you as his dad?"

"And you as his mum." I lean over the bed rail to kiss them both. "I'm so proud of you, El. You were amazing."

"I just kept telling myself to power through it so I could meet my baby. Look at him! He's so perfect."

"He is indeed." He couldn't be more perfect, with a light dusting of blond hair, a button nose and a little bow mouth. I've already taken inventory to confirm he has ten toes and ten fingers.

"What's his name?" Stella asks, dabbing at tears.

I nod to Ellie to tell her mother the name we've chosen for him.

"Harrison Godfrey Kingsley."

I use my mother's maiden name of Autry professionally, but I'll give my son my legal name.

"We're going to call him Harry," Ellie adds as she gazes at the baby, who settled the minute he was given to his mother.

"I love it," Stella says. "Welcome to the world, sweet Harry."

CHAPTER 21

Marlowe

Thankfully, they don't take us back to the concrete room. In fact, they don't seem to know what to do with us now that I've agreed to help the niece of our kidnapper. He never did give me his name, which I suspect is intentional.

"We're hungry." It has to be at least a full day since they took us, and we haven't been given anything to eat in that time. I can't imagine what Sebastian and Emmett and the others are going through, but I have no doubt they've marshaled the full resources of Quantum to find us. Any minute, I expect them to come bursting into the room, guns blazing.

The black-eyed kidnapper picks up the phone and tells someone to bring us food.

While we wait, I stare him down, refusing to blink. "You've gotten what you want from me. Why don't you let us go?"

"I need insurance. What's to say you won't renege on your agreement to help Ariel the minute you leave here?"

"You have my word. I won't renege. I'll give you my phone number. She can call me to arrange a meeting."

"And you'll take her calls?"

"I swear to God on the lives of everyone I love that I'll take her call and do everything I can to help her."

He thinks about that for a minute before walking to a desk and returning with a notebook and pen that he hands to me. "Write down your number."

I do what I'm told, trying to remember my new phone number. Whatever it takes to get us the hell out of here.

"How about you call her now and get the ball rolling?"

"Fine by me."

He puts through the call. "Hi, love, it's Uncle T. I have a very special surprise for you." He hands the phone to me with a menacing look that puts me on notice that I'd better not fuck this up.

"Hello, Ariel, this is Marlowe Sloane."

The girl lets out a high-pitched scream that has me holding the phone away from my ear.

"Are you *kidding me right now?*"

"No, it's really me." I tell myself that the girl has no idea her uncle is holding me and my friend hostage and forcing me to make this call. She's an innocent bystander. "Your uncle showed me your video. You're very talented."

"Oh my God! I'm going to faint. I can't believe Marlowe Sloane thinks I'm talented! My whole life… I've just wanted to find a way to touch people." Her voice is heavy with emotion that reminds me of how I felt before I got my big break. I remember the almost painful yearning to use my gifts to connect with people. There's nothing she could say that would convince me more that her passion is legitimate. I vow in that moment to keep my promise to her uncle, regardless of whatever else might happen.

I talk to Ariel for the twenty minutes it takes for the food to arrive. The smell of pizza makes my mouth water. "I have to go now," I tell her, "but let me give you my number. Call me next week, and we'll make plans to get together."

"You'll never know what this means to me."

"I think I know. I was once right where you are with a dream and a heart full of ambition. People helped me get where I am, and I'm happy to pay it forward with you."

I can hear her softly sobbing through the phone. "Thank you so much."

"My pleasure. I'll talk with you soon." I end the call, stand, hand the phone to T and help myself to pizza for myself and Leah. After I've eaten two slices and consumed an entire bottle of water, I confront T. "May we go now?"

"I'll see you out, assuming I won't have any problems with the police or your security if I let you go."

"You'll never hear from me again as long as you leave us both alone." I can't promise he won't hear from the police, so I don't speak for them.

"Keep your promise to my niece, and I'll have no further business with you."

"I give you my word."

He signals to another man, who's been guarding the door. "See them out."

"We need our phones and Leah's car."

"We'll get them to you."

"See that you do."

I grab Leah's hand and hold on tightly as we follow the other guy down the metal stairs and through a series of corridors. At the end of a long hallway, he pushes a door open.

The burst of bright sunlight temporarily blinds me, but I push forward, towing Leah with me while taking deep breaths of fresh air. We break into a jog and then a sprint, rounding a corner where we encounter a massive police presence.

I've never been so happy to see cops in my life.

Sebastian

They're safe. The second I hear that news, my chest finally relaxes enough for me to take the first true deep breath I've had since I learned they were missing. In the next second, I'm sobbing uncontrollably. I make for the stairs and take them down to the lobby, where I use the palm scanner to gain access to the club. Only when I'm sealed away in my office do I allow myself to give in to the emotions that overtake me.

My phone chimes with a text from my mother, who's jubilant to hear the news that Marlowe and Leah are on their way home. Hayden must've told her.

I'll respond to her later, after I get my shit together.

I'm not sure why I came down here. What I really need to do is get the fuck out of this building. I should go home, pack some clothes and leave town before I'm forced to confront things that're better left alone.

I grab my phone and keys off the desk and head for the elevator. It opens in the lobby just as Marlowe and Leah are walking in the main door, surrounded by cops. For a second, I'm so overwhelmed by the sight of her that I can't make myself move or breathe or do anything other than drink her in. She's safe, and so is Leah. That's the only thing in this entire world that matters in this moment.

Marlowe walks over to me, puts her hand on my chest and backs me into the elevator. The doors close, silencing the police officer who was telling her they need a statement.

She looks up at me with a smile on her face, her eyes dancing with delight. "Going somewhere?"

What the fuck is wrong with her? She got kidnapped by one of the most ruthless gangbangers in LA because of me. So why is she looking at me that way?

She takes a step forward.

I take a step backward and hit the wall. "Are you hurt?" I have to know.

"Not physically."

"What the hell does that mean?" I'll fucking kill him if he touched one red hair on her head.

"Interesting guy, your friend."

"He's not my friend. He was *never* my friend."

"I know." Still with that sexy, knowing smile, like she's got a secret she's not ready to share with me. "You want to know what else I know?"

Desperately. But then I remember my plan to get the fuck out of there, and I try to step around her.

She's not having it. She blocks me. "Whatever you're thinking, knock it off. Whatever you're planning, your plans have changed. I'm in charge now."

In the scope of ten seconds, I go from flight mode to hard as a fucking rock.

She nods toward the open elevator doors. "Move it."

"I have somewhere to be."

"Not anymore you don't." Before I can anticipate her next move, she has my phone out of my back pocket and powers it down. She sticks it in her shirt, where I assume it's found a home in her bra.

I swallow hard. There's no way I can touch her if I still plan to get out of there. If I touch her, I'll never leave, and that's what I need to do. She can do so much better, and I want that for her. I want the best of everything for her.

She grabs me by the shirt and tugs me along with her through the double doors that lead to the club. When we're inside, she turns the lock that only I ever use when I'm there alone and want to keep it that way.

"What're you doing?"

"Don't talk to me unless you're asked a direct question. What's your safe word?"

I scoff. "I don't need one."

"Oh yes, you do."

I realize she isn't fucking around. She's in full-on Domme mode and so unbearably sexy as she orders me around that I nearly swallow my tongue. It takes effort, the kind normally expended in the gym, to resist the overpowering desire to haul her into my arms and devour her. My gratitude is so profound. He took her, but he didn't harm her, at least not physically. Good thing, because I didn't have murder on my to-do list today.

I want to know if she was harmed, but she's told me to shut up. After the ordeal she was subjected to because of me, it seems like the least I can do to let her play this out her way. When she's through with me, I'll make my escape.

I'm stunned when she heads straight for the dungeon. The last time we were there, I was rescuing her after Rafe's attack.

She points to the stairs. "Move it."

"Marlowe—"

"Shut the fuck up, Sebastian."

I'm aroused to the point of madness. I stumble down the stairs.

She follows me. "Strip."

I turn to her. "We need to talk."

She laughs. "The time for talking was when he first called and told you to ask me for a favor. That was the time for you to say, 'Hey, Mo. I need a favor.' So no, we're not going to talk now."

"You don't understand—"

"Oh yes, I do. I understand everything now, and you will, too. But for now, you're going to do what you're told. Remember how we agreed to take turns being in charge? It's my turn. So shut your mouth and take off your clothes. *Now.*"

"I… uh…"

"You sure you don't need a safe word?"

"Fuck no." I can handle whatever she dishes out. I'm certain of it.

"Fine, then shut up and strip."

I can't believe that my hands actually tremble when I start to unbutton my shirt. My dick is so hard that it's a struggle to unzip my jeans.

She watches my every move and licks her lips when my cock springs free of my pants. "He's missed me."

I'm not supposed to say anything, so I don't. But if I could speak, I'd tell her that every part of me missed every part of her.

"I missed him, too." She curls her hand around my cock and begins to stroke me the way I showed her I like it.

I'm on the verge of coming within seconds.

Of course she knows that. "Don't come. Your orgasm belongs to me."

I experience a moment of pure panic. As a Dom, I pride myself on my unbreakable control. Surely I can't be on the verge of losing control this easily. I fight it off, gritting my teeth and trying to think about anything other than the desperate need ripping through me.

She releases me suddenly, and I take a step back, nearly knocked off my feet by the change in plans. "Up on the cross. Hurry up about it. I don't have all day."

I see now. She's going to teach me a lesson and get on with her life. The disappointment is almost as powerful as the desire, but what did I expect? I got her freaking kidnapped by a gangbanger. What did I think was going to happen when she came home? That we'd live happily ever after behind a white picket fence? The idea of that is so preposterous as to be laughable.

"Something funny?"

I didn't mean to laugh out loud. "No, ma'am." I step up onto the platform where the St. Andrew's Cross is located. "Front or back, ma'am?"

"Let me have your back first."

I assume the position with my hands grasping the leather straps. I hear rustling behind me, but other than that, nothing happens for quite some time—long enough that I begin to sweat from the heat in the dungeon. My dick leaks from being so fucking hard it aches.

When she joins me, her naked body brushes against mine, drawing a gasp of pleasure from my tightly clasped lips. She affixes Velcro straps to my wrists and ankles, making it so I can't move and leaving me completely at her mercy.

I'm not afraid of her in any way, but I'm afraid I won't actually be able to take it like a man. I've seen Marlowe reduce her subs to sniveling shells of their former selves. She wouldn't do that to me, would she?

"Tell me something." She runs her fingertip straight down my back, into the crease between my cheeks until she's pressing against my back entrance. "Has anyone ever plugged you?"

"No, ma'am." I don't want that, but I can't very well say so unless I want to put a stop to everything.

"Hmm, interesting. Let's do that."

Fuck. How can my dick get any harder than it already is? It's going to explode.

She leaves me and returns with lube that she applies to my ass with two very insistent fingers.

I've done some ass stuff here and there, but receiving has never been my thing. Giving is where it's at. When her fingers fully breach me, my natural inclination is to try to get away, but there's nowhere to go with the shackles firmly in place. I grit my teeth, close my eyes and focus on breathing through the discomfort. And is it possible that she's intentionally trying to make it hurt? I wouldn't put it past her after what she endured because of me.

She withdraws her fingers before sending them into me again. This time, the fit is even tighter, which leads me to believe she's added a third finger. Fuck, that hurts. She goes at me hard, stroking in and out in swift movements that I've got no choice but to take. When she reaches around me with her free hand to stroke my cock, I explode, coming so hard, I nearly black out from the painful pleasure that rips through me like a tidal wave.

"What a naughty, *naughty* sub you are."

She sounds delighted, which irks me.

So she bested me this time. Now that she's taken the edge off, I won't be so easy to break. I feel an intense pressure against my anus. Holy fuck, she's using the biggest of the plugs. A cold sweat overtakes me. What if I can't do it? I try to remember the things I tell my subs when they insist they can't take me in their asses. *Breathe. Push back. Try to relax.* As if that's possible when your body is being stretched and invaded. I have a whole new appreciation for what my subs endured when they tried to take my cock this way.

Only two ever succeeded.

Payback is a bitch, I think as she pushes the plug relentlessly into me until my body yields to allow it in. By the time the plug is fully inserted, I'm as hard as I was before I came. The plug sits snug against my prostate, so snug that the slightest movement is going to set me off again. When the plug begins to vibrate, I shout from the sensations that have my entire body seizing from the orgasm that hits me like a tsunami this time. It comes from nowhere and leaves me gasping in the aftermath.

"You suck at being a sub."

I'm too spent to fire back, not that I can anyway. I'm not supposed to talk. I'm supposed to just stay still and take whatever she's dishing out.

"You've earned two punishments."

I can tell by the tone of her voice that she's thoroughly enjoying this. And when the first lash of the flogger hits my ass, my dick gets hard all over again.

My groan lets her know how totally she's winning this game of ours.

CHAPTER 22

Marlowe

I've got him right where I want him as I lash his ass until it's fiery red. I want him to feel it every time he sits down for the next few days. I want him to remember this and me and what he's going to learn while he's at my mercy.

"When did you know you were in love with me?" I ask him between lashes.

He's breathing harder, but otherwise has had no noticeable reaction to the flogging. I'm watching him closely, as I always do during scenes. I take my job as a Domme very seriously. My subs may get very, *very* uncomfortable, but they never get hurt. "What're you talking about?" His voice is tense and strained.

I give the plug a gentle tug and then push it back into place.

His body goes rigid in reaction.

This is fun—for me. Not so much for him, I think. Oh well. Too bad he didn't tell me the truth the other day. None of this would've happened. "Answer the question. When did you know?"

"I'm not in love with you."

I laugh—hard. "Liar."

"You're going to tell me how I feel now?"

"Want to know when I knew for sure that you love me?"

"Knock yourself out."

"When my kidnapper... what's his name anyway? I never heard."

"Turk," he says, snarling over the name.

"When Turk told me what he wanted with me. Two things became very clear to me right then and there—that you ran because he asked you for something from me and that you ran because you love me."

"No, I don't."

"Yes, you do. What I want to know is how long have you loved me?"

He's stubbornly silent.

I pull on the plug, withdrawing it until the widest part stretches him obscenely. *"How* long?"

He sags into the restraints, his shoulders slumping. "I've always known. Long time."

"Why didn't you tell me?"

"Because."

I lash him harder than I have yet.

He cries out. "I didn't think I was right for you."

"And I got no say in that?"

"I didn't get past me not being right for you. Look at me. I'm scarred from the fights I was in as a kid, covered in stupid tattoos that I got before I knew they should mean something, and you just got kidnapped and threatened because of me. And you wonder why I think I'm not good enough for you?"

I lash him another dozen times, until he's panting and sweating. But then I stop myself, because one of the cardinal rules of our lifestyle is to never act from a place of anger. I'm furious that he thinks so little of himself.

"You know what bothers me more than anything?"

"What?" he asks in a low growl.

"You're a Dom. What's the most important element in a Dom/sub relationship?"

"Communication."

"Bingo. And what did you do when Turk called you and asked you for something?"

"He didn't ask *me* for something. He wanted it from *you*."

"And that was unacceptable to you?"

"Fuck yes, it was! I don't want that scumbag anywhere near you."

"How'd that work out for you?"

The sound that comes from him is nearly inhuman. "I fucked up, all right? Is that what you want me to say?"

"It's a good start." I rub the redness on his ass.

He moans.

"What're you going to do if something like that happens again?" I slip a cock ring around his balls and smile when his backbone goes completely straight in reaction to the tight rubber around his most sensitive parts.

"It's not going to happen again."

"Sure, it will. Your woman is a big star."

"You're not my woman."

"Oh yes, I am, and you'll be glad to know I've decided to give you another chance."

He grunts out a laugh. "What makes you think I want another chance?"

I place a soft, tender kiss square in the middle of his back. "Because you love me enough to leave me to keep me safe." I lean my forehead against him and wrap my arms around his midsection. This moment is about love, not sex or domination, and I fully luxuriate in the awareness that I've found *him*, the one I've hoped to find, the one who completes me and makes me whole.

That he's been right under my nose all along makes it even better than it would be with someone new. I know this man. I know his heart, and I'm starting to understand what drives him. He cares so much about the people he loves that he'd sacrifice himself if it meant saving them.

I kiss him on either side of his spine. "I don't need you to protect me."

"Too bad."

"If you feel such a burning need to protect me, could that be because you love me?"

"Stop it. We had fun. That's all it was."

"Bullshit." I wrap my hand around his cock and squeeze hard.

He hisses out a deep breath.

"Stop lying to me and yourself."

"I'm not lying. I don't want this."

The words hit me like a fist to the gut. I was so sure I had him figured out. Maybe I'm wrong, but I don't think so. When we were together, before Turk called and ruined everything, nothing had ever felt more perfect or more right. I know he felt the same way, and that's why I'm pushing him so hard.

If I can't bring him around in here, I fear he'll run away from me and never come back. That can't happen. Now that I've had a taste of perfect, I want to gorge on it—and him. I reach up to remove the restraints on his wrists. Then I free his ankles. I take his hand and lead him to the chaise in the corner that I requested when we built the dungeon.

"Sit."

He sits gingerly due to the plug and the ring.

I straddle his lap, forcing him to look at me. "Have you ever felt anything better than what's between us?"

"Sure I have." He feigns a casual tone, but I see the truth in his black eyes. "Lots of times."

I rock back and forth over his cock. "I never took you for such a liar."

"I'm not lying."

"Yes, you are." I align his cock with my pussy and face the usual battle to allow him in. I go for maximum impact as I slowly but surely sink down until he's in as far as he can go. With my hands on his shoulders, I study the planes and angles of his arresting face. He's beautiful in a fierce, sexy sort of way. "You work so hard to be strong for everyone else. Who's strong for you?"

His hands curl around my hips, and his fingertips press into my flesh. "I don't need anyone to be strong for me."

"So much bullshit, Sebastian. I never knew you were such a coward." Oh, he doesn't like that! I'm delighted by the foul look he gives me. If he didn't care, he wouldn't get pissed. I tilt my hips and begin to ride him slowly, loving the way his eyes roll back in his head.

Gotcha.

I turn on the vibration in the plug, and he goes crazy, hammering into me until I'm sure I'll never walk straight again.

That's fine with me.

Everything is fine as long as I have him—and he has me.

Emmett

They told me I needed to stay here and chill until the cops brought Leah and Marlowe to us. Actually, the words Flynn used were "chill the fuck out." I'd like to see how he'd handle it if Natalie had been the one taken. I pace from one end of the lobby to the other more times than I can count. I've never noticed that it takes roughly one hundred steps to walk across the lobby, probably because I've never had any reason to count them before now.

At least I don't feel like I'm having a heart attack anymore.

She's safe. She's on her way back to me. Everything is all right. Except it won't really be all right until she's back in my arms where she belongs. It's ridiculous how essential she's become to me. A few months ago, I was describing her as a pesky fly buzzing around my head, making me crazy with her silly legal questions, perky tits, hot-as-fuck ass and endlessly witty commentary. I wanted to strangle her almost as much as I wanted to fuck her.

Now…

Well, now I can't seem to breathe properly when she's not around, and I can barely function when she's in any kind of danger.

I'm kind of pissed, actually. My life was perfectly fine until she upended everything. How dare she do this to me? Does she have any idea what she's put me through over the last thirty hours without her?

The elevator dings before it opens, and then there she is. I'm so happy to see her sweet face that I don't even care that she's ruined my life.

I rush toward her and lift her right off her feet.

She wraps her arms around me and sobs into my neck.

I carry her straight to my office, ignoring the cops who're saying they need to talk to her. They can fuck right off. I kick the office door closed behind me and drop to the sofa, cuddling her into my chest. "Shhh, it's okay. Everything is okay now." I say that to her as much as to myself. We both need the reassurances.

"I thought I'd never see you again."

"I'm so sorry you were scared." I tip her chin up so I can kiss her.

She clings to me, her mouth opening to my tongue, and before I know what's what, I'm stretched out on top of her, our legs are intertwined, and I'm so hard for her, I'm afraid I might burst from the need that pulses through me like a separate heartbeat that belongs only to her.

Only when I have to breathe do I break the kiss and drop my head to her chest. "You can't ever do this to me again."

She sinks her fingers into my hair. "It's not like I set out to make you nuts."

"Well, you did."

"You were nuts?"

I raise my head so I can look down at her. "I was out of my mind. You've burrowed your way so deep inside me that I can't live without you."

"Does that mean we're in a *relationship*?" Her saucy smile is much more "her" than the heartbroken tears could ever be.

"Shut up."

"Make me."

"Happy to." I kiss her until I'm about to come in my pants. I reach down to free myself, and after pushing her clothes aside, I slip inside her. It's like coming home, every damned time. How and why it's so different with her, I'll never know. It just is, the same way her eyes are blue and her little tits are incredibly sensitive and her pussy is so tight, it makes me want to howl from the pleasure.

I can't do that here. But when I get her home… There might be howling. "I love you so much, my sexy little pit bull. So fucking much, it made me crazy to know you were in danger. This is the second time you've done this to me. You gotta stop scaring me. If anything ever happened to you…" I'm horrified when my voice catches and my eyes fill.

Leah frames my face in her hands and brings me in for a sweet, tender kiss that nearly unmans me. "I'm fine. I'm right here with you, exactly where I've wanted to be since the day I started at Quantum and you and your big brain nearly made me come in the conference room."

Even when I think it's not possible to laugh, she proves otherwise.

"And I love you, too. So much." She caresses my face with a tender touch. "All I could think about the whole time we were gone was if you were okay."

"I wasn't. I wasn't okay at all." I hold her and kiss her and make love to her. "I need you to marry me, Leah. Marry me and be with me and just be mine."

"Are you really proposing to me while we're having sex?"

"I guess maybe I am. Why? Did you need some fancy romantic proposal?"

She shakes her head. "This is just fine."

"Is that a yes?"

"Yes, Emmett, I'll marry you."

I love the blissed-out smile on her sweet face. "I hope you're happy that your evil plan to fully infiltrate my life has been so successful."

"I'm very happy."

I hold her as close to me as I can get her. "That's the only thing that matters."

CHAPTER 23

Sebastian

Is it possible to die from too much sex or to become dehydrated from coming so many times, you lose count of how many orgasms there've been? If so, I'm knocking on death's door as Marlowe completely and thoroughly uses me. I honestly can't believe we're still here. It has to be hours after this started. The club is due to open shortly, but the main door is locked. What will the employees do when they report to work?

There's nothing they can do. I have the only key to that door, and it's on the floor of the dungeon in the pocket of my jeans.

I want to ask her how long we're going to do this, but I suspect I already know the answer to that question. My chest aches from the pressure building in the area of my heart. I can't give her what she wants, as much as I might wish otherwise.

She once again turns on the vibration in the plug, and like every other time she's done that, I come like an inexperienced teenager in the throes of first lust.

"*Jesus*, Marlowe. What the fuck do you want from me?"

"Everything."

"No."

"Yes."

"I can't."

"Bullshit."

"I don't *want* to."

"Bullshit."

"So what? We're going to do this until I give you the answer you want?"

"We're going to do this until you give me the *truth*."

"Aren't you getting sore?"

"Funny you should ask. I was just thinking I should switch locations."

"What..." Before I can gauge her intent, she's moved my cock so it's pressed against her ass. "Marlowe, don't. You need to be prepared for that."

"You're not in charge here, remember?"

She strokes lube onto my cock, which is hard—again. How is that even possible?

"You're going to hurt yourself."

"What do you care?"

"I care." I care too much, and that's the problem. I never again want to feel as helpless as I did knowing she was in danger because of me, and there wasn't a damned thing I could do about it. As good as the good times with her were—and they were better than it's ever been with anyone—I can't risk something happening again or that she'll wise up in a year or two and realize she can do way better than me.

After hearing me say I care, she pauses. "What do you care about?"

"You. Of course I care about you. We've been friends for years."

She scowls and continues on her misguided plan to initiate herself into anal sex.

"You're going to hurt yourself. You need to be prepared, especially to take... well, me."

"Fine, then prepare me." She lifts herself off me and stands next to the chaise, gesturing for us to switch places.

"You haven't had enough?"

"Obviously not."

"Marlowe..."

"Prepare me. Now."

I don't want it like this. "I'm not sure I can."

She glances at my hard cock and raises a brow.

"I'm kind of sore from what we've already done." I'm quite certain I've never had this much sex in such a condensed time period, and I really am sore.

Her eyes shoot fire at me, but her chin wobbles. "Fine. Forget it. Just forget the whole thing." She walks over to where our clothes lie scattered about on the floor and gets dressed, her movements jerky and rushed, as if she can't wait to get out of there and away from me.

I start to get up to go to her, but my legs feel like overcooked spaghetti noodles. It takes me a second to get my shit together, and by then, she's heading for the stairs. I gently grasp her arm to stop her. "Don't go."

"Why not?"

"Because."

"That's all you've got?"

It's time to put up or shut up. I get that. But the words... They're stuck inside me, wedged behind an unbreakable wall of fear.

She twists her arm free of my grasp. "Let me go, Sebastian. You've made it perfectly clear that you don't want what I do."

"That's not true."

"Whatever."

"Marlowe."

Probably only because we've been friends for so long does she turn to look at me.

"I'm afraid." It takes every ounce of courage I can find inside me to admit that.

Her expression doesn't change. "Of what?"

"Of this, of you, of how I feel when I'm with you, of what it felt like to know you were in danger because of me, of losing you after what we've had. All of it. It's terrifying."

She takes a deep breath and lets it out slowly before closing the distance between us and laying her hands flat against my chest. "I love you."

"I know, but—"

"Sebastian."

I look into the lovely green eyes that are looking at me with affection and humor and love, so much love. "I'm *in* love with you. I think perhaps I have been for as long as I've known you."

"You... I... *Really?*" My voice breaks on that last word, the way it did when I was twelve and going through puberty.

"Really."

I shake my head. "You shouldn't love me like that."

"Kinda too late." She flashes the toothy grin that made her a superstar. "I already do. I've made a lot of really bad decisions because I refused to acknowledge what was right in front of me for years. Are you going to make bad decisions, too?"

"You got kidnapped because of me."

"I know, and guess what? I survived it because of *me*. I'm right here. I'm safe and sound and telling you I'm in love with you."

"You can do better."

Her disappointment is obvious. "I guess I'll see you around, then."

"Wait."

She stops but keeps her back to me.

"You bring so much to the table, and I..."

She turns to face me. "Do you love me, Sebastian?"

When she looks at me that way and asks me point blank, I find I can't deny it. I don't want to. "Yeah, I love you." Some of the tension in my chest eases when I say those words.

"That's the only thing I need you to bring to the table. I don't want or need one single other thing from you besides that. Well, I need your exceptional cock once in a while, too."

"He kinda comes with the package."

"It's a very appealing package, and you don't even know it. You're the most loyal person I know. Do you have any idea how important that quality is to someone like me, who frequently sees the worst of people in this business? You're the best friend anyone could ever hope to have. There's nothing you wouldn't do for any of us, and we all know it. I've seen your heart, and I love your heart."

"You humble me."

"You thrill me."

My heart, the heart that belongs only to her, skips a crazy beat, the same way it would if I were about to step off a cliff into a free fall. Isn't that exactly what I'm doing? "Are you absolutely sure this is what you want? That I'm what you want?"

"One million percent sure."

"And you won't change your mind in a year or two when someone better comes along?"

She puts her arms around my waist and gazes up at me. "There is no one better than you."

When she says it with such conviction, I start to believe that maybe it's true. There might be better men out there, men who've never broken the law or done the things I've done, but no one will ever love her more than I do. That much I know for certain. I wrap my arms around her and bury my face in her soft, fragrant hair. "Are we really going to do this?"

"Only if it's what you want, too."

"It is. It's what I've always wanted but was too afraid to reach for."

"And now that you have it within your grasp, what do you plan to do with it?"

"Keep it." I tighten my hold on her. "Forever."

EPILOGUE

Marlowe

It's Oscar night, and I'm nervous. Not about the awards or the show, but what comes after. Over the last week, Sebastian has been preparing me to finish what we started in the dungeon that day. Tonight, under the copper-colored Dior gown that was made just for me, I'm wearing the largest of the plugs he procured for me.

When I think about the battle it took to insert that plug, my body tingles with anticipation and a healthy dose of fear. Sebastian is twice the size of the plug. There's a very good chance I won't be able to handle him there, but I'm determined to try.

How am I supposed to think about anything but what's coming later while we're at the show?

He walks into his bedroom and stops short at the sight of me in the gown that perfectly complements my coloring. Wearing an Armani tuxedo, he's absolutely devastating.

"Let me see the front," he says gruffly.

I turn to show him the plunging neckline—if you want to call it that. It leaves the middle of me completely bare. The daring look required double-stick tape to keep my nipples from popping out, but Tenley has assured me I'm a slam dunk for a best-dressed nod, not that I care about that.

I do care about the heated, desperate, possessive way Sebastian studies me. "What do you think?"

"There's too much of you showing."

I *knew* he'd say that. "All the important parts are covered."

"All your parts are important."

I crook my finger at him. "Come here and let me see you."

He crosses the room to me, and I smooth my hands over the fine fabric of his jacket. "You look gorgeous."

"So do you."

I hook my arm through his and turn us to face the full-length mirror Tenley brought when she learned that Seb didn't own one. "How can men live this way?" Tenley asked.

I tip my head to lean it on his shoulder. "We look pretty good together, don't you think?"

"We look incredible together."

Ever since he decided to let go of the fear and take what he wants, he's been like a whole new and improved version of his already awesome self. He's all in, and all-in Sebastian is a force to be reckoned with. He tells me he loves me no fewer than a dozen times a day. He wants to talk about our future—where we'll live and whether we should sell his place and live at mine at the beach or buy something new together.

He won't let me pay for anything. "I've got it, babe" is his regular refrain.

I let him pay because I understand that he needs to take care of me, which is fine with me. What do I care who pays as long as we get to do everything together?

Turk was arrested about an hour after we walked out of the warehouse. My statement and Leah's helped to build the case against him. I've kept my promises to Ariel and have plans to meet her for lunch this week. She had nothing to do with what her uncle did, and if I can help her get ahead in this cutthroat business, why wouldn't I? Somehow the cops managed to keep my name and Leah's out of the public statements about Turk's arrest, and for that I'll be eternally grateful. I've had more than enough publicity lately.

Turk has been charged with multiple felony counts of kidnapping, false impris-onment and extortion. His chop shop was raided, and the guys who worked for him were arrested, too. Leah and I think it's kind of cool that we helped to shut down their entire criminal enterprise.

Speaking of Leah, she and Emmett are *engaged*! We're all so thrilled for them. I love the way she's totally transformed Emmett's life and given him something he didn't even know he was missing until she showed him that there could be so much more. And the rock he put on her finger? Holy statement, Batman. The man is smitten, and that's plainly obvious to anyone who spends even five minutes with the two of them.

She and I are closer than ever since our ordeal with Turk, and I was delighted when she asked me to be in her wedding party.

Sebastian's hand on my ass takes me out of my thoughts and back to reality when he presses on the base of the plug. "Everything still a go for later?"

"Yep."

"You're not going to wimp out on me, are you?"

"I really hope not."

He carefully puts an arm around me and kisses the top of my head. "It's okay if you do. After you plugged me, I have a whole new appreciation for what it's like to be on the receiving end."

"No, you don't. That plug was nothing compared to the beast in your pants."

His gruff laughter warms me all the way through. It's so perfect with him. He's everything I ever wanted and more. That I can be completely and totally myself with my friend Sebastian, who is also my love, is the greatest gift in an already blessed life.

"We need to go."

"I still can't believe I'm your date to the Oscars."

"Believe it. You're my date to life."

"I still can't believe that either."

"Is your mom going to watch?"

"Yep, with my dad, apparently." No one is really clear on how the relationship between his parents works these days, but whatever. It works for them, Sebastian says, and that's what matters.

A chauffeur-driven black Bentley, the same model as my white one, delivers us into town for the show. I'm meeting my Quantum partners there and looking forward to a big night for all of us with *Insidious* the front-runner for best picture. Winning two years in a row would cement our place as the top production company in Hollywood.

Because of that, I'm almost more excited for the best picture category than I am for best actress. Although, it would be nice to win for acting again. It's been almost twenty years since I took home the best supporting actress statue for my first film. I also received an Oscar as a producer for *Camouflage* last year.

More than anything, I'm excited to have the man I love as my date to the biggest event of the year.

My cell phone rings, and I take the call without checking the caller ID, certain it's one of my partners. It's not.

"Marlowe. Please don't hang up."

Rafe. "How'd you get this number?" I can't imagine how he would've gotten my new number.

"It doesn't matter. I need to talk to you. You have to do something. Everywhere I go, the women… They throw things at me. One of them threw hot food on me in a restaurant!"

I roll my lips together so I won't be tempted to laugh.

"They hit me and slap me. You have to call them off!"

"Why should I? After what you did to me and twelve other women, it's the least of what you deserve."

"I said I was sorry."

"I don't believe you. I think you're sorry you finally got called out for your bad behavior. Here's a piece of advice—stay home. No one can throw things at you or slap you if you don't go out. Also, you might want to stay out of the US since there's a warrant for your arrest. And here's my final piece of advice. If you call me again, I'll press charges for harassment in addition to the assault charges."

"Marlowe, please…"

I end the call and block the number.

"So fucking hot." The low rumble of Sebastian's sexy voice makes me want to fan myself.

"You think so?"

"Oh yeah. My woman is a *badass*. Nobody better fuck with her."

"That's right."

"Damn straight."

"They're throwing food at him in restaurants."

We lose it laughing.

And when the phone rings again, I scowl in anticipation of another call from him. This time, I check the caller ID and see Flynn's name pop up.

"Mo," he says before I can even say hello. He sounds frantic. "Nat's in labor."

"*Already?*" She's not due for another month.

"Yeah, we were all ready to leave when her water broke. We're on our way to the hospital."

"What does Dr. Breslow say?"

"That she's okay to deliver at thirty-five weeks, but…"

"She'll be fine, Flynn. She's young and strong, and the baby is totally fine. I know it."

"Mo." He manages to convey a world of fear in the way he says my name.

"You want me to come to the hospital?" I'd do it in a second if he asked me to, and he knows it.

"Absolutely not. It's going to be a big night for you and for Quantum. I hate to jinx myself this way, but will you accept for me if I win?"

With his superstitions, it's a huge thing for him to even acknowledge the possibility that he might win. "I'd love to. Can I tell them where you are?"

"Yeah, why not? I'm gonna be a dad."

The wonder and amazement in his voice move me to tears. "Yes, you are. The best dad ever. We love you both. Let us know how she's doing?"

"I'll text you."

"Give Nat our love."

"Will do."

"Keep breathing, Flynn."

"Trying. I'll be in touch."

The line goes dead, and I glance at Sebastian. "Do you think I should go to the hospital?"

"We'll go by after the show."

"We have plans after the show."

"They'll keep until we check on our friends."

We arrive a short time later at the Dolby Theatre in Los Angeles and wait in a long line of other cars offloading celebrity cargo.

"You ready for this?" We'll officially go public with our relationship at this event, and I've tried to prepare Sebastian for how things will change for him. He says he gets it, but how could he until he's chased from a coffee shop or grocery store by camera-wielding paparazzi? Sure, he's spent time with all of us and seen how it can be for us, but it's different when the focus is on you—and the focus *will* be on him once the media figures out that we're together.

He kisses my hand and gazes into my eyes. "I'm ready for anything if it means I get to sleep with you every night and wake up with you every morning."

Swoon. "I love you."

"Love you, too, babe. Let's go knock 'em dead." He gets out first and reaches for me.

I take hold of his hand and let him help me out of the car.

The crowd goes wild when they see that it's me, and we're momentarily blinded by the flashes of a thousand cameras recording this moment. I hear the buzz: *Who is he? Do we know him? Haven't we seen him before?* It won't take long for them to figure out who he is. I've instructed Liza not to give them anything. Let them figure it out for themselves.

I wave to my adoring fans who call out to me from the bleachers as we walk the red carpet, stopping for several interviews with the big entertainment shows.

As we planned, Seb waits for me outside the shot so he won't be forced to answer questions. I talk to the interviewers about the movie, tell them who I'm wearing and make small talk while avoiding the one question they most want answered: Who is he, and what does he mean to me?

Soon enough, they'll know. He's Sebastian Lowe, and he's everything to me.

Sebastian

The awards show is surreal. What the fuck am I doing in a three-thousand-dollar tux, hobnobbing with Hollywood royalty? When Marlowe looks over at me and flashes that irrepressible trademark grin, I remember what I'm doing here. I'm here for her, because there's nowhere I'd rather be than wherever she is.

A week after sealing my fate in the dungeon, I wonder why I bothered to resist her. My resistance was as futile as metal would be avoiding a magnet when the two are on a collision course with destiny.

She is my destiny, and for some reason that I'll never fully understand, I'm hers.

After our stroll down the red carpet, we're shown into the theater, where the Quantum team is seated in the first two rows. When the producers are informed that Flynn and Natalie won't be attending, there's a scramble to fill their seats. Marlowe agrees to fly solo for the presentation of the best original screenplay award they were supposed to do together.

Everyone wants to know where they are. Other than our Quantum family, we tell no one why they're missing the biggest night of the year. Only we know that this could be the biggest night of their *lives*, and the reason has nothing to do with awards.

It takes forever, or so it seems, to get to the awards we came for. Jasper wins the Oscar for cinematography on *Insidious* and goes up to accept his award.

"This means so much to me." His voice is thick with emotion as he stares down at his second consecutive Oscar. "A year ago, I was a footloose bachelor without a care in the world other than my work and my friends. Today… Tonight, I'm eternally thankful to my beautiful wife, Ellie Godfrey, who made me a dad last week when our son, Harrison, was born. Ellie and Harry are watching from home, and I want to thank them both for giving me a life I could've only dreamed about before they came along. To my partners in crime at Quantum… During the most difficult days of my life, you stood by me, you raised me up, and you gave me the courage to fight for the life I wanted. I love you all so much. Thank you to the Academy for this incredible honor."

We're all in tears as we stand and cheer for Jasper, Ellie and baby Harry.

After a few more awards are presented, we get to best actress. When her name is read as one of the nominees, Marlowe gives me a goofy grin and squeezes my hand.

"And the Oscar goes to Marlowe Sloane."

She won! Holy shit, she won! And when she leans in to kiss me tenderly before getting up to receive her award, my heart swells with a love so big, it can't be contained. I walk her to the stage and hold her hand as she goes up the stairs on impossibly high heels. I let go only when I'm confident she's got it from here.

"Wow, thank you so much to the Academy and everyone who voted for me. I'm thrilled to be recognized for this role and this character and the important light it shines upon the work of mental health professionals. I want to thank Flynn for being my partner in this film, as well as my best friend and the beloved brother of my heart for all these years. My love and thanks go to Hayden, who gives his heart and soul to everything he does, to Jasper, who makes us all look good on film, and Kristian for juggling the details. I wouldn't want to do this life or this job without you guys and our entire Quantum family. I want to thank my mom…"

Her voice goes soft, and her eyes fill with tears. I'm unbearably moved by her.

"None of this would've happened without her fierce belief in me and the many sacrifices she made to bring me to LA to chase the dream. I owe everything I have to her." She takes a breath and looks at me. "You all know what happened to me recently, but what you may not know is that one of the worst days of my life was also one of the best days because it led me to where I should've been all along, with my friend and forever love. Sebastian, I'm not sure what I ever did to get lucky enough to spend this life with you, but I'll be grateful for you every day that I have left. I love you so much. Thank you again for this incredible honor."

Tears roll down my face as I applaud and whistle and generally make a scene. I'm so fucking proud of her. And what she said about me? I still can't believe she loves me like that, but thank God she does.

She comes back out to accept for Flynn when he wins the Oscar for best performance by an actor in a leading role. "I'm delighted to accept this award on behalf of my best friend, Flynn Godfrey, who is, at this very moment, helping his beautiful wife, Natalie, welcome their first child."

The crowd goes wild, cheering for that news.

"Flynn would want me to tell you that it meant the world to him to bring this particular character to life, to shine the light on the scourge of opioid addiction in this country and to show that it is possible to fight your way out of the pits of hell to find help and a new life after addiction. To everyone who's currently struggling, you have our hearts and our support and our love. Thank you for recognizing Flynn's amazing performance with this award."

I can't seem to contain the tears that flow as each of my closest friends is recognized for their amazing gifts.

Hayden is next when he receives the award for best director.

He takes the stairs two at a time, which makes us laugh. I love seeing my usually stoic, focused, moody friend glowing with happiness. He's my brother from another mother, and I'm filled with pride as I watch him on stage.

"Thank you to the Academy for the overwhelming recognition of *Insidious*. We struggled to name this film. We wanted to call it *Addict*, but the studio thought we could do better, and they were right. *Insidious* is the perfect title for this film that tells the heartbreaking story of our times. This new age of addiction isn't limited to rich people who can score a pricey hit. This wave is indiscriminate. It touches every city and town, every economic level. It is indeed insidious. It was my honor, and the honor of everyone associated with Quantum, to tell this story. I want to thank my partners at work and life—Flynn, Marlowe, Jasper and Kristian, as well as the amazing team that supports us every day. And I want to thank my beautiful wife, Addison, for coming up with the title of *Insidious* and saving our asses, but for also saving my ass by loving me and marrying me. I have no idea who I was before I had you, sweet Addie, but all I know is that everything is better now." He holds up the statue. "Thanks again for this incredible award."

It surprises no one when *Insidious* completes the sweep and wins for best picture. Kristian accepts for Quantum.

"Thank you to the Academy and everyone who felt our film was deserving of this honor. We're so fortunate to get to do this work, to tell important stories and to do it with the people we love most in the world. The second-best thing I ever did was say yes to Flynn and Hayden when they asked me to join their team at Quantum. The very best thing I ever did was fall for my sweet fiancée, Aileen, and her kids, Logan and Maddie, who're now my kids, too." He looks at Aileen and the kids, who're decked out in formal attire for the big night. "The three of you have given me more than I ever hoped to dream possible, and now..." Kristian pauses for a second to get himself together. "We've recently found out that our foursome will be a gang of five by the end of the year."

We all go wild clapping and whistling as Aileen sobs and smiles and laughs at our reaction to their news.

"Our family is the best award I could ever be given. Love is the best award, but best picture is a pretty close second. Thank you again for honoring *Insidious* with this award. It's my pleasure to accept it on behalf of the entire Quantum team."

My hands hurt from clapping, and my voice is hoarse from all the cheering and shouting I've done in support of my family. Watching them on the stage, arms linked, beaming with happiness, I'm so proud, I could burst.

After the show, we skip the parties and head right to the hospital, bringing Oscars and ball gowns and excitement to the maternity waiting room where several other expectant family members are stunned to realize who's joined them. We're there a long time, so long that the other families leave. Tuxedo jackets and high heels are discarded, enormous amounts of junk food are consumed, and the Oscars we brought to show Flynn and Nat are lined up like forgotten toys on a side table.

I love that everyone is far more concerned about Flynn, Natalie and their child than they'll ever be about those statues. They know what matters in this life, and their priorities are firmly in order. Max Godfrey is here, as are Flynn's other sisters, Annie and Aimee. Stella is in the room with Flynn and Nat.

Flynn finally comes in around four in the morning, weary and teary and glowing with happiness. "She's here. Cecelia Estelle Godfrey. Seven pounds, six ounces, nineteen inches. We're going to call her Cece. Nat was amazing." He breaks down, and his father is right there to hug him.

Max pats his son on the back. "Congratulations, Dad."

"Nat said to bring you all in to see her and Cece so you can go home and get some rest."

The entire gang of us follows him back to the room, toting parts and pieces of formal wear as well as a whole new collection of Oscars.

Marlowe hands Flynn his. "Congrats."

Flynn takes it from her, smiles, gives it a passing glance and places it on the counter next to the window before going back to sit with Natalie and the baby.

Nat looks tired, gorgeous, happy and content as she holds her baby daughter.

"She's beautiful, guys," Marlowe declares.

"Well done," Jasper says.

"Thank God she looks like Natalie." Hayden's comment earns a scowl from Cece's father.

We visit with the new family for half an hour before we notice Natalie trying not to yawn.

"We're going to go and let you get some rest," Marlowe says. "We'll check in with you in the morning, or I guess later this morning."

"Thanks for being here, everyone," Natalie says. "It means the world to us that you were here to welcome our Cece."

We hug and kiss them both before leaving together, a bedraggled group that barely resembles the well-put-together contingent we were earlier. Marlowe and Hayden create a stir among the doctors, nurses and other hospital personnel as we head for the main doors, but they ignore the attention they get everywhere we go.

Since we let our driver go, Marlowe and I hitch a ride back to Malibu with Hayden and Addie, who drop us at my place just as the sun breaches the horizon.

"What a night." I follow Marlowe into my condo and straight to the bedroom that's become ours, where we drop our clothes on the floor in our haste to get horizontal. Then I remember our plans and the plug, and a dastardly, evil idea comes to me. I find the remote in my pants pocket and wait until she's gone into the bathroom to brush her teeth to turn it on.

She lets out a shriek. "Sebastian! *Shut that fucking thing off!*"

It's all I can do not to roar with laughter. "That's not my name right now."

She comes to the door, gloriously naked, her red hair a disheveled mess after being taken out of the elaborate style she wore to the awards ceremony. She has a toothbrush in her mouth as she glares at me. "Stop."

"No. Hurry up and get your *ass* in here." I'm in full Dom mode when I stare her down, letting her know I'm taking the lead.

That's how we've worked things out. Sometimes she's in charge, other times I am. Since we're both totally fine with submitting to the other, we've found our groove. If there are "rules," per se, they're simple. When one of us indicates a desire to be in charge, the other is expected to go along with it. Only a safe word can stop the train once it's left the station.

She's tired. I can tell that just by looking at her. She's drained from Oscar night and the extended visit to the hospital. And maybe she's a tiny bit afraid of what we're going to do. But she gives me a defiant look and turns to go finish brushing her teeth.

My cock is rock hard thinking about what's about to happen here. I go to my bedside table for lube and then to the closet for a spare towel. I'm ready for her when she emerges from the bathroom and stands before me with her fingers linked and her head down in supplication. She's brushed her gorgeous hair, and it hangs in shiny lengths. I'm transfixed by the sight of her nipples peeking through her hair.

I go to her, drawn so powerfully by the need for her that seems to grow exponentially with every passing day. She's become so essential to me that I'd go without food and water before I'd go without her. I used to laugh at guys like me, even my own friends, who became such pathetic slaves to the women they love, but now I get it. I'm her slave, her faithful servant, anything she wants me to be.

"Is my little sub nervous?"

"Yes, sir."

"How come?"

"Um, hello?" She gestures to my fully erect cock.

"You know I'd never hurt you, right?"

"Not intentionally."

"Not at all. Ever."

She gives me a saucy, defiant look that I love. "And how do you propose to do what we're going to do with that *thing* without it hurting at all?"

I'm a little offended on behalf of my *thing*. "I didn't say it wouldn't hurt at all. I said I wouldn't hurt you."

"Are you splitting hairs?"

I smile. "No more talking unless you need your safe word."

"Yes, sir."

Those words coming from her go straight to my heart. Before we do anything else, I need her to know what she means to me. I can tell I take her by surprise when I put my arms around her and hold her as close to me as I can get her. I smooth my hand over her silky hair, down her back, and cup her sweet ass. "I love you, Marlowe. I was so proud of you at the Oscars, I thought I might burst from it. I'm so honored that you picked me to spend your life with, and I just want you to know that I'll never take for granted the amazing trust you've put in me."

To my complete horror, she sniffles.

I draw back to find her face awash in tears. "What?"

She laughs—at me, not with me. "Don't panic. These are good tears."

"There ought to be a fucking law against girl tears."

She cups my face and runs her thumb over the scruff on my jaw. "Sorry about the tears, but what you said... It's your fault."

I glower playfully at her. "How so?"

"I've waited my whole life to find someone who would say what you just did to me and truly mean it. Someone who would love me for me and not for the illusion of me."

"I know exactly who and what you are. I couldn't give the first fuck about your fame, your money or all the bullshit that comes with you. I just want you."

"Have me, Sebastian."

Marlowe

It hurts. I'm not surprised, because I knew it would, but it's not as bad as I thought it would be. He prepared me well and goes slowly, giving me his cock in small increments as my body adjusts to the invasion. I've heard that it gets better... Any time now. I'm waiting and breathing and focusing and trying not to think about anything other than what's happening right here and now.

We discussed the best position and agreed I should be on my back so we could see each other.

"Talk to me." His voice is strained, and his jaw is tight with the tension of trying to make this good for me.

"*Ungmw.*"

"That's not a word."

I arch my back, telling him without words to give me more.

He does.

I cry out from the shock of painful pleasure. My nipples and clit throb, and my skin is alive with sensation that makes everything more intense.

Sebastian dips his head and takes my left nipple into his mouth, sucking and tugging and biting, just enough to draw my attention away from what's happening below—until he sinks farther into me. It's all I can do not to scream.

"Is that it?"

"That's half."

"Jesus."

"I've told you before it's *Sebastian*, but I can understand how you'd make that mistake."

How can I laugh when I'm being invaded by that *monster?*

He presses his thumb against my clit, and a sound I've never made before comes from deep inside me.

I've been told anal is the most intense experience there is, but I had no idea how intense it would be. Time seems to stand still as he withdraws and returns, giving me more each time, until finally, somehow, I manage to take all of him. I'm having one orgasm after another, my entire body thrashing and reacting to the nuclear-level thrill of taking him this way.

I feel a ridiculous sense of accomplishment.

"You feel so good." His lips skim my ear as he speaks in a gruff whisper. "So hot and tight and sexy. Tell me it's good for you."

"It's getting there."

"Tell me when you're ready for more."

"You said I had it all!"

"You do, but that's only part one."

"Oh my God. You're going to kill me."

"Never." He kisses my lips, my throat, and pays homage to my right nipple. When he switches sides, I squirm, looking for something more.

He pushes himself up on his arms. "Hold on to me."

I grasp his biceps, trying to brace myself, but nothing I could do would've prepared me for the ride he takes me on. Powerful is the only word I can think of to describe the connection I feel to him as he surges into me over and over and over again until I'm coming harder than I ever have before. He's right there with me, groaning through his release.

Afterward, I drift on a sea of pleasure and aftershocks and emotion. It's such a fucking relief to have found *him*, the one who's meant to be mine. I put my arms around him, holding on tight to him, to this, to us.

"Are you okay?"

"Yeah. You?"

"I'm so good. Never better." He withdraws from me, slowly and carefully, and gets up to use the bathroom.

I hear water running before he returns with a warm washcloth that he uses to clean me up. He drops the washcloth on the floor and sits on the edge of the bed, an arm propped on either side of my hips, gazing down at me. "You sure you're okay?"

"Yep."

"Further proof that you're a total badass. You're only the third one who's ever been able to do that with me."

"Where are the other two so I can have them killed?"

His smile lights up his beautiful black eyes. "You have nothing to worry about where they're concerned. I wouldn't know them if I fell over them. That was years ago." He twirls a strand of my hair and lets it slide through his fingers. "There's no one else but you, my sexy badass superstar. You ruined me for anyone else years ago."

I flash him my trademark goofy grin. "Excellent." I give him a tug to bring him back into bed with me and curl up to him, my head on his chest, my arm across his abdomen and his arms tight around me.

We have so much to look forward to—Kristian and Aileen's wedding in a few weeks, Leah and Emmett's wedding in the fall, watching Logan and Maddie and Harry and Cece and God knows how many other kids grow up, maybe having a few kids of our own…

"Do you want kids?"

His body goes completely still. "Do *you?*"

"Maybe."

"Huh."

"What does that mean?"

"It just never occurred to me that you'd want a family."

"Why not?"

"You're so focused on your career most of the time."

"I have been in the past, but now I've got other things I want to focus on."
I smooth my hand over his muscular abdomen. "I didn't really want kids until I
had someone in my life to have them with."

"You think I'd be a good dad?"

"You'd be a great dad. They'd be so lucky to have you."

"What if I screwed them up or they got into trouble or found out about
the shit I did when I was a kid?" He raises his head to look at me. "Are
you *laughing*?"

"I'm not laughing *at* you."

"Well, I'm not laughing, so you're not laughing with me." He pokes my belly,
and I laugh harder.

I clear my throat and force myself to be serious because I know he's legitimately
concerned. "Do you honestly think that any kid of mine is going to be allowed to
run wild and do the things that you did?"

"No, but—"

"No buts. We've got this, Seb. We'll be great parents, and we'll raise wonderful,
well-behaved kids who'll be so focused on school and sports that they won't have
time for anything else."

"Are you sure we can do that?"

"I'm very sure we can do anything if we do it together."

"You promise you're not going to suddenly wise up and realize you could've
done way better than me?"

"If you ever say that again, I have permission to stab you."

His delicious lips curve into a sexy smile. "Such a badass."

"And don't you forget it. I love you. I will *always* love you. And the only thing
you have to do to keep me forever is love me back."

His dark eyes sparkle with happiness that looks so good on him. He kisses
me, lingering for several delicious minutes. "Done."

***

If you or someone you know is a victim of domestic violence, please contact the National Domestic Violence Hotline at 1.800.799.7233 or visit their website at *https://www.thehotline.org.*

And that's a wrap, as they say in show business. Eight books later, the Quantum family is set to live happily ever after as they continue to work and play together in Hollywood. I like to think of them at birthday parties and soccer games for each other's kids and still doing what they've always done now that they've all found their bliss. I hope you enjoyed Marlowe's long-awaited story and love her with Sebastian as much as I do. I always pictured them ending up together once they both were in the right place to see what was possible for them. Every time someone objected to my plan to end Quantum with Marlowe's story and said WHAT ABOUT SEBASTIAN, I wanted to giggle. I always had a plan for him.

Make sure you check out the audio edition of FAMOUS, starring the amazing Sebastian York as our Sebastian and Emma Wilder as Marlowe. Join the FAMOUS Reader Group at *www.facebook.com/groups/famousbook8/* and the Quantum Reader Group at *www.facebook.com/groups/QuantumReaders/*.

Some of you have asked if I'll revisit the Quantum world in the future, and all I'll say to that is maybe. I never say never to anything, but I do plan to move on from here with more books in my other series and hopefully some new things coming down the road. I'm very proud of the Quantum series, which fell far outside my comfort zone and challenged me in many different ways.

Mostly, I'm proud of the epic romances contained in this series, which includes some of my all-time-favorite moments. Will we ever forget Hayden banging on the glass at Club Vice, trying to get Addie's attention before she did something that couldn't be undone? Or Leah and the butt plug or Fluff biting Flynn's ass or Jasper fighting for the life he desperately wanted with Ellie or Aileen finding Kristian in the closet? Every moment with these characters was a delight for me, and I'm thrilled that so many of you loved them as much as I do.

As a special THANK YOU to the Quantum Series fans, I've written a special bonus epilogue to this book called PRECIOUS, that'll take you to Kristian and Aileen's wedding. To find the link, go to the FAMOUS page on my website at *https://marieforce.com/famous* and click on the link to the bonus epilogue, PRECIOUS. We'll ask for your email address to add you to my mailing list if you're not already there (if you are, you won't be added again), and then you'll have immediate access to the epilogue.

I've also included the short story JOYOUS that was published as part of the Naughty & Nice anthology late last year for those who didn't get to read it then. Turn the page to read JOYOUS. In the audio edition of FAMOUS, JOYOUS is done by Cooper North, who played the part of Flynn in the first three Quantum books.

A huge thank-you to the team that supports me every day: my husband, Dan, as well as my HTJB team, Julie Cupp, Lisa Cafferty, Holly Sullivan and Nikki Colquhoun. Thank you to my awesome publicist, Jessica Estep, my fabulous editors Linda Ingmanson and Joyce Lamb, and my longtime beta readers Anne Woodall and Kara Conrad. A special thanks to the Quantum beta readers: Katy, Heather, Tammy, Molly, Marla, Sherri, Julia, Phuong and Mona.

Finally, to all the readers who've embraced this series from the second Flynn met Natalie in a New York park in 2015, thank you from the bottom of my heart. You have made this such a rich, rewarding ride for me, and I'll be forever grateful for your support.

Much love,
Marie

Turn the page to read JOYOUS, A Quantum Christmas…

JOYOUS
A QUANTUM CHRISTMAS
BY: MARIE FORCE

Flynn

Christmas has never been my favorite holiday. Probably because it's also my birthday—a year of buildup for one big day that's over in a blink. When I was a kid, I'd get so excited for my big day only to experience massive letdown on the twenty-sixth, knowing I had a full year to wait for my big day to come around again. I also hated that my sisters got presents on *my* birthday. Sure, I knew it was Christmas and everyone got presents, but I didn't think it was fair that there wasn't *one day* that belonged only to me like their birthdays belonged to them.

I know, I know. I sound like a spoiled brat, but that's how I felt back then. And I *love* my sisters. Always have, even if they're royal pains in my ass most of the time. They're the reason the fame and success I've had as an actor never made me into a world-class jerk. They wouldn't have stood for it, and I'm thankful for their influence on me even when they're driving me nuts.

As an adult, Christmas and my birthday have been just another day—especially since my nieces and nephews began arriving and the day became even less about me. This is the first year in forever that I genuinely care about Christmas, but it's not because of me. Nope, it's all about my beautiful, sweet, sexy wife. Now that I have Natalie in my life, every day is like Christmas, and I want to put in the effort to make sure she has the best holiday ever. She was separated from her family when she was only fifteen, so it's been nine years since she had a family to spend the holidays with. I want her to have the most amazing, special Christmas of her life, but I'm stumped as to how to pull that off.

Because I suck at this crap, I've brought in the expert—Addison York Roth, my faithful assistant, the little sister I never had and my business partner Hayden Roth's new wife. Addie is the most organized human being on earth, and she loves Nat almost as much as I do. She knows all about the nightmare Natalie endured at fifteen and the resulting estrangement from her parents and sisters, so Addie will fully appreciate my desire to give my beautiful wife a Christmas she'll never forget.

"I don't give a flying fuck about my birthday," I tell Addie. We're in my Los Angeles office at Quantum Productions, the company I founded with Hayden, one of the top directors in Hollywood. We've since added superstar actress Marlowe Sloane, cinematographer Jasper Autry and producer Kristian Bowen as partners in the company—and in life. The people I work with are also my closest friends. "Don't let anyone make it about me. I want this Christmas to be all about *her.*"

Addie, still tanned from her three-week honeymoon in the Adriatic, has her iPad ready to take notes. "What do you have in mind?"

"I don't know. That's the problem. I want it to be amazing for her, but I can't for the life of me figure out what that should entail. That's where you come in."

"I need consultants on this one." She gets up to use the office phone. "Can you come into Flynn's office? Bring Leah, too." After a pause, she nods. "Thanks."

"I assume that was Aileen?" She's engaged to Kristian. My sister Ellie is having a baby with Jasper, and Leah is hot and heavy with Emmett, our general counsel. It's been one hell of a year for the Quantum family, and we need a Christmas that does justice to the changes we've undergone. I want it to be perfect, which means it'd be a total clusterfuck if I tried to do it myself. With Addie overseeing the plans, however, there's reason for hope.

Whatever. As long as I'm with Natalie, it'll be perfect. The rest is just details. Or so I tell myself. I'm not sure why I'm so stressed about a holiday I normally don't give two shits about.

"Are you listening to me?"

Addie's question cuts through the nonsense in my always-busy mind.

"Of course I am."

She gives me a skeptical look. "I was saying we should go to Aspen."

I toss the idea around in my mind. Natalie and Ellie, both of whom are pregnant, are safe to fly the two hours it takes to get to Colorado. The house is huge. It would easily accommodate the Quantum crew as well as Nat's sisters, my sisters, their families and my parents—all the people we'd need to make this the perfect Christmas for Natalie. "That could work." I just hope that everyone else will agree with the plan.

Aileen comes into my office. "What could work?"

Addie fills her in. "Christmas in Aspen. Flynn's house there is enormous and close to skiing, shopping, five-star restaurants and anything else we could want or need."

"Ohhhh." Aileen's expressive eyes glitter with excitement. "Sign me up. The kids would love to have snow at Christmas. It was so hit or miss when we lived in New York."

The more I think about Aspen, the more I love the idea. Could it really be that simple? Leave it to Addie to cut to the chase.

Aileen, who was Nat's friend in New York, offers a shy smile. "I don't mean to imply that we're invited."

"Of course you are. It wouldn't be Christmas without everyone there." Aileen and her kids have made Kristian so happy. There's nothing I wouldn't do for her or the kids. They're family to me now. That's how it works with us.

Addie frowns. "Do we have to invite Rafe?"

Leah comes into the room, scowling at the mention of Rafe. "Don't you mean he-who-shall-not-be-named? Maybe he'll go home to France for Christmas and we won't have to invite him to whatever we're doing."

"Christmas at Flynn's place in Aspen," Addie tells her.

Leah plops down in a chair. "Hell yes. That sounds awesome, but Marlowe will want to bring him." As Marlowe's assistant, Leah has the 411 on her boss.

"Ugh." None of us can stand the guy that Marlowe is crazy about, which puts me at odds with one of my best friends for the first time in the nearly fifteen years we've been close. None of us get what she sees in the smooth-talking Frenchman. Natalie tells me I don't need to get it. According to my wife, Marlowe is the only one who needs to get it. Which is fine—until I have to spend Christmas with him.

"Time with my love in Aspen, sign me up." Leah blinks and seems to snap out of her fantasies of alone time with Emmett in Aspen. "But it'll be fun to have everyone else there, too."

Addie cracks up laughing. "Nice save."

Leah smiles. "I can be diplomatic when I need to."

That makes me laugh. Diplomatic is the last word I'd use to describe Leah, one of the funniest people I've ever known. She'd been Nat's roommate in New York when I first met them, and it'd been Natalie's idea for Marlowe to hire Leah as her assistant. And now Leah is madly in love with Emmett, who walks around with a dopey grin on his face these days, all thanks to Leah.

Love has been in the air in the Quantum Productions office this year. Each of my friends and partners has ended up with someone I would've hand-chosen for them, except for Marlowe, that is. I keep hoping she'll see the light with Rafe and dump his pretentious ass. I swear he's dating her more for what she can do for his career than because of the magnificence that is Marlowe. He works for the company that distributes Quantum films in France, which is how she met him.

There's just something about him that seems off to me, and I know Hayden, Kristian, Jasper and Emmett feel the same way. If I can prove he's using her to get ahead, I swear to God I'll bury him. Maybe the time in Aspen will give me more info to build my case. Not that I want to be the one to clue her in, but I'd rather it come from a friend who loves her than the media or someone who'd be looking to exploit her celebrity for their benefit.

As the women discuss the details of Christmas in Aspen, I ponder the added benefit of a few days with Rafe and the chance to look for a crack in the armor. It's there. I'm convinced of it.

"Flynn."

Addie's exasperated voice snaps me back to the meeting. "What?"

"You're daydreaming today. I asked if we're in agreement about Aspen? If so, we'll take it from here and make the plans."

"Absolutely yes to Aspen." A week in the mountains with my love and our favorite people? Suddenly, I can't wait for Christmas.

Natalie knows we're going away for the holiday, but other than telling her to pack for cold weather, I haven't given her any info and have asked the others to help keep the secret.

"It's not fair that everyone else knows where we're going, and I don't."

"I love that pout, love, but it's not going to break me."

She gives me a sly, sexy look. "I have other ways to break you."

And I'm hard. That's all it takes when it comes to her. "Is that right? I'd love to see you try."

She rubs her hands together gleefully. "Ohhh, a challenge. I *love* a challenge." Before I can gauge her next move, she's up and out of bed—and with the growing baby belly, she's been moving slower lately. But that doesn't stop her now. Before I know it, she's standing on my side of the bed, her dark hair shining after a shower and blow dry, her lips soft from the balm she applies at bedtime and her curves more luscious than ever as she incubates our baby. I can only stare at my lovely wife.

Mine. Forever. Best words ever.

"Sit up."

Those words are pretty good, too. "Is my little sub trying to dominate her Dom?"

"Nope. In this case, she's after information."

Amused and aroused, I sit up, swing my legs around so my feet are on the floor. "Give it your best shot."

She grabs a pillow off the bed, puts it on the floor and drops rather inelegantly to her knees.

"Nat…" I worry constantly now that she's pregnant, and some of the biggest fights we've had have been about my overly gentle treatment of her. She's gotten used to the dominant sex I introduced her to and is constantly annoyed with me for insisting we take it easy while she's pregnant.

"No talking unless you're going to tell me what I want to know."

"I'm not going to tell you."

"Then be quiet."

God, I love her. I love that she couldn't care less about who I am to the rest of the world. She's the first woman who truly loves me for me, not for what my parents or I can do to boost her career, not for the money or the adulation that's such a big part of the celebrity culture. For Natalie, it's never been about any of those things, which make her different from everyone else from the beginning. It's so fucking *real* with her and has been from the first second I saw her when she crashed into me during a shoot in a New York City park—and then her old wildebeest dog, Fluff, bit me. Best day of my life, hands down.

Fame, fortune and Oscars have nothing on winning the love of the most extraordinary woman I've ever met.

At the moment, my extraordinary wife is out to wreck me as she runs her hands up the insides of my legs, setting every nerve ending in my body on fire as I wait to see what she has planned for me. I'm so hard, I'm leaking copiously, but she ignores that part of me to focus all her attention on other parts of me, making me burn for more.

"*Natalie.*" My teeth are gritted, my hands are curled into fists and my heart is beating so hard, I can hear the thundering echo of it ringing in my ears.

"Shhhh. You're not talking, remember?"

I want to tell her revenge is a bitch, but she knows that. She loves my form of revenge, which is another reason I love her. She accepts every part of me, even the part that needs dominant sex. But I'm not the Dom right now. My sub is making me her bitch as I fight the urge to explode all over her pretty face. I wouldn't do that to her, no matter how much she tortures me. And dear sweet baby Jesus, her tongue on my balls is pure torture.

After nearly a year together, she knows all my hot spots, and she exploits every one of them as she tries to drive me crazy.

With a hand on my chest, she pushes me back so I'm lying on the bed. Then she arranges my legs so they're splayed open, my feet propped on the edge. Christ have mercy… If she so much as breathes on my cock, I'm going to lose it.

"Are you ready to tell me where we're going for Christmas?"

Right about now, I'd sign over my entire fortune to her if it meant she'd put me out of my misery and suck my dick. But I can't be that easy. "No."

"It's not fair that all my friends know, and I don't." Her lips are so close to my shaft that I can feel her hot breath wash over my sensitive skin.

I break out in goose bumps.

She sees that and smiles triumphantly.

I love her madly, desperately. I've gotten to the point that I can barely remember life without her. I've started turning down parts that would take me away from her for even one night. The only way I'll work anymore is if she can come with me. With a baby due to arrive early next year, work is on hold while I give her my full attention. The only thing I'm bothering with professionally is the passion project I'm spearheading to bring Natalie's story to the big screen. Otherwise, I'm all about her.

And none of these thoughts are able to distract me enough to control the explosive orgasm that's about to boil over. "Natalie…" She knows me well enough by now to understand the warning I'm offering. If she doesn't do something—soon—I can't be responsible for what happens next, which is an entirely new phenomena that's all her fault. Before her, control was never a challenge for me. With her, it's a constant, delightful struggle. With her, everything is different, better, *more*.

She runs her tongue over my cock, and I jolt. "You're sure you can't tell me *anything* about what you've got planned?"

"Yeah." The single word emerges on a gasp when she wraps her hand around the base and teases the tip with her tongue. "Babe."

"Yes, Flynn?"

My little minx is enjoying this, but then again, so am I. If she's in the room, I'm happy. At times like this, I'm downright delirious because she's all mine and I'm the only man in the world who will ever know this sexy, seductive, mischievous side of her. I'm about to spill the beans on the plan for Aspen when she sucks me into her mouth and finishes me off. I come so hard, I see stars, and she never misses a beat as she swallows every drop. She does it so well that I'm still hard when it's over.

"I thought I could break you."

I hate that she sounds disappointed in herself, and that's what finally breaks me the way nothing else ever could. Extending my arms, I encourage her to join me on the bed.

She curls up to me, and I hold her close. "We're going to Aspen with the whole gang. Your sisters, too."

"Oh, Flynn! Really?"

Nodding, I run my fingers through her silky dark hair, loving the way her green eyes dance with joy. "I wanted you to have a big family Christmas to make up for all the years you were alone for the holidays."

I'm horrified when her gorgeous eyes fill with tears. She knows I can't handle it when she cries. It makes me insane. After the pain she endured as a teenager, I never want her to be sad or upset again, even if I know that's an unrealistic goal.

"Don't do that." I wipe away the tears that spill down her cheeks. She's been a regular waterworks since she got pregnant, which I'm told is perfectly normal even if every one of her tears is like a razor to my heart.

"Can't help it." She leans in to kiss me. "You're so sweet."

"I am *not* sweet." My inner Dom cringes at that word she tosses around a little too often for my liking.

"Yes, you really are."

"I'll show you sweet." I move so I'm on top of her, but I'm careful not to put any weight on the baby bump. I arrange her legs so they're propped on my hips and slide into her slowly and carefully so I won't hurt her or the baby. I'm always so afraid of hurting her that our sex life has become downright vanilla since she got pregnant. I'll indulge in the occasional spank or surprise her with a toy every now and then, but the kinky business is on hold until after she gives birth.

It's funny that I don't even miss it. Before Nat, I would've been bored without it. With her, it doesn't matter what we do as long as we do it together. I watch her closely, looking for any sign of discomfort. I'm big, she's tight, and the baby is taking up a lot of room in there.

"Okay?"

She nods, looking up at me with those bottomless eyes that see straight through to the heart of me, the heart that belongs to her and only her. I knew the first day I met her that there'd never again be anyone else for me, and a year later, I only want her more than I did then, if that's even possible.

She reaches up to run her fingers through my hair, her touch sending a shiver down my spine. "Why do you look so serious?"

"Making love to my wife is very serious business."

"Stop worrying about hurting me. It feels amazing as always."

In her second trimester, we've discovered that being pregnant makes her super horny and orgasmic, two things I'm happy to indulge whenever she snaps her fingers. I'm her slave, and she knows it, but I'm always careful with her.

We've argued about that. She doesn't want me treating her differently because she's pregnant. I can't help my need to protect her and the baby from anything that would harm them, even me. So I give her easy when my inclination is usually fast and hard. We'll get back to regular programming after our bundle of joy arrives. For now, slow and easy is the routine. She doesn't seem to mind as I can feel the almost constant grip of her internal muscles massaging my cock as one orgasm rolls into another.

Since she took the edge off for me, I can wait her out, keeping up the pace until I sense her beginning to tire. That's another thing that happens far more easily since she's been pregnant. When I feel her starting to come again, I let go and allow myself to join her because she needs her rest—not because I've had enough. I'll never get enough of her.

I stay deep inside her as I gaze down at the face that changed my life. "I can't wait to spend Christmas with you."

"I can't wait either. And it's your birthday."

"It's not about me. It's all about you."

"It's about *us* and the people we love best."

Her eyes are heavy, and her lips are slightly swollen from the blow job. She's stunning. "The only thing I want for Christmas or my birthday is you."

"I can do better than that."

"No, you can't."

She falls asleep with a small, contented smile on her face. Sometimes I still can't believe that this is my life now, that *she* is my life now. If you'd told me this time last year that I'd be so completely in love with someone that I'd actually marry her and start a family, I would've laughed in your face. After the disaster that was my first marriage, I'd publicly sworn off matrimony and anything that smacked of commitment. And then there was Natalie and her bitchy little dog and that face... Dear God, that face. I run my fingertip lightly over her cheek.

The best part of the plan for Christmas is a full week with her. I can't wait.

Ten days later, a boisterous group arrives at LAX for the flight to Aspen. The only thing detracting from my euphoric mood is the weather forecast coming from Aspen, where a blizzard has been threatening all week. We're leaving a day earlier than planned, hoping to get there before the storm materializes, but the predictions keep changing and the various models are giving differing information. My parents and sisters Annie and Aimee as well as their families will be flying up on Christmas Eve, the same day Natalie's sisters are due to arrive.

My stomach is in knots. I'm not a huge fan of flying in the best of conditions but knowing we could be flying into a storm doesn't sit well with me, even if I trust the pilots who've worked for us for years. They moved up our time of departure hoping to outrun the storm.

Natalie, who cuddles Fluff on her lap, senses my anxiety and keeps a tight hold on my hand, even after we're buckled into our seats. "Relax. You're on vacation, and everything is going to be fine."

All around us, happy-sounding voices discuss plans for skiing, snowboarding, sledding, snowman-making and other winter activities. Aileen's kids, Logan and Maddie, are so excited for Christmas and the trip that Kristian warns us they might spontaneously combust. Maddie was concerned about Santa finding them in Aspen, but Kristian assured her that Santa always knows where she is. Aileen and Kristian shipped gifts to the house in Aspen on Santa's behalf. Like me, he's looking forward to his first Christmas as a family man, and we're all excited about having the kids with us for Christmas morning. Next year, we'll add two more little ones to the family—ours as well as Jasper and Ellie's. Those are the two we know about so far, but with everyone in our group pairing off and falling in love, the baby boom is apt to continue for quite some time to come.

Fine by me. More people to love.

Across the aisle from us, Addie is cozied up to Hayden, who has an arm around her. I keep waiting to hear that she's expecting, too, but so far, there's no news on that front, and Nat tells me I'm not allowed to ask her. Behind us, Leah and Emmett are giggling and whispering the way they do these days, and in the last row, Sebastian, who is Hayden's childhood friend and the manager of our BDSM club, sits alone, gazing out the window. He jokes about being the eleventh wheel with us, but claims he has no desire to be attached to anyone. I don't see him settling down any time soon, even if the rest of us are. His philosophy has always been why would he want just one woman when he can have *all* the women? That used to be my philosophy, too, until I found *the* woman in the most unlikely of places. I run a finger over the small scar on my arm where Fluff bit me that first day. I wear that scar like a badge of honor, a reminder of how life can change in a matter of seconds.

"Where the hell is Marlowe?" Hayden asks.

"She said she'd be here," Leah replies.

"We're on a time crunch with the storm looming." I glance at Leah over the top of my seat. "Will you call her?"

"Yep."

If she doesn't arrive soon, we're going without her. She can catch up when lover boy arrives from France. I can hear Leah's side of the conversation and catch enough to know they're coming.

"Five minutes," Leah confirms. "Rafe's flight from Paris was late getting in."

I hate that he's coming with us, but I'd never say so to Marlowe. I just keep hoping she'll realize she can do much better than a phony charmer with a French accent and a questionable past. And yes, I had Gordon, our director of security, look into the guy and didn't like some of what he uncovered, especially the part about his ex-wife claiming he was violent with her during divorce proceedings. He was never actually charged, but somehow Gordon found out about it, telling me it's not something that would be revealed in a routine search, which I've also done.

In order to bring this info to Marlowe, I'd need to confess to having had her boyfriend investigated. No one else knows I did that, not even Natalie, who'd be pissed with me for butting into Marlowe's life. But with every instinct I have telling me the guy is no good, I have no regrets about having Gordon take a look at him. Rather than start an international incident with one of my best friends at Christmas, I've decided to take a wait-and-see approach. I'm living proof that people can grow and mature over time, and I want to give Rafe the benefit of the doubt for Marlowe's sake. I hope I'm wrong about him.

Marlowe comes up the stairs and onto the plane, red-faced and out of breath from the dash through the airport. Unfortunately, Rafe is right behind her, equally winded and red-faced.

"So sorry to hold you all up." His English heavily accented with French inflections. "All my fault."

It's telling that none of us have anything to say to him. I wonder if she notices that or if she's so besotted, she can't see the forest through the proverbial trees. He's been in France the last three weeks, and she's been looking forward to his

OTHER TITLES BY MARIE FORCE

Erotic Romance

The Erotic Quantum Series

Book 1: Virtuous *(Flynn & Natalie)*

Book 2: Valorous *(Flynn & Natalie)*

Book 3: Victorious *(Flynn & Natalie)*

Book 4: Rapturous *(Addie & Hayden)*

Book 5: Ravenous *(Jasper & Ellie)*

Book 6: Delirious *(Kristian & Aileen)*

Book 7: Outrageous *(Emmett & Leah)*

Book 8: Famous *(Marlowe)*

Contemporary Romances

The Gansett Island Series

Book 1: Maid for Love *(Mac & Maddie)*

Book 2: Fool for Love *(Joe & Janey)*

Book 3: Ready for Love *(Luke & Sydney)*

Book 4: Falling for Love *(Grant & Stephanie)*

Book 5: Hoping for Love *(Evan & Grace)*

Book 6: Season for Love *(Owen & Laura)*

Book 7: Longing for Love *(Blaine & Tiffany)*

Book 8: Waiting for Love *(Adam & Abby)*

Book 9: Time for Love *(David & Daisy)*

Book 10: Meant for Love *(Jenny & Alex)*

Book 10.5: Chance for Love, *A Gansett Island Novella (Jared & Lizzie)*

Book 11: Gansett After Dark *(Owen & Laura)*

Book 12: Kisses After Dark *(Shane & Katie)*

Book 13: Love After Dark *(Paul & Hope)*

Book 14: Celebration After Dark *(Big Mac & Linda)*

Book 15: Desire After Dark *(Slim & Erin)*

Book 16: Light After Dark *(Mallory & Quinn)*

Book 17: Victoria & Shannon (Episode 1)

Book 18: Kevin & Chelsea (Episode 2)

A Gansett Island Christmas Novella

Book 19: Mine After Dark *(Riley & Nikki)*

Book 20: Yours After Dark *(Finn & Chloe)*

Book 21: Trouble After Dark *(Deacon & Julia)*

The Green Mountain Series

Book 1: All You Need Is Love *(Will & Cameron)*

Book 2: I Want to Hold Your Hand *(Nolan & Hannah)*

Book 3: I Saw Her Standing There *(Colton & Lucy)*

Book 4: And I Love Her *(Hunter & Megan)*

Novella: You'll Be Mine *(Will & Cam's Wedding)*

Book 5: It's Only Love *(Gavin & Ella)*

Book 6: Ain't She Sweet *(Tyler & Charlotte)*

The Butler Vermont Series
(Continuation of the Green Mountain Series)

Book 1: Every Little Thing *(Grayson & Emma)*

Book 2: Can't Buy Me Love *(Mary & Patrick)*

Book 3: Here Comes the Sun *(Wade & Mia)*

Book 4: Till There Was You *(Lucas & Dani)*

The Treading Water Series

Book 1: Treading Water *(Jack & Andi)*

Book 2: Marking Time *(Clare & Aidan)*

Book 3: Starting Over *(Brandon & Daphne)*

Book 4: Coming Home *(Reid & Kate)*

Historical Romances

The Gilded Series

Book 1: Duchess by Deception

Book 2: Deceived by Desire

Single Titles

Five Years Gone

One Year Home

Sex Machine

Sex God

Georgia on My Mind

True North

The Fall

Everyone Loves a Hero

Love at First Flight

Line of Scrimmage

Romantic Suspense

The Fatal Series

One Night With You, *A Fatal Series Prequel Novella*

Book 1: Fatal Affair

Single Title

ABOUT THE AUTHOR

Marie Force is the *New York Times* bestselling author of contemporary romance, romantic suspense, historical romance and erotic romance. Her series include the indie-published Gansett Island, Treading Water, Butler, Vermont and Quantum Series as well as the Fatal Series from Harlequin Books.

Her books have sold more than 9 million copies worldwide, have been translated into more than a dozen languages and have appeared on the *New York Times* bestseller list 30 times. She is also a *USA Today* and *Wall Street Journal* bestseller, a Speigel bestseller in Germany, a frequent speaker and publishing workshop presenter.

Her goals in life are simple—to finish raising two happy, healthy, productive young adults, to keep writing books for as long as she possibly can and to never be on a flight that makes the news.

Join Marie's mailing list on her website at *marieforce.com* for news about new books and upcoming appearances in your area. Follow her on Facebook at *www.Facebook.com/MarieForceAuthor* and on Instagram at *www.instagram.com/ marieforceauthor/*. Contact Marie at *marie@marieforce.com*.

CPSIA information can be obtained
at www.ICGtesting.com
Printed in the USA
FSHW011533111019
62934FS